PRETTY
LITTLE
KILLERS

PRETTY LITTLE KILLERS

The Keepers, Book 1

RITA HERRON

Montlake
Romance

Text copyright © 2018 by Rita Herron

Published by Montlake Romance, Seattle

www.apub.com

Amazon, the Amazon logo, and Montlake Romance are trademarks of Amazon.com, Inc., or its affiliates.

ISBN-13: 9781542049849
ISBN-10: 1542049849

Cover design by Damon Freeman

Printed in the United States of America

PRETTY
LITTLE
KILLERS

PROLOGUE

Five-year-old Korine Davenport climbed into her father's lap and wrapped her arms around his neck. He was big and sweet and wonderful.

"Tell me I'm pretty, Daddy."

Her daddy lifted the lid of the music box he'd just given her, and a soft melody began to play. It was the same song from the movie they'd watched last night. The ballerina with the fluffy tutu danced and twirled on the pink satin as her father sang, "You're so pretty, oh, so pretty, so pretty and witty and bright . . ."

Korine planted a big wet, juicy kiss on her daddy's cheek. Then he helped her onto his feet, and they began to dance.

This was the best day ever! Tonight, Santa would come.

But she'd already gotten what she wanted—the music box *and* a new doll. The porcelain doll she'd seen in the store the other day that had red hair like hers and blue eyes that looked like the violets her mother grew in the garden. She was going to name her Ruby.

"Look at me and Daddy dancing, Ruby," she said as they danced through the study. Stars twinkled and glittered through the window, bright against the night sky.

Her father scooped her up and swung her around. She giggled, and he rubbed his thumb down her cheek, then over the waist of her pink satin dress. "Merry Christmas, sweetheart. You know Daddy loves you, don't you?"

She bobbed her head up and down. "I love you, too."

Another spin and her hair swirled around her face. She felt light and beautiful, like the ballerina. She was Daddy's special girl!

"You're so pretty, oh, so pretty . . ."

The door screeched open. Daddy had closed it when they'd come into his study. Something shiny glinted against the darkness.

Her daddy didn't seem to notice. He spun her around again. Her dress whirled around her, the petticoat beneath crinkling.

A loud popping noise made her jump. Her father stumbled and jerked his head toward the door with a frown. The popping sounded again, and his eyes widened.

Korine clung to him as he swayed and staggered all over the room. He bumped his recliner and the piano, and then the two of them went tumbling to the floor. She tried to hold on, but he lost his grip on her.

She slid from his arms, flailing to hold on to him. Something crashed on the floor. Ruby . . . no . . . her face was broken!

Korine's head hit the corner of the coffee table. Pain shot through her temple, and stars swam in front of her eyes.

Her daddy fell backward, his mouth open. He called her name, but his voice sounded garbled, like he had seashells in his throat.

She rubbed at her forehead and felt something sticky. When she pulled her hand away, her fingers were red.

A croaking, froglike sound came from her daddy. She tried to scream, but her voice wouldn't work.

He laid his hand on his chest, and blood oozed through his fingers. His white shirt turned red.

She cupped his face in her hands. "Daddy," she whispered.

The music box continued to play, but her daddy's ragged breathing puffed out, drowning the melody.

Tears blurred Korine's eyes. Daddy couldn't leave her.

She glanced back at the door, but it was closed again.

A second later, her father's eyes rolled back in his head. A coldness washed over her. She cried out and shook him. But he didn't move.

She had to get help. She tried to stand, to run.

But her legs gave way as she slipped in the blood.

CHAPTER ONE

Twenty-five years later

Korine Davenport would never stop looking for her father's killer.

She traced her fingers over her FBI badge as she glanced around the office of her Savannah row house. It was a fixer-upper in a transitional neighborhood, but she'd gotten a good deal on rent. She didn't care about fancy furniture or expensive things.

This house was just a place to hang her hat—no, her gun—at night, not a home. And she was determined to live on her salary, not her inheritance.

Money left for her in a trust fund from her father's will. Money she didn't want to touch because it would mean she'd profited from his death.

His unsolved case was one reason she'd gone into law enforcement.

Night was falling, gray clouds adding a creepiness to the property. The real estate agent had hinted that the place was haunted.

Ghost stories didn't frighten her. Not when there were real live monsters out there, predators who hunted both day and night.

Notes on unsolved cases were stacked on her desk, a testament to the fact that she was obsessed with cold cases and kept up with the ones she'd worked at the police departments in Atlanta and then Savannah before she'd applied to the FBI. A whiteboard on the wall held names of murder victims that needed attention.

The need for answers kept her awake at night. And when she finally succumbed to exhaustion and fell asleep, nightmares of victims' faces haunted her.

Criminology books, forensics materials, and research on serial killers dominated her sideboard, while photos from articles on crimes covered another wall, at odds with the porcelain doll on the mantel. Esther Ray—the first one her father had given her.

She'd left the others in the curio at her mother's house.

She'd stopped playing with dolls a long time ago.

She gritted her teeth, battling the bittersweet memories. Christmas had just passed, a reminder of the day she'd lost her father. She'd never been able to decorate a tree, listen to Christmas carols, or enjoy the festivities, not when Christmas Eve had been the worst day of her life. She ran a finger over the rosewood music box her father had given her, but she couldn't bring herself to open it.

Still, the chorus to "I Feel Pretty" played softly in her head, mingling with the sound of the gunshots.

Her throat tightened, panic rising in her chest.

She took several deep breaths. For God's sake, she wasn't a five-year-old traumatized child anymore.

She couldn't allow emotions into her work.

She checked her phone—no text about an assignment yet. The director would probably assign her some menial tasks, although Blaine Hamilton, her father's lawyer and her mentor, had connections and had called in favors to get her assigned to Savannah. Hopefully, his pull and the reputation she'd earned in Atlanta and Savannah would help land her an active investigation.

She'd hoped to get a call today. Now, night loomed, dark and lonely.

She might as well visit her mother. Get it over with.

Dread knotted her stomach as she stepped onto the front stoop of her house. The wind howled, shrill and harsh, the dark clouds overhead casting an ominous gray over the brittle grass.

A movement caught her eye. She froze, pivoting to search the bushes to the right. Just as it had a dozen times this week, the hair on the back of her neck prickled.

Someone had been watching her.

One hand on her weapon, she eased down the steps and inched toward the red-tipped shrubs. The bushes rustled; then she heard another movement. Someone running into the woods behind her property.

All her life she'd been paranoid that her father's killer would come back for her.

Maybe this time he had . . .

◆ ◆ ◆

Special Agent Hatcher McGee climbed in his SUV, flexed his fingers, and stared at them, disgusted at himself. His hands were shaking like a willow tree in the wind.

Even though it had been six months since he'd killed the monster who'd murdered his wife, he could still feel the man's blood on his hands. See the blood staining his fingernails.

He wanted a drink, bad.

His mama and daddy's voices echoed in his head. They were good people. Honest. Hardworking. They'd raised him on family values and love. They'd died and left him alone, on his own, at seventeen. Still, their teachings had stuck.

Except for the night Felicia had died.

He'd crossed the line.

Although technically he'd rammed the knife in the bastard's belly in self-defense, his actions had come under scrutiny, and he'd almost lost his FBI badge.

If he had to do it over, he'd still kill him. His wife hadn't deserved to die so young. Especially not in such a violent way.

Worse, she'd died because of *him*.

Because of his job. Because he tangled with evil every day. Because he'd been screwing another woman.

That guilt and evil had touched him inside and out. Putting the maniac who'd taken her life in the ground had felt damn good.

Too good, maybe.

His parents were probably rolling over in their graves.

His choice had nearly cost his partner, Wyatt, his life, too.

It had also allowed another sadistic man, the second Skull, to escape.

Felicia's ghost hovered in front of the window, mocking him.

She couldn't rest. Couldn't move on or find peace.

She blamed him. She had every right to.

Only working could dull the pain, make him forget for a little while.

He started the engine, then sped down the graveled road leading from his cabin on the marsh to the Coastal Highway. Palm trees and sea oats dotted the islands here in South Georgia, where the summer heat could be oppressive and mosquitos and gnats fed on locals and tourists like kids devouring ice cream at Seahawk Island Sweet Shop.

Although he'd hidden out in his cabin with a bottle most of summer and fall, away from the tourists—and work.

The downside to going back today: he was being assigned a new partner. A rookie female agent.

Korine Davenport.

The very woman he'd spent the night with when he should have been home, protecting his wife. Granted, he'd been on the verge of divorce, but . . . still . . . *Damn*.

Thankfully, his superior didn't know he had a personal history with Korine Davenport, only that he'd helped train her.

If Bellows knew the truth, he'd never pair them together. In fact, he'd probably send Hatcher back to the shrink.

An image of Korine's fiery red hair and sexy blue eyes taunted him.

She was another line he'd crossed. He and Felicia had been separated when he'd agreed to teach a class at Quantico. The first time he'd laid eyes on the young trainee, he'd nearly choked on lust.

Her pale skin framed with that dark-red hair had been his undoing. Her strength, sass, and vulnerability were a potent combination that he hadn't been able to resist.

One night after a heated training session, they'd had drinks and . . . the best damn sex he'd ever had in his life.

It had been so hot and steamy that he'd ignored his phone ringing. Ignored the fact that his wife had called, terrified she was being stalked. Even if he had answered, he probably would have blown her off.

Felicia had always had a dramatic flair and had liked attention. He'd thought she'd made up the stalker. She'd fabricated lies before to seduce him, then more to make sure he came whenever she called. She'd cried wolf so many times he'd finally gotten fed up with her and told her he was done.

Unfortunately, that last time he'd been wrong.

She'd died because of it.

A part of him had died that day, too. He'd climbed from the bowels of hell into the bottle.

And now he was making a comeback. By God, no one would stop him.

Not even Korine Davenport.

Adrenaline kicked in at the thought of finally being in the field again, and he gripped the steering wheel of his SUV tighter as he veered onto the causeway leading to Seahawk Island. Located about forty miles from Savannah, the island drew vacationers from across the South, especially Atlanta and Athens, Georgia.

He drove past the village, the heart of the island with its pier, shops, restaurants, and bars. During the summer, fall, and spring, tourists congregated on the island, crowding the establishments. Walkers, joggers, bikers, and sightseers filled the sidewalks and streets. Fishermen and crabbers gravitated to the pier for the day. The park, with its massive, ancient oak trees and picnic tables, was packed with families and couples enjoying the sunshine and fresh air. Squeals and laughter echoed from the playground and putt-putt golf course. In summer, the pool would be packed but was closed for the winter.

Although some visitors came for recreation, others wanted to climb the lighthouse that was supposedly haunted or tour the fort where numerous soldiers had died in the Civil War.

The kids flocked to the pirate ship to explore the nooks and crannies and history of the pirates who'd shipwrecked here during a storm over a hundred years ago.

Now everything appeared deserted.

January had rolled in with a bang. Winter robbed the warmth of the sun and cast a grayness over the marshes and sandy shores. The festive Christmas lights that had sparkled and adorned the town during the holiday were gone, and a few windows remained boarded from the recent hurricane damage. Sea oats and palm trees swayed in the gusty breeze, and rental places sat vacant, giving it a ghost-town feel.

He wiped sweat from his forehead. He'd never believed in ghosts until he'd lost his wife. Now he saw her spirit everywhere he went. In the bedroom at night. In the graveyard where he'd buried her. In the streets of Savannah, and hovering over the sea and marshland.

Even now in the seat beside him.

Hatcher blinked to clear his vision, and she was gone. He wished he could go back and change things.

His mouth watered for a drink as he passed The Buoy, a local bar. He tossed a stick of gum in his mouth and chewed vigorously in an attempt to stifle his craving.

Today was a new start. Drinking wasn't on the agenda. If he wanted to work again, and he desperately *needed* to work to keep his sanity, he had to stay sober and keep his temper under control.

He slowed as he passed the ancient church on the edge of the marsh at the corner of the turnoff for Sunset Cove. In the waning light of day, the gravestones in the cemetery stood like shadowy, spiked monuments in a sea of ghosts. Locals claimed the cemetery screamed with the tortured spirits of those who'd died in battles fought in the Civil War. The Confederate soldiers had burned down the first lighthouse on the island because they didn't want the Union to use it to guide them.

Hatcher's heart pounded with anticipation, the old familiar adrenaline surge at the beginning of a case heating his blood as he veered down a side street.

His phone buzzed just as he parked. His director, Roman Bellows. He punched "Connect." "Yeah, I'm here."

"Listen, Hatcher, we need to regroup. I think I should assign someone else to this case."

"No." Hell no. He couldn't yank him away without giving him a chance. "I can handle it."

"You don't understand. I just talked with the local police chief on the island, who called us for help, and the woman who reported the murder—it was Tinsley Jensen."

Hatcher's pulse jumped. "Tinsley Jensen?"

"Apparently she rents a cottage in the cove." Director Bellows's breath puffed out, ragged and riddled with anxiety. "She has serious emotional issues," he continued. "She never leaves that cottage. Never."

Good God, who could blame her? She'd been held hostage and tortured by a maniac.

Still, he'd had no idea she was agoraphobic.

Hatcher broke out in a sweat triggered by another heaping mound of guilt. It was his fault the woman had gone off the grid. His fault because he and Wyatt had been tracking down the maniac who'd kidnapped Tinsley when Hatcher got a lead on the man who'd abducted Felicia.

His fault for leaving Wyatt alone to face the sadistic man—his fault the Skull had escaped and Tinsley was still in danger.

CHAPTER TWO

Korine flipped on the radio as she drove to her mother's house, her nerves on edge. Visiting her mother was painful, but she couldn't desert her. Her mother needed her, even if she didn't act like it.

The newscaster from the local public radio station broke into her thoughts. *"The safety app, thought to be a lifesaver to some by alerting people of crimes in their area, has come under serious scrutiny. Yesterday three people in the Savannah airport jumped a man they believed to be the mugger targeting tourists in Savannah's City Market. The man turned out to be an undercover officer. He suffered a broken arm and dislocated shoulder in the assault."*

Korine shook her head at the irony. The designer of that app had good intentions. Korine had thought of a dozen ways she could use it. Women, college coeds, and teens could be alerted of a crime being committed and avoid that area. People near a crime scene would know to watch out for a perpetrator and help the police by reporting it.

But there were obviously kinks to work out.

She turned down the drive to the big Georgian home where she'd grown up, her emotions warring inside her. Morbid, but her mother had refused to sell the house after Korine's father was murdered. She claimed she couldn't leave the memories behind.

Although those very memories had stolen her will to live. Depression had plagued her for years until the point where she'd slipped into a catatonic state.

Korine had hoped her promise to find her father's killer might spark life back into her. Instead, her mother had worsened and stopped talking.

Saying a silent prayer that her mother at least recognized her presence today, Korine parked and rang the doorbell, then gently eased open the door.

"Mom, it's Korine."

Esme, her mother's caretaker, appeared with a wary smile. "Hi, sweetie."

"How's she doing today?" Korine asked.

Esme shrugged. "Not a good day." She gestured toward the study. "She hasn't spoken or eaten anything. She's been playing that CD over and over."

Korine paused in the hallway, hearing the faint notes of the song that had been playing when her father was murdered through the closed door.

A chill slithered through her. Why was her mother listening to it?

Korine's gaze shot to the curio holding the porcelain dolls her father had given her. They were beautiful, but unlike her mother, she needed to leave the memories behind. Surrounding herself with them only intensified her grief.

She braced herself as she opened the door and peeked inside. "Mom, it's me, Korine."

The familiar dark wainscoting and crown molding looked as stately today as it had twenty-five years ago. Although hardwood replaced the carpet that had once covered the floor, she could still see the blood flowing onto the white Berber and staining it dark crimson.

Worry seized Korine. Her mother was sitting so still it looked as if she weren't even breathing.

Over the past few years, her mother had gone from bouts of anxiety and agitation, where she'd toss her husband's CDs and medical journals all over his study, to being unable to get out of bed all day.

She'd also fussed at Korine for not taking care of her brother. Kenny was four years older than Korine and had been in and out of trouble and drug rehab since he was a teen.

Korine knelt in front of the wheelchair and pulled her mother's hands in hers. "Mom, let's go to the sunroom and have a cup of tea."

"I'll make a pot," Esme offered behind her.

Korine gave her an appreciative smile as the woman disappeared.

But her mother didn't respond. She stared into space, her fingers tapping the arm of the wheelchair. Esme had suggested the chair as a way to move her mother from one room to the other after her mother started staying in bed all day.

Korine's cell phone buzzed on her hip. She snatched it and checked the number. Her boss, Director Bellows.

"I need to take this."

Again, no response from her mother. Korine stepped over by the window and connected. "Agent Davenport."

"It's Director Bellows. I know you trained with Special Agent Hatcher McGee at the academy and he praised your work. His partner is out recovering from an injury, so I want you to work with him temporarily."

Director Bellows knew they'd worked together. But thankfully, he didn't know the whole story.

"Of course, sir. What's the case?"

"Homicide—Sunset Cove, Seahawk Island."

"I'm on my way."

Korine's pulse hammered as she ended the call—she finally had a case. A real case.

She had to leave.

She walked back to her mother and gently rubbed her back. "I'm afraid I'll have to skip the tea today. I have to go now."

Her mother's chin quivered slightly, and for a moment, Korine thought she might say something. But then her face became a blank mask again.

She wanted to scream in frustration. But she'd done that before, and it did no good.

Esme stepped back into the room, her brow furrowed. "Ms. Korine?"

"I'm sorry. I have to go to work," Korine said.

Esme nodded as Korine rushed toward the door.

Still, she couldn't shake the sound of that blasted song from her mind as she started the car.

She had to focus, though. She was going to work with Hatcher McGee. God . . . he was legendary for solving hard cases.

And for being a hothead.

He was also damned hot in bed.

But no one knew about their indiscretion except the two of them. At least she didn't think he'd told anyone.

Director Bellows wouldn't have partnered you with him if he knew.

No doubt Hatcher would be pissed to be assigned a rookie like her. A stupid rookie who'd believed him when he said he was single.

If he'd been home with his wife instead of with her the night they'd fallen all over each other in bed, his wife might still be alive.

She wouldn't make the mistake of sleeping with him again.

She'd prove to him that she could contribute to the case. That she was a professional. That this time, she wouldn't succumb to his sexy body and rugged charm.

That their one night of passion meant nothing to her. That it hadn't haunted her with what-ifs and fantasies about a repeat experience.

The tune from her music box chimed in her head as she drove toward the cove, a reminder that the most important case of her life remained unsolved. That she'd trained to become an agent so she could rid the world of crime.

That sex and romance had no place in her life.

"Sometimes it's better not knowing," her mother had once said.

Korine didn't believe that for a minute. The only way she could find peace was to arrest her father's killer.

Hatcher spotted the police officer's flashlight beam before he saw the cop. The thin stream of light washed over the edge of the dock, illuminating the body propped against the post holding up the rails.

His first thought was why hadn't the killer shoved the body into the water? If he or she had, the body might not have been discovered for days.

Unless the killer had been interrupted or . . . he wanted the victim to be found.

Hatcher's boots dug into wet sand as he left the parking lot and crossed to the dock. Sea oats and grass jutted up in irregular patches. He walked through the opening of the seawall created to keep the tidewater from reaching the houses in the cove.

Hurricane Matthew had caused erosion and washed debris, shells, driftwood, and seaweed onto the shore. Some of the residents and businesses were still struggling to clean up fallen trees and to repair the shattered roofs and flood damage.

Thankfully, the low tide had saved them.

Two days later, if the storm had struck during the full moon and King tides, the situation could have been devastating. Half the island might have been washed away.

Birds cawed as they flew overhead. A faint light from the lighthouse at the pier a half mile away blinked, looking almost eerie in the distance but still working, orienting ships to the port in Brunswick.

The officer glanced up and saw Hatcher, then walked toward him. "Officer Leeks," the man said.

Hatcher shook his hand and introduced himself, wondering why the locals had called in the Feds. They didn't always welcome the FBI, but Savannah was short on cops, and Hurricane Matthew had stretched the island's small officer pool thin. Sad, how looters took advantage in the wake of disaster. "Your chief asked us here?"

The officer nodded. "Yeah. Come take a look."

He should probably wait on his new partner, but he was the senior agent, and he wanted to get started.

Hatcher's boots pounded the wood as he followed the officer to the end of the dock. The scent of death rose in the salty air, acrid and strong, swirling in the mist. Birds had already begun to swoop down to pick at the carcass, nibbling at the flesh, the pigeons flocking. Officer Leeks lifted a bottle of water and sprayed it toward the pigeons to shoo them away.

Hatcher removed his flashlight and shined it over the body. "What do you know so far?" he asked.

Officer Leeks plugged a handkerchief over his nose and mouth as if he was about to gag. "Not much. Woman who lives in that house there"—he pointed to the small yellow clapboard house facing the cove—"said she saw someone dragging a body onto the dock."

Hatcher's pulse clamored. That house was where Tinsley Jensen lived. Where she'd made a prison for herself.

Focus, man, focus. He'd convinced his superior to let him continue working the case, and he couldn't let him down.

He'd have to talk to Tinsley, but first he wanted to assess the situation. "When did the report come in?"

The officer checked his watch. "About an hour ago."

Judging from the stench, though, the man had been dead for hours. "Have you spoken with the woman?"

"Not yet. I rushed out here first, just in case the victim was still alive."

The rotting wooden railing of the dock looked as if it might give way, but it was keeping the dead man's body from tumbling into the murky water.

Hatcher stooped to examine the victim.

White male, close-cropped brown hair, midfifties. Skin was wrinkly and discolored.

His head had been smashed in.

He wore dress pants and a white shirt. Expensive shoes and watch.

His clothes were intact, suggesting he hadn't been sexually assaulted, but Hatcher wouldn't know for certain until the autopsy.

Both pants and shirt were drenched in blood from the beating he'd taken.

Hatcher raised the flashlight to study the victim's face again, and his heart hammered. *Shit.*

This was no accident or random crime. It was intentional.

And probably the reason the local sheriff had asked for the FBI.

The killer had left them a message—a pair of intertwined SS on the victim's forehead, painted in blood.

Korine's phone trilled just as she reached the island and turned onto the road leading to the cove. Director Bellows again.

"Agent Davenport, sir. I'm about to park at the cove."

"Good." His breathing sounded heavy. "I wanted to ask a favor of you."

Korine frowned, nerves fluttering. "I'm listening."

He wheezed a breath. "Hatcher McGee is—was—the best agent I've ever had."

Was?

"Go on."

"At Quantico, I'm sure you heard that his wife was murdered."

She wiped perspiration from her neck. "I did, sir. That was a shame."

"Sure as hell was. Worse, McGee blamed himself. He crossed the line. When he finally tracked down her killer, he ripped the man apart. It was brutal. Pure revenge fed by an alcoholic rage."

He was a drinker? Disappointment flared. She'd had troubles with her brother on that front. "He was cleared of any charges, wasn't he?"

"Only because I vouched for him during the investigation. After it was over, he sank back into his whiskey. I thought he was lost forever."

Korine took a deep breath. "I don't understand."

"He's been badgering me to put him back on active duty," Bellows continued, "so I went to bat for him over that, too, but I stipulated that he had to quit the booze."

She slowed her car, eyes narrowing as she scanned the dock and cottage in the cove.

"What I'm trying to say is that my ass is on the line. I need you to watch McGee and make sure he's ready to be back. If he's drinking or goes rogue, I want to know."

He wanted her to spy on Hatcher McGee? *Jesus.* That wouldn't sit well with Hatcher if he found out.

"Agent Davenport, do you hear me?"

"Yes, sir."

"Are you on board?" Bellows barked. "Can you handle the job?"

An image of Hatcher's heated eyes as he drove his cock inside her taunted Korine.

Then the photo she'd seen of him at his wife's funeral.

Grief stricken, guilt ridden, and . . . alone.

She'd wanted to comfort him, but she'd been too furious when she'd discovered that he was still married.

That he'd lied to her.

So she hadn't attended the funeral. The last thing she wanted was to appear needy or unprofessional.

No way she'd attempt to try to fill his wife's shoes.

"Agent Davenport?"

"I can handle it, sir."

"Good." Relief tinged his voice. "I know you're a by-the-book agent; that's why I chose you."

He ended the call, and Korine pocketed her phone, his words echoing in her ears. Director Bellows had no idea how badly she'd messed up before.

She couldn't mess up again.

CHAPTER THREE

The Keeper raised her hands and stared at the blood dotting her palms and fingernails.

His blood.

She hadn't meant to get it on her. To taint herself with his evil.

But she hadn't been able to resist. His blood meant he was dying. Suffering.

As he should.

She tossed the gavel into her bag. She'd take it to her secret place later.

Hands shaking, she turned on the hot water and shoved her hands beneath the spray. For some reason, she didn't want to wash off the blood.

But she had to.

The police had found his body. They'd investigate. Hunt down his enemies as if they needed to get justice for his killer.

Bitterness swelled in her chest.

He deserved what he'd gotten. No one on this earth would mourn his loss. Except maybe his wife. And she was just as bad as him. She should have stood up to the man and convinced him it was criminal to allow so many predators to walk free.

The crimson blood mingled with the warm water and swirled around and around like a river in the sink before it disappeared down the drain. Her nails looked ragged, stained, and dirty.

A sardonic laugh caught in her throat. Tomorrow, she'd get a manicure. Then no one would ever know.

Heart racing, she closed her eyes and relived the past few hours. The adrenaline rush from knowing she was finally getting justice. The way his voice had quivered with fear at the last moment. The way he'd begged as if he'd thought that would make a difference.

A laugh bubbled inside her as she envisioned the shock on the bastard's face when she'd tied him down. He hadn't believed she would actually hurt him. Had pegged her as a weak female.

He'd finally understood the depth of his mistake.

He was just as bad as the evil men he allowed back on the streets.

For a moment when she'd watched his life force flow from him, she'd felt powerful. Not helpless anymore. Not wounded. Not invisible.

Or alone.

Breathing easy for the first time in months and filled with optimism for the future, she dried her hands.

The stories awaited. All those people who sympathized with her pain.

Who'd understand what she'd done if she told them.

But she didn't have time for that now.

It was time to go to work.

CHAPTER FOUR

"What do you think that bloody SS means?" Officer Leeks asked.

Hatcher didn't want to freak the young guy out, but a mark like this was symbolic and suggested premeditation. It also suggested that this crime was not an isolated murder.

That there would be others.

"Agent McGee?"

"It's the justice symbol," Hatcher said.

A car engine rumbled from the street. Hopefully, the FBI evidence response team—ERT—and medical examiner.

He turned and spotted a black sedan rolling into the cul-de-sac where he'd parked. *Damn, not them. Probably Korine Davenport.*

Knowing he had to play nice and ignore the fact that they'd slept together—and that despite his wife's death, he'd fantasized about having her again—he walked toward the vehicle. If this wasn't his new partner and someone had gotten wind of the murder and come to gawk, he'd make sure they didn't contaminate the crime scene or take pictures and blast them all over social media before the police informed the family.

Moonlight shimmered, barely visible through the dark clouds, but just enough for him to get a look at the driver as she climbed from her car.

Definitely female.

Long legs that seemed endless appeared. The dark pants and jacket she wore suggested that she was an agent. His gut pinched as she slammed the car door and started toward him.

That fiery red hair that had tortured him in his dreams escaped some kind of clasp that was supposed to hold her hair back but failed. Five six, slender, with an angular face that looked feminine in spite of her square jaw, she should have looked all businesslike.

Except he knew every inch of skin beneath that boring suit, every inch from her voluptuous breasts and coral-colored nipples down to the butterfly tattoo on her inner thigh.

Fuck. He had no business remembering that.

Irritated that he had, he clamped his jaw tight and braced himself to deal with her. Hopefully, this partnership would be short-term. Wyatt would come back. Unless Wyatt refused to work with him.

He wouldn't blame him if he did.

Korine picked her way through the brush, her eyes widening as she looked up at him. Even in the dark, he noticed her lift her chin stubbornly, as if she knew their interlude had been a mistake. Or maybe she was needy like Felicia had been and wanted more.

It didn't matter.

He had nothing to give. Especially to her, the woman who'd torn him away from his wife when she'd needed him the most.

Anger coiled inside him. Bellows had probably told her to watch *him.*

Fuck that. He was the lead here, and he'd make sure she knew it. He extended his hand, determined to maintain a professional demeanor. "Agent Davenport, good to see you again. I just took a look at the body."

Her hand felt small and delicate as she shook his, and reminded him of how erotic her fingers had felt around his cock.

She tensed, as if irritated he hadn't waited on her. "I got here as fast as I could. You want to show me the crime scene and catch me up?"

He gestured toward the dock and indicated she should go first. "Woman in that cottage called it in. Victim is a white male, fifties, bludgeoned to death."

"Bludgeoned?"

"ME will have to confirm that was the COD, but that's the way it appears. Haven't found the murder weapon yet."

"ID?"

"No ID yet either."

A gusty wind picked up, shaking the trees, and she shivered as if chilled. "Then we should get to work."

He didn't like the way she said *we*. This partnership was temporary, not long-term.

And he refused to take orders from her.

He folded his arms, the breeze from the ocean swirling sand around their feet and bringing her sweet aroma to him—lavender. He'd tried to erase it from his mind, but it had tortured him anyway. He'd even bought a damn lavender-scented candle and burned it while he drank.

He'd get rid of it tonight. Throw it out with the booze.

She brushed a strand of hair from her face and stared at him expectantly.

Annoyed but anxious to focus on work, he led the way to the body. Officer Leeks looked as shaky as the railing he gripped, as if he was barely hanging on to his dinner.

Hatcher quickly made the introductions. "You've been very helpful in securing the crime scene," he told Leeks. "Why don't you wait in the cove for the evidence response team and the medical examiner?"

The man looked visibly relieved, then practically ran down the dock.

Korine frowned. "What's wrong with him?"

"Squeamish, I guess. Probably his first murder." Hatcher lifted his head and pinned her with a stare that was half dare.

Her gaze flickered with understanding, then amusement. "Good thing you don't have to worry about that from me."

He arched a brow. "Good thing."

She'd been tough in training and had experience with sex crimes, but this was a dead body. The blood and smell alone might get to her.

But she showed no sign of it as they approached the victim.

Seagulls swooped over the edge of the water, pigeons flocking again.

Seemingly unbothered, she waved them away with one hand, her gaze darting to the water and beach, then to the victim. She halted, her posture ramrod straight, then pulled a small flashlight from her jacket pocket and shined it on the body.

He almost taunted her about getting sick when she'd just criticized the other cop.

But the stark expression on her face made him pause. "What?" he asked.

"I know who he is," she said bluntly.

He glanced at the body, then back at her. "You know the victim?"

"Not personally, but I recognize him." This time, she pinned him with a challenging look. "You're telling me you don't?"

The derision in her voice made him grit his teeth, and he studied the man's face. Flat nose. Long chin. Split lip and bruises all over his face.

"Just spit it out," he said, his voice tight. "Who is he?"

She leaned forward for a moment, raking the flashlight beam over the dead man's face. A second later, she looked up at him, her expression unreadable.

"His name is Lester Wadsworth." She paused, both brows arched. "*Judge* Lester Wadsworth."

The name sifted through the cobwebs in Hatcher's brain. The media coverage surrounding the recent case the judge had presided over had garnered national news. Hatcher had watched bits and pieces of the news stories from a bar stool through blurry eyes and a blurry brain with his best friend, Jack Daniels.

"He presided over the River Street Rapist trial," Hatcher said.

Davenport nodded, her look full of derision. "He dismissed the case on a technicality so the bastard is free to rape again."

Which had triggered mountains of protestors and media attention on the victims who'd suffered horribly at the man's hands. Victims who felt the justice system had failed.

Maybe one of them had killed the judge. That would fit with the justice symbol painted on his forehead.

◆ ◆ ◆

Sympathy for the judge failed Korine. She'd not only followed the trial but also been first on the scene when one of the rapist's victims had been found.

She'd never forget it. She had just transferred from Atlanta to be closer to her mother.

She and her partner at the time had been called to an alley where a young woman had been discovered near the dumpster out back of a local bar, beaten and bloody, nearly unconscious.

The young coed, Andi Rosten, had been hysterical. It had taken an hour to calm her down enough to describe the attack and her attacker.

Later she'd fallen into a deep depression and had tried to commit suicide. Now she lived with her parents and struggled daily to regain control of her life.

Knowing the man who'd hurt her was behind bars would have gone a long way toward Andi's recovery. With him at large, she was obviously terrified he'd track her down and rape her again—or kill her for testifying against him as he'd threatened.

"I remember the trial, very emotional. That reporter, Marilyn Ellis, stirred up panic with her story about the rapist's release," Hatcher said in a gruff voice. He gestured toward the intertwined SS. "The symbol of justice is significant."

Korine's heart pounded. "The killer wants us to know that he exacted justice because we failed." It also meant that each person affected by one of the cases the judge tried had to be questioned.

And treated like a suspect.

That didn't sit well in her gut.

She stooped down, aimed her flashlight on the man's face, and examined it. "Did you find the murder weapon?"

He shook his head. "You think the killer used a hammer?"

She shrugged. "Maybe. Could have been a rock." She leaned closer and with a gloved hand, traced a finger around a dark circular bruise. "Although the shape and size is larger than a hammer head . . . it might have been a gavel. Maybe one of the judge's. I heard he has a collection."

"We'll look for it," Hatcher said.

The wind picked up, swirling the acrid odor of death and blood through the air. A boat puttered somewhere in the distance. The clouds shifted, covering the moon, leaving the area almost pitch-black.

The sound of cars parking in the circle at the entrance to the cove alerted him to the fact that help had arrived.

"We'll have to look at all of Judge Wadsworth's enemies," Hatcher said. "That could be a long list."

"The killer might not even be on it," Korine said. "More than a hundred protestors gathered outside the courthouse during that trial." Andi had definitely been in the courtroom that day. So had the two other victims.

Other women had come from all over the South to support the victims and protest. Any one of them could have decided to get revenge. So could have a family member, friend, husband, or boyfriend.

"I'll ask Cat to pull the security footage at the trial and start sifting through the feed and names."

Cat Landon was an analyst at the bureau, a quirky young woman with a photographic memory. She was also a computer whiz and had a criminology background. Korine had met her and admired her work. Both obsessed with death and with cold cases, they'd connected and shared drinks and dinner a couple of times.

"We'll need a list of all the judge's cases, his enemies, and any hate mail he received." She lifted the judge's jacket sleeve, exposing abrasions on his wrists. "Looks like he was tied up. He's a big man. Somehow the killer overpowered him, maybe had a gun or Taser, or he could have drugged him."

Hatcher shifted. "Means whoever it was got close to him. Maybe the judge even knew the unsub."

Korine snapped a photograph of the body, then took a close-up of his bloody face and his wrists. "At the courthouse, the judge was always guarded, surrounded by cops. A security detail followed him home at night."

Hatcher snapped a picture of the dock, then pointed to the walkway, where blood dotted the rotting wood. "This is not the kill site. The unsub dragged him out here for a reason. When we find the place he was murdered, we might learn more."

Korine scanned the area. Why had the unsub dumped his body in plain sight instead of pushing him into the marshy water and letting the tide carry him out to sea? Or why hadn't he left the judge where he was murdered?

"Someone wanted him to be found," she said, the truth dawning. "But why here?"

An odd look twisted Hatcher's face. "Good question." He furrowed his brow. "You worked sex crimes. Do you know any of the River Street Rapist victims?"

Korine sighed. "I answered a call to one of the victims and took her statement."

"Maybe you should excuse yourself from the case," Hatcher suggested.

"I did my job. It wasn't personal." Although taking Andi Rosten's statement had been grueling. "If you want to know if I was upset over the judge's ruling, of course I was. But I joined the bureau because I believe in the system." If she'd killed anyone, it would have been the rapist. But after the trial he'd disappeared.

He was probably lying low until the dust settled, then he'd stalk another victim and continue his reign of terror.

Voices sounded, and members of the ERT walked toward them. Another man wearing a lab coat followed.

"Judge Wadsworth also tried a guns dealer," Hatcher said, cutting into her thoughts. "Put him away for life. Dealer could have hired someone to off the judge as revenge."

"Why not shoot him? It would have been faster." She retrieved her pocket notepad and made a list of what they needed to do. "Whoever did this wanted him to suffer. And if he—or she—used a gavel, it was a statement just as the justice symbol was."

"Good point." Hatcher greeted the ERT and medical examiner.

The gray-haired man in the lab coat offered his hand. "Dr. Dillard Patton, Medical Examiner."

Korine shook it and introduced herself. "I'm Agent McGee's new partner."

"For now," Hatcher said bluntly, earning him a curious look from Patton and a frown from Korine.

A middle-aged, heavyset guy introduced himself as Supervisory Special Agent Roger Cummings, the lead of the ERT. Two agents with him were Tammy Drummond and Trace Bellamy.

"What do we know so far?" Cummings asked.

Korine filled them in on the judge's suspected identity.

"My guess is he's been dead since last night," Dr. Patton said. "The unsub must have kept him somewhere then dumped him this evening."

"We need to find the murder weapon," Korine said. "Get someone to search the water. Killer could have thrown it in."

Hatcher shoved a hand through his tousled black hair as he glanced at the cottage in the center of the cove.

Korine had tried not to look at him. She didn't need a reminder of how handsome the damn man was. Something about his intense, brooding masculinity drew her like a siren's call.

Those mocha-colored eyes looked pain filled and soulful and dangerous at the same time. His big body was dangerous to her, too. Thick muscles strained against his shirt, which hid washboard abs beneath. Sex appeal at its most potent.

Instead, she scanned the property, looking for places a predator could hide. Judge Wadsworth wasn't a small man. Dead, he would have seemed even heavier.

It took someone strong to haul him across the dock.

The ERT needed to search the sand, the shells, and the seagrass for drag marks and forensics. Maybe they'd find footprints . . .

A gray cottage sat to the left of the one the caller lived in, and a white one stood to the right, although they appeared deserted. The cove was named Sunset Cove because of its magnificent sunsets, but the sun had long faded. Shrouded by palm trees and sea oats, and bathed in darkness, the houses looked spooky.

"Do your thing here," Hatcher said to the ME and ERT. "I need to question the woman who reported the body."

He'd said *I*, but Korine ignored it. He obviously didn't want her along, but he was stuck with her. And she would pull her weight.

She wanted to hear what the caller had to say. Maybe she'd witnessed something helpful and could give them a lead.

♦ ♦ ♦

A boat puttered by, barely discernible in the dim light, slowed, then sped up. Hatcher watched it disappear into the inlet and wondered whether the killer could have come in by boat instead of by car. If the killer was in that particular boat, he might be watching to see that the body had been found.

But if the judge's murder was related to the River Street Rapist, why dump the body here instead of River Street, where the victims had been snatched?

Hatcher angled his head toward Dr. Patton. "I'm assuming cause of death was from head trauma."

Dr. Patton glanced up from where he was examining the corpse. "I'd say so, but I'll do a full autopsy and let you know time of death, COD, and anything else I find."

"Be sure to check for drugs," Korine said. "We need to know if he was subdued before he was beaten."

"I always run a tox report," Dr. Patton said, irritation lining his face as if he didn't need Korine to tell him how to do his job.

Hatcher thanked him, then turned to go to the cottage. As much as he dreaded it, he had to talk to Tinsley Jensen, find out how she was involved in this.

It was too coincidental that she'd been a victim in one crime and was now a witness to another.

He didn't like coincidences.

Korine joined him as he strode up the seashell-lined walkway to the cottage. Shells and gravel crunched beneath his boots. Even though he was at least eight inches taller than his new partner, she kept up with him.

Just like she had in bed. He'd never met a woman so adventurous and passionate . . . or so tender that she'd made him want to hold her forever.

Not even his wife had stirred that kind of emotion. Theirs had been an odd match, one shaped by too much booze and her lies . . .

Fish-shaped wind chimes that resembled sea glass dangled from the porch awning, dancing in the breeze and tinkling softly, dragging him back to the case. A hand-painted sign crafted from driftwood hung on the door and read, THIS IS MY HAPPY PLACE.

He doubted Tinsley Jensen was happy.

White Adirondack rockers stood vigil on the porch, facing the ocean, offering a reprieve from the sun during the hot part of the day and a view of the beach and sunset.

It looked peaceful and relaxing, as if the owner were here on vacation.

Only he knew better.

"The caller lives here?" Korine asked.

"Yes."

"What exactly did she see?"

He inhaled sharply, then knocked on the door. "We'll find out. But I should warn you: she may not be amenable to talking to me."

Korine scowled. "Why not?"

"Because she was a victim in the last case I worked. And her kidnapper got away."

Recognition dawned in Korine's expressive eyes. "Tinsley Jensen?"

He gave a nod.

A voice echoed from the opposite side of the door, and the covering for the peephole slid open. "Who's there?"

Korine stepped up so Tinsley could see her through the peephole. "We're here about your nine-one-one call."

The door squeaked open a fraction, and Tinsley's pale, frightened face appeared. Anger followed, streaking through her eyes and slamming him in the gut with its brutal honesty.

"Tinsley?" Hatcher's voice sounded rough, unsure. Guilty.

"I don't want to talk to you, Hatcher." She started to close the door in his face, but Korine caught it with her foot.

Korine flashed her badge. "Then talk to me," she said softly. "There's a dead man out there. We need to know exactly what you saw."

Tinsley pressed her lips into a thin line, then gestured toward Korine. "Okay, I'll talk to you." She shot Hatcher a look of disdain. "But not him."

Hatcher folded his arms. He wanted to argue. To declare that he was lead on this investigation. That Korine was a damn rookie.

But he kept his mouth shut.

CHAPTER FIVE

Compassion for Tinsley filled Korine. She couldn't imagine living every day terrified that a sadistic man like the unsub who'd held the young woman hostage might return to hurt her again.

No doubt Hatcher harbored guilt over that.

The fact that Hatcher's deceased wife and this woman had been friends complicated matters more. If Tinsley knew about Korine's night with Hatcher, she probably wouldn't want to talk to her either.

Tinsley stepped aside, and although she'd said she didn't want to talk to Hatcher, she allowed them both entry.

Korine scanned the foyer—a distressed white hutch held shoes, umbrellas, beach bags, and sun hats, all signs of home and a relaxing getaway.

Apparently, though, the woman never left the house to enjoy that ocean or the sand and sun and beach.

She and Hatcher followed Tinsley to a small den that looked cozy and quaint. A seashell lamp and photos of the beach, sea turtles, crabs, and the sunset added to the beach theme. A wall above her desk held sketches of the trees on the island that had been hand carved with images of soldiers who'd died in the area.

At odds with the serene blue-and-white decor, built-in shelves held dozens of books and magazines on the historic graveyards, ghosts, and hauntings in Savannah. Another book featured stories about the

Day of the Dead celebrated in Mexico. After Tinsley's abduction, the Feds had speculated that the Skull had adopted his disguise from the sugar skulls used in the Day of the Dead traditions. Although with the island's famous Skull's Crossing, where human skulls had been found mired in the marshland years ago, and three more skulls found recently, it was possible that the unsub had used the skull image because of that case.

Or that the unsub might have killed the victims, dumped their bodies in the ocean, and the skulls had floated to the surface after Hurricane Matthew.

A pair of binoculars sat on a table by the window that overlooked the cove, as if perched there for quick use. A picture window also overlooked the ocean, although sheers were drawn, blocking the view.

Tinsley's way of keeping anyone from seeing into her private world from which she kept everyone locked out.

The den adjoined a kitchen with a breakfast bar and island, providing an open-concept design.

A parakeet was perched in a birdcage in the corner. The bird was so motionless and quiet that it almost didn't look real. The door to the cage stood ajar, but the bird remained inside.

Tinsley reached for a china cup filled with what Korine guessed was tea and took a sip as she sank onto the sofa.

The cup and saucer rattled in her hands as she set it back on the wicker coffee table. "So what I saw was real?"

"I'm afraid so," Korine said. "Tell us exactly what happened. Everything you saw. What you heard."

Tinsley wrapped her arms around her waist as if she needed to hold herself together. A petite blonde with bangs framing enormous violet-blue eyes, she was as beautiful and as delicate as one of the sea-glass treasures one might find washed up on the shore after the storm. Yet she was also frail, with dark circles shadowing her haunted eyes.

"I was on the computer when I heard a noise," Tinsley said. "I checked all the windows and doors, then looked outside and saw a figure dragging something along the dock."

"Could you tell if it was a man or a woman?" Korine asked.

She shook her head. "Not really, the sun had already set. It was too dark."

"Did he come from the street?" Hatcher asked.

Tinsley massaged her temple with long, slender fingers. "I don't know."

Korine offered her an encouraging smile. "Did you hear anything? A car? A boat maybe?"

"I told you I don't know. I was on the computer and listening to music when I heard the sound." She reached for the tea again with hands that trembled.

"Where exactly was the figure when you saw him?" Korine asked. "Near the entrance to the dock or the cul-de-sac?"

"He was just there," Tinsley cried. "I can't tell you anything else."

Korine squeezed Tinsley's arm. "I understand this is difficult, especially after all you've been through. It was brave of you to call the police."

Tinsley's face blanched. "You know who I am?" Then she made a sardonic sound. "Of course you do. I'm famous, aren't I?"

Korine understood the anguish in the young woman's voice. As a child, she'd hated when people recognized her from the news stories about her father's murder. "I study crimes. That's how I recognized the victim. His name is Judge Lester Wadsworth. He ruled over the—"

"River Street Rapist trial," Tinsley said, her voice shocked.

"That's right," Korine said. "Did you follow the trial?"

Tinsley clamped her teeth over her bottom lip. "I watch the news. I keep hoping that . . ."

"That the man who took you will be found," Hatcher filled in.

Tinsley gave Hatcher a wary look but nodded.

"Is there anything about the figure you saw outside that seemed familiar?" Korine asked, steering them back to this case. "Anything that stood out?"

Tinsley rubbed her temple again, her eyes darting around nervously. "Not that I recall."

Korine hated to pressure her, but sometimes witnesses forgot details until they were pushed to remember. "Did he have a limp? Was he short? Tall? Heavy?"

"I don't know, it was too far away to tell," Tinsley said.

Korine offered her a sympathetic smile. "I understand you don't want to come to the station, but we could bring mug shots here for you to look at."

Tinsley lurched up and motioned to the door. "I told you I didn't see his face. And I don't want to look at any mug shots. Now please leave."

Korine glanced at Hatcher, who shrugged. She slipped a business card onto the coffee table. "All right, but my work and private number are on there. Call me if you think of anything, or if . . . you just want to talk."

Tinsley's gaze met hers, the pain and fear so deep that it nearly stole Korine's breath.

Tinsley rushed them to the door, a desperate fear in her jittery movements. Although the parakeet remained inside the cage, it had hopped to the edge near the open door, feathers ruffled.

"We'll find him," Hatcher said as he and Korine stepped onto the porch.

Tinsley's only response was to slam the door in their faces. The sound of half a dozen locks being clicked and shifted echoed from the inside.

CHAPTER SIX

Fog fell like ghostly fingers across the cove, misty rain splashing onto the sand and palm trees, spreading into the mercurial water of the Atlantic as if the shadow of Tinsley's past had followed her to Sunset Cove.

She couldn't escape it, no matter how far she'd run. And she *had* run, dammit.

She paused by her parakeet's cage, reached a finger inside, and stroked his head gently. When she'd finally come home, she'd been relieved to know her neighbor had taken care of Mr. Jingles. But she'd churned over the fact that she was keeping the bird locked in a cage. During her abduction, she'd learned what it felt like to be trapped. That night she'd moved Mr. Jingles with her to the cottage and opened his door, giving the bird its freedom.

Mr. Jingles used to talk and sing tunes from TV commercials all the time—the reason she'd given him the name. Now, he sat quietly and stared at her as if he were angry because she'd abandoned him for so long. She'd hoped allowing him to fly around the house freely would soften his attitude, but he'd yet to venture outside the cage.

This place—the cove with its spectacular sunsets, the beach, the view from her cottage—was supposed to give her solace and peace. It was supposed to help her recovery process. To make her forget the helplessness and pain she'd experienced and move on with her life.

Yet tonight the ocean, vast and wide, loomed beneath the inky sky like an endless tomb of nothingness without light.

All because a dead body had been left on the dock in front of her house.

She closed her eyes and envisioned the beauty of the twinkling stars and the vibrant reds and oranges and yellows of the sun as it faded each night.

When she opened them, the dreary blackness outside chilled her to the bone. The sound of her own screams the night she'd been abducted reverberated in her ears and drowned out any pleasant sounds, a reminder that evil had stolen what constituted her normal life at twenty-nine.

Afraid she was bordering on psychotic with her morose thoughts, she turned to her blog. At her therapist's advice, she'd started journaling her thoughts about her abduction, her attacker, and the fact that he'd escaped. Surprisingly her entries had incited others to share their stories of being victimized and of the injustices that had cost them their sense of security, their happiness, and . . . their future.

She'd named the blog *Heart & Soul* because that's what she did—she poured out her heart and soul in the words that filled the screen. She'd been surprised at the interest the site had drawn.

The blog had brought her friends, a support group, a way to not feel lonely when she was a prisoner in her own house—and very much alone.

The photo of the sandy shore dotted with broken shells and sea glass to her right made an ache stir deep within her. She wanted to be part of the world again, to comb the shore and search through the broken shells and find the one or two that had survived the tides undamaged. To recover the bits of sea glass that she'd collected as a child and craft them into jewelry to wear as a reminder that beauty still existed in the world.

She wanted to feel the sunshine on her face and hear the children's laughter as they chased the waves, not be an outsider watching through locked windows and closed doors.

Rain drizzled down, pattering the tin roof and splashing raindrops against the weathered glass windows.

Not that it mattered whether the sun was shining or the heat was unbearable, or whether it was cold outside or there was a hurricane.

Not when she was trapped inside these walls.

It was a prison she'd made for herself—to keep safe.

Only she didn't feel safe. Or alive.

Each day blended in with the others—the monotonous routine of climbing from bed for morning coffee, then checking the news to see how many innocents had become victims, how many criminals had escaped, how many times the system had screwed up and another man who'd hurt someone walked the streets, free and able to hunt again.

Each time she posted to *Heart & Soul*, she was flooded with tales from soul sisters who understood and shared her fears and pain. Ones who wanted justice for the innocents as much as she did.

She inhaled and took a sip of tea, then settled down to write. Her fingers moved over the keyboard, and she lost herself in pouring out her turmoil:

I want to leave the house, to walk along the surf, to sift my toes through the sand and feel the gentle waves lapping at my feet, the sun warming my skin, and the breeze ruffling my hair.

But I am trapped. A hostage who may never know that freedom again.

He kept me inside a cage like an animal. Inside a small room with dark walls that had been scratched by others he'd caught. Each one of us marked the days we were held with fingernail claws into that wall, as if we were animals ourselves.

Little did he know that we were—I was—simply sharpening my claws and waiting on a time I could use them on him and escape.

But even when I did, he got away. And I was trapped again.

This time I locked myself away.

I mark the wall with the days—ninety-two now—that I have hidden in this place. Too afraid to step foot outside the door. Too afraid to walk on the beach or venture into town to shop or go to a restaurant to have a meal.

Too afraid of dying to really live.

Yes, I am an agoraphobic.

While he is running free, I'm chained to him, to his voice, his touch, the things he did to me. To the memories that choke me and sometimes make me want to die.

The only way I escape is in my head and my dreams.

Yet too many times I am tormented by the nightmares, and he is chasing me again.

It will never end.

Unless she ended it.

Five minutes later, responses from her followers flooded the screen. Some were sympathetic and offered hope. Others poured out their own horrid experiences. Two women had been victimized by the River Street Rapist, who'd terrorized Savannah's college coeds for the past year. Another at the hand of her own husband. Then a post from a mother who'd killed her boyfriend to stop him from molesting her son.

Most of the comments were anonymous.

The victims connected and didn't need names.

Sometimes it hurt more to read the other women's sorrowful accounts than it did to think of the inhuman way *He* had treated her. She didn't know his real name and refused to say the name he'd called himself.

She slipped open the desk drawer and stared at the knife inside. The ivory handle felt cold. Slick. Foreign. Yet the blade comforted her as she ran her finger over the sharp edge.

Sweat beaded on her neck. Her hand trembled.

Relief was only seconds away.

She envisioned raising it to her wrist and slicing the pale skin. Blood would flow, freeing her of the burden of living each day when she wasn't really living at all.

It would feel too good to be free of the pain.

To know that *He* wasn't keeping her hostage.

But killing herself wouldn't be killing him. It would mean *He'd* won.

She shoved the drawer closed.

A light outside the window flickered in the dark, distant and foggy in the rain. Pulse hammering, she stood and moved to the window.

The police—Hatcher—and that other agent had left.

But someone was out there. More police or investigators? Had Hatcher returned?

Or was it *Him*?

Terror made adrenaline shoot through her veins, and she grabbed the knife from the drawer. She wouldn't use it on herself.

But if he came after her, she would use it on him.

CHAPTER SEVEN

Hatcher scanned the area as he veered onto the mile-long drive to Judge Wadsworth's house. Live oaks dripping with Spanish moss flanked the drive, the giant branches of the trees curling and bending as if linking arms across the plush acreage to protect its residents.

Yet the Spanish moss looked brittle and dry, like an old woman's scraggly hair, casting an eeriness to the area and reminding him of the legend of Skull's Crossing, the place where he'd lost his wife.

Rumors claimed that two women were murdered there years ago, their bodies dumped in the ocean for the sharks to finish off. Yet the tides had tossed pieces of their remains in the marsh, drawing the gators as well. The women's souls were caught between land and water, in limbo between heaven and hell. They haunted both the sea and the marsh, their cries echoing at low tide.

In the past months, three more skulls had been found at the same place—three that had never been identified. Three suspected to be victims of the Skull.

The wind whistled off the sea, the dry brush and sea oats a testament to winter and a reminder of death.

But the judge's body hadn't been left at Skull's Crossing.

Instead, it had been left on the dock in clear sight of Tinsley Jensen's cottage.

But why? The judge had nothing to do with Tinsley's case or the fact that her abductor had escaped. But it had to have been left there for a reason . . .

He heaved a breath, then climbed from his SUV, the loamy scent of the marshland behind the judge's house assaulting him. Or maybe it was the scent of death.

The sound of a car motor rumbling echoed behind him, and he stood by his SUV with arms folded and waited for his new partner to climb from her vehicle. He didn't want to work with Korine. But he had no choice.

The breeze snatched a strand of her hair and sent it flying around her face. She swiped it away from her cheek as if annoyed at the intrusion. Her gaze skated over the house and property, but instead of looking impressed, she showed no reaction.

A gray Mercedes was parked in the circular drive in front of the mansion. Through a window in the detached brick garage, he spotted a BMW convertible.

"Wonder where the judge's Lincoln is," Korine said.

He arched a brow. While he'd buried himself in the bottle, she'd been honing her skills and studying cases big time. "You did your research?"

She barely gave him a glance as she started toward the house. "I told you I followed the River Street Rapist trial." Her grim tone matched the severe frown on her face. "His wife drives the Mercedes, his son, Theo, the Beamer. He also has a tech-savvy daughter, Serena, who lives in Savannah."

Seashells crunched beneath his boots as he followed her up the path to the front door. She paused before ringing the bell. "Wife Annette is known for being meek, submissive."

He bit back a comment. She was showing off, but any information she had about the family could save time.

Besides, he'd have to pick his battles. He didn't want her tattling to Bellows that he was difficult to work with.

"Any more insight?" he asked.

In spite of trying to maintain a professional tone, he realized he'd sounded petulant.

She raised a brow. "Son is a bit of a rebel. Some kind of artist, I think."

"And the daughter?"

"Ironically, she created a phone app to alert people of crimes in progress. She also attended the trial for the River Street Rapist. When the bastard was released, the press tried to interview her. But she refused to talk to them."

"She didn't defend her father?"

Korine shook her head. "She gave no comment."

Which meant she could have agreed or disagreed with her father's ruling.

Korine rang the doorbell. Hatcher straightened to his full six two and braced himself to deliver the bad news about the judge's death.

He hated this part of the job.

But he had to be alert and study the wife's reaction. She might be weak and submissive, but everyone had their limits.

If she'd reached hers, she might have snapped and killed her husband.

Korine inhaled a deep breath. Although she'd disagreed with the judge's ruling, she hadn't wanted to see the man dead.

She would have preferred for him to apologize to the River Street Rapist's victims and do something to make sure the bastard didn't hurt anyone else.

The door opened, and a woman wearing a maid's uniform and nametag reading "Hilda" greeted them. Korine introduced them. "We need to talk to Mrs. Wadsworth."

Hilda adjusted the collar of her uniform. "May I tell her what this is about?"

Korine softened her tone. "Actually it's personal, but it's very important."

Hilda motioned for them to follow her. "I'll tell her to meet you in the parlor." She escorted them to a room decorated with antiques, oriental rugs, and expensive paintings. The heavy velvet drapes were drawn, the dark paneling and colors of the room regal but oppressive.

The maid gestured toward the sitting area. "Have a seat. I'll be right back." Her heels clicked on the marble foyer as she hurried toward the winding staircase.

Curious, Korine crossed the room to the corner where a glass curio cabinet held the judge's collection of gavels, some made of expensive wood with gold trim, some bearing intricate carving. The front row showcased plaques correlating with gavels that had been used in the judge's most famous trials.

It didn't appear that any were missing.

"Anything else you want to share before we interview her?" Hatcher asked.

Korine tensed. "Mrs. Wadsworth appeared to be the doting wife on her husband's arm at social functions, but she avoided the press. One reporter speculated that she was afraid of the judge."

"I am not afraid of him."

The woman's voice startled Korine, and she realized the judge's wife was standing in the doorway. She looked elegant in black pants and a gold jacket, her diamonds glittering. She wore her brown hair in a perfectly coiffured bob and her nails were manicured, her makeup flawless.

Mrs. Wadsworth tugged at the neckline of her turtleneck, and Korine thought she spotted a bruise on the woman's neck. The judge's wife had frequently worn high-necked blouses and long sleeves when she'd been photographed. Maybe the rumors were true.

"Is that why you insisted on seeing me?" Her sharp tone reeked of disapproval. "You're chasing gossip about my husband and me?"

Damn. She'd just screwed up. "No, and I apologize for my insensitive remark," Korine said.

Hatcher offered his hand and introduced them both, obviously trying to smooth over Korine's gaffe.

The woman didn't look appeased. Instead, Mrs. Wadsworth speared them both with a condescending look. "If you're here about one of my husband's trials or cases, I have no comment. He doesn't discuss his work with me."

A muscle twitched in Hatcher's jaw. "I'm sorry, ma'am, but it's important that you speak with us."

Mrs. Wadsworth toyed with the gold chain around her neck. "Then by all means, come in and sit down." A wary look tugged at the woman's face as she claimed a leather wing chair in front of the fireplace and folded her hands in her lap. "All right. Now what is so important?"

Korine gestured for Hatcher to speak. She'd already alienated the woman.

"When was the last time you saw or spoke to your husband?" Hatcher asked.

Mrs. Wadsworth twisted her fingers together. "I . . . don't understand. Why do you want to know?"

Hatcher crossed his arms. "Please just answer the question, ma'am."

She sucked in a sharp breath. "He phoned and left a message with Hilda about seven last night. Said he'd be working late."

"Was that unusual?" Korine asked.

Mrs. Wadsworth shook her head. "He often stayed late to review trials, transcripts." She lifted her chin. "Why are you asking?"

Hatcher shifted. "Were you aware that people were upset over his recent case and the fact that he released a suspected rapist?"

She shot up from her chair. "Of course. I do read the paper and watch the news." She straightened her jacket. "It wasn't his fault that the lawyers didn't do their jobs." She gestured toward the door. "Now, I have a headache. I'd appreciate it if you left."

Hatcher lowered his voice. "I'm sorry, but we can't do that. Not yet."

"Why not?" Mrs. Wadsworth snapped.

Korine took the initiative and coaxed the woman to sit again. "Because we have bad news. I'm sorry to have to tell you this, Mrs. Wadsworth, but your husband is dead."

Mrs. Wadsworth's face turned ashen, and she pressed one diamond-studded hand to her chest. "What? That can't be true."

Korine slid into a seat beside her. "I'm afraid it is, ma'am."

"What happened?" Mrs. Wadsworth asked in a strained voice.

Korine gave her a sympathetic smile, although there really was no way to soften the blow.

"Tell me," the woman shrieked.

Korine cleared her throat. "We don't have the official autopsy report, but we believe he was murdered."

Hatcher paused to give the woman time to absorb the news. Her eyes widened in shock for a millisecond. But the shock quickly faded, and she wet her lips with her tongue.

"How did it happen? Do you know who killed him?"

"We're investigating—that's why we're here," Hatcher said.

Mrs. Wadsworth angled her head toward Korine, then back to him. "I wish I could help, but I can't."

Hatcher patted her hand, and she flinched, a telltale sign that the bruise on her neck was probably just as he expected—the judge had a heavy hand with his wife.

Anger coiled inside Hatcher's gut. He had no tolerance for a man beating up on a woman.

He'd have Cat check hospital and doctor records as well as police reports to see whether any domestic-abuse issues had ever been raised.

"Considering your husband's position on the bench, I'm sure he made enemies," Hatcher said. "Do you know of anyone in particular who would hurt him?"

She settled a solemn gaze on him. "He made enemies, but he didn't bring that part of his work home with him."

Maybe not. But he took his anger and frustrations out on his wife.

"Did he ever mention being threatened?" Korine asked.

The judge's wife pushed up from her chair, her breathing unsteady. "I already told you, we didn't discuss work. I'm sure his personal assistant at the courthouse will be able to assist you."

Footsteps sounded, then a man's voice. "Mother?"

A second later, a thin man in his midtwenties appeared, his hair styled and his designer shirt, slacks, and polished Italian loafers expensive. He looked like a male model.

"In here, Theo." Mrs. Wadsworth fiddled with the neck of her shirt as her son entered the room. "The police are here."

"I know. Hilda phoned me." Theo froze in the doorway, one hand gripping the edge. "You're with the police?"

"FBI." Korine stepped forward and introduced them.

Theo glanced at his mother. "What's going on, Mom?"

Hatcher wanted to pull the guy outside and question him before his mother broke the news, but he was walking a fine line. She didn't give him time to protest before she blurted out the reason for their visit.

"Your father was murdered," she said in a choked whisper.

Emotions flashed in Theo's eyes.

"We are sorry for your loss." Hatcher paused a second, then fisted his hands by his sides. "We were just asking your mother if she knew anyone who would want to hurt your father."

"I told them your father and I didn't discuss business," Mrs. Wadsworth said quickly.

Hatcher shifted. "Theo, do you know anyone who would kill your father?"

Theo pulled at his chin. "A lot of people hated my father. People he put behind bars. Victims who didn't get the justice they wanted. Families of those victims." Theo drummed his fingers on his thigh. "His personal assistant, Gretta Breer, should be able to give you a list of his enemies."

Mrs. Wadsworth had also pointed them to the assistant—maybe mother and son had practiced their stories.

Korine offered Theo a sympathetic look. "When did you last talk to your father or see him?"

A wariness settled in Theo's eyes. "You aren't implying that my mother or I had something to do with Dad's death, are you?"

Hatcher maintained a neutral expression, while Korine shrugged. "You know how the system works. We have to question everyone who knew your father, get alibis, eliminate the family."

Theo studied them for a long minute, his posture rigid. "My father and I spoke yesterday morning on the phone, just briefly. I had an appointment and told him I'd talk to him later."

"*Did* you talk to him later?" Korine asked.

Theo shook his head, regret flashing on his face. "Now I won't get to."

"What was the call about?" Hatcher asked.

"Dinner. He wanted me to come this Sunday."

"What did you tell him?" Hatcher asked.

"That I had work to do and I'd see."

Hatcher sensed something was off. That Theo didn't want to have dinner with his father. "Did you and your father get along?"

Theo gave a quick look at his mother. She hung close to him, clutching his arm. "We had disagreements just like every family does," Theo said. "He was a . . . hard man."

Mrs. Wadsworth bit down on her lower lip and averted her gaze.

Korine picked up a framed photograph on the mantel and studied it. "You weren't close to him, were you?"

"Why do you ask that?" Theo said.

"Both you and your sister look uncomfortable, as if you don't want to be in the picture."

"It was Christmas last year," Theo said. "My date was waiting, and Serena and Dad had argued again about that damn app she created. He told her it was dangerous."

"App?" Hatcher asked.

"Yeah, the crime-share one that lets citizens post when a crime is occurring. It's supposed to alert bystanders so they can clear an area or warn them to pay attention so they can help identify a criminal. But some people have misused it."

Hatcher had heard the story. The app was a good idea, but it had problems, too.

"Where were you last night, Theo?" Hatcher asked.

The man was fast on his feet, but his mother beat him by answering first. "Theo was here with me all night." She aimed a conspiratorial smile at her son. "Weren't you, darling?"

Theo's eyes darkened, but he gave a quick nod. "We had dinner, then Mother retired for the night and I did some work."

Convenient. "What kind of work do you do?" Hatcher asked.

Theo made a low sound in his throat. "I'm an artist. Wood carvings."

Korine raised a brow. "You carved a gavel for your father, didn't you?"

His eyes widened. "How did you know that?"

"The press."

"He didn't appreciate it, though, did he?" Hatcher asked.

Anger slashed Theo's features as he shook his head. "I thought he might finally understand what my art meant to me. But he refused to put the gavel in his precious case. He . . . called it trivial, thought I should be doing something more worthwhile with my life, like following in his footsteps."

A motive? Killers had murdered for less.

"I suppose Hilda will corroborate your alibi," Hatcher said.

Mrs. Wadsworth fidgeted. "Of course. Now, I need you to leave. This news has been most upsetting, and I'm sure you have other people to interrogate."

"One more question," Hatcher said, since neither the wife nor the son had asked how the judge was killed. "Do you have that gavel, Theo?"

A muscle jumped in Theo's jaw. "I ground the damn thing up in the wood chipper." Theo gestured toward the door. "I think it's time you leave. My mother has suffered a shock and needs time to process this."

"I'm sorry," Hatcher said again. "But I'm sure you both want to find your father's killer. You can help by allowing us to search your father's home study and computer. We might find something about one of his cases or a threat that would lead us to his killer."

Theo's jaw tightened. "He didn't bring work files home. You won't find anything in there."

Hatcher used his height to intimidate the man. "I need to look."

Theo didn't seem intimidated. "Then get a warrant," he said. "And don't question my mother again without me or her attorney present. She's suffered enough without being treated like a suspect."

Hatcher met the man's steely gaze with one of his own. Theo was hiding something. And so was the mother.

CHAPTER EIGHT

Korine contemplated Mrs. Wadsworth's reaction and her relationship to her son as she walked to her vehicle.

Hatcher paused beside his SUV, his gaze pensive.

"They're hiding something," Korine said. "I think the judge abused his wife."

Hatcher hit the key fob to unlock his vehicle. "I agree. The son is protective of her."

"I have a feeling he and his father didn't get along. In the family photographs, they were never together. It was always the daughter with the father and the son with the mother. They must own a place on Seahawk Island, too, close to Tinsley's. Several of the pictures were near that cove."

"I'll get Cat to find out," Hatcher said. "We need to speak to the daughter."

Korine raised a brow. "Tonight?"

"We don't want to give her too much time. The mother probably called her as soon as we left to give her a heads-up."

True.

Family members were always primary suspects in a homicide investigation. Eliminating them was part of the job. To do that, it was helpful to catch the family before they had time to compare stories.

Korine climbed into her car and followed Hatcher to a townhome in Savannah a few miles from Korine's house, although these townhomes had been remodeled and were more expensive. She loved the old architecture of the buildings, the graveyards and ghost stories, the rich history of the city.

It was nearly ten o'clock, but on Friday night the town came alive, especially the restaurants along River Street. The holidays had brought tourists, but winter had set in and the streets were quieter, a testament to the lull between Christmas and the big Saint Patrick's Day celebration.

She and Hatcher parked on the street and met at the door to Serena's townhome. Korine rang the doorbell, and seconds later the judge's daughter, an attractive brunette with shoulder-length, wavy hair answered.

Her eyes looked red-rimmed, and she clutched a tissue in her hand. Interesting that so far, she was the only one who'd shed a tear over the judge's death. "My mother called. You must be the agents who talked to her and my brother."

Korine nodded and introduced herself and Hatcher. "I'm sorry for your loss."

"We understand that it's not a great time, Miss Wadsworth," Hatcher said, "but we really need to talk."

A wary look passed over Serena's face, but she gestured for them to come in. They followed her through a narrow hall to a living room/kitchen with a large center island. Unlike her mother's place with its antiques and expensive furnishings, Serena's furniture was modern with clean lines.

Korine scanned the mantel for photographs but saw none of her and the judge or any member of the family.

"My mother said that Dad was murdered." Serena sank onto the big club chair by the fireplace. Gas logs flickered, throwing out heat into the space, but Serena dragged a plush gray afghan over her as if chilled. "When?"

Korine and Hatcher exchanged looks, and he indicated for her to take the lead. "We don't have a definitive time of death yet, but it happened sometime last night."

"Where did you find him?" Serena asked.

"Sunset Cove on Seahawk Island. Do you know the place?" Hatcher asked.

She rubbed her fingers over the afghan, her brows furrowed. "Our family used to vacation there when we were little."

Now that was interesting. And just as Korine suspected from the photographs. "Did your family own a cottage there?"

"We used to, a little cottage in that cove. But my father sold it when we were teenagers."

Korine's instincts kicked in. Was that the cottage where Tinsley Jensen lived? Had something happened to the unsub at that cove?

If so, that could have been the reason the killer left the judge's body on the dock.

◆ ◆ ◆

Hatcher studied Serena Wadsworth with a critical eye. She was in her early thirties, attractive. In the photographs at her parents' house, her father had appeared to dote on her.

But she was also the opposite of her mother. Not meek or mild. Instead of waiting on a man to come to the rescue, she'd invented a crime app to help protect people.

"Tell us about your family," Hatcher said. "We met your brother."

Her mouth tilted into a smile. "Ahh, Theo. He's smart, and Mother's pet."

He arched a brow. "Do I sense sibling rivalry?"

She shrugged. "Dad doted on me when we were little, so Mother made up for it with Theo."

"You and your father were close?" Korine asked.

"Not really. He wanted a little princess to show off. I was a big disappointment."

"That's hard to believe," Korine said. "I'm sure he was proud of you and your accomplishments."

"My father lived in the Dark Ages. He thought women should be arm candy—quiet and obedient. He wanted a ballerina, but I was a tomboy. He wanted a daughter to do as he said, and I had a mind of my own. We disagreed over almost everything. Some of his judgments, how he treated women, and my brother."

"Did he talk down to women?" Hatcher asked.

She nodded. "He expected women to be obedient."

"And your mother was obedient?" Korine asked softly.

Serena shifted uncomfortably. "Most of the time."

"Was your father abusive to her?" Korine asked.

Serena's face paled. "Not so much when I was little, at least not physically, although his looks and tone could cut through you like a razor-sharp knife." She paused, and Hatcher and Korine both remained silent, waiting. "The last few years, when Theo chose his own path, Dad's temper got the best of him."

"What do you mean, 'when Theo chose his own path'?" Hatcher asked.

Serena laughed softly. "Dad wanted Theo to attend law school and marry a socialite who would be the appropriate wife, who'd look good beside him and serve Theo as Dad expected my mother to serve him."

"Theo didn't go for that?" Hatcher asked.

"Theo doesn't go for women," Serena said bluntly.

Now Hatcher got the picture.

"Let me guess," he said. "Your mother defended Theo's lifestyle choice. That's when your father hit her."

Serena nodded. "When I saw the bruises, I threatened to report Dad if he touched her again. Then my mother defended him. Can you believe that?"

"Unfortunately, that's common with domestic and spousal abuse," Korine said.

Serena chuckled bitterly. "Maybe, but the last time was too much. Dad said awful things to Theo, then hit him. Said he was going to teach him to be a real man."

"Real men don't hit women or their children," Hatcher said firmly.

Serena smiled. "I agree. And for once, Mom became a bear and fought back. But Dad broke her arm and two ribs. Needless to say, he and I haven't spoken since."

She had just given herself motive. But was her relationship with her father adversarial enough for her to commit murder?

Hatcher had to push. "Did you talk to your father or see him yesterday or anytime this week?"

She sighed. "I didn't see him, but he phoned and left a message, ordering me to get my people to take down my app. The message wasn't pretty." She shrugged. "I didn't return his call."

Hatcher traded looks with Korine. "Where were you last night?"

She clenched her jaw. "After my father called, I went for a run. It's the best way for me to relieve stress."

"You run alone?" Hatcher asked.

A frown marred her forehead. "I did last night. I realize that means I don't have an alibi, but trust me, I didn't kill my father."

"But you hated that he was hurting your mother?" Korine said.

"I tried to convince her to leave him, but she wouldn't. She loved the stubborn, demanding old fart." She tapped her chest. "Me? I wouldn't risk my future to get rid of him. He had enough enemies that I figured one day karma would catch up with him."

And it had.

Still, she'd shed tears over him.

Hatcher carefully chose his words. "Tell us about Theo and your father. They had a falling-out that night when your mother defended Theo?"

"That's putting it mildly. Dad threatened to cut Theo out of the will."

"Theo must have been angry," Korine said sympathetically.

"He was more hurt than anything." Serena twisted a loose thread from the afghan around her finger. "But if you think that Theo killed my father, you're wrong. He doesn't have a mean or violent bone in his body. He didn't care about the money or his inheritance."

Maybe not. But one thing Hatcher had learned from his job was that, if pushed too hard, anyone was capable of violence.

Maybe Theo didn't care about the money. But he was protective of his mother. Perhaps the physical abuse had triggered Theo's instinct to protect her.

And get rid of the source of both their problems.

♦ ♦ ♦

Korine offered Serena her business card. "Again, we're sorry for your loss. If you think of any information that might help, or of anyone who might have wanted your father dead, please give us a call."

Serena took the card with a sad smile. "I will."

She walked them to the door and said good night with a calmness that was unsettling.

"What do you think?" Korine asked Hatcher.

"An interesting family," Hatcher said. "But I don't see her as a killer."

"Neither do I."

Hatcher stopped beside his vehicle and glanced at his watch. "Hopefully tomorrow we'll have time and cause of death and can get warrants for the judge's files. We also need to question the victims of the River Street Rapist."

Korine's lips slanted into a frown. "I know. Although after the way they've suffered, they don't deserve to be treated as suspects."

"But they do have the strongest motive," Hatcher pointed out.

Korine unlocked her car. He was right.

That didn't mean she liked it.

God, she'd held Andi's hand while she sobbed her heart out in the hospital. She'd helped her through the rape exam, had seen her bruises and pain.

That night she'd wanted to hunt the bastard down and kill him herself.

Hatcher unlocked his SUV. "We'll need a warrant for the judge's files. And I'll ask for help to analyze them. We need to prioritize suspects and follow up on the judge's cases and any threats against him."

"I can question Andi Rosten in the morning while you handle that," Korine offered.

A muscle jumped in Hatcher's jaw. "We do the interviews together."

Korine raised a brow. "Don't you trust me to get a read on her?"

He hissed between his teeth. "You may not like working with me, and I don't particularly want to be partnered with you either, Korine, but we are partners for a reason. To watch each other's backs."

"You just want to make sure I'm tough enough on Andi," Korine said through gritted teeth.

"Don't make this personal," Hatcher said.

Anger shot through her. "Like you did on the last case?"

His cold look had her regretting those words.

"I'm sorry," she said. "That was out of line."

He didn't comment, simply gave her another icy stare.

Korine sighed, determined to get back on track. Hatcher was the senior agent. If she pissed him off, he might talk to Bellows, and she'd be sidelined.

At least if they talked to the rape victims together, she could make sure Hatcher didn't push them too hard.

She also needed him to attest to the fact that she was impartial in this case.

And she would be impartial.

Although she wouldn't blame Andi or any of the rape victims if they celebrated the judge's death tonight.

Because of Judge Wadsworth's ruling, the man who'd violated them was still on the loose.

Milburn had sworn when he raped the women that he'd come back after them if they talked. He'd made that same threat in court.

Those three women would live in terror until he was behind bars for life.

♦ ♦ ♦

Hatcher phoned about the warrants as he drove to his bungalow on the outskirts of Savannah.

Korine thought he didn't care or that he wouldn't sympathize with the rape victims.

He probably sympathized too damn much.

But he had to do his job, and that meant questioning them.

Although if one of them had killed the judge, he wasn't sure he could make the arrest.

After the trial and the judge's decision, the press had run stories with both slants—one that the judge was a hard-ass and shouldn't have let the sadistic, maniac rapist off. The other, that the judge hadn't had a choice, that the cops hadn't done their jobs, and that the judge had to take the fall because they'd fucked up.

Either way, it didn't give the victims any comfort. They wouldn't have relief until Milburn was in prison.

Just like Tinsley Jensen wouldn't have peace until the Skull was caught.

He parked at his rental house, agitated about both the case and Korine.

The marsh loomed, dark and desolate, its silence a welcoming retreat yet haunting at the same time. He'd chosen this location so he could escape the hub of Savannah and the tourists.

So he could be alone.

His boots dug into the dry grass as he strode to the side door and let himself inside. The old furnishings in the house gave it a musty feel. The odor of empty booze bottles added to the rancid smell.

He hadn't noticed before because he'd been dulling his pain with the stuff.

The fact that he had to question rape victims in the morning made him crave a drink. But he bypassed the bottle on the kitchen counter, grabbed the bag full of empty bottles, and carried them outside to the recycling bin.

When he came back in, he poured himself a glass of water and chugged it down.

Felicia's picture mocked him from the mantel as he stepped into the den. He'd left her photograph there as a reminder that she was dead.

It should have been him instead.

CHAPTER NINE

Beverly Grant hurried into her town house and made a beeline for the bathroom. She'd forced herself to attend a special counseling session her friend Liz had organized for first responders and others who worked with violent crimes, but it hadn't helped. She was still wound up and sick to her stomach.

Five years she'd worked as a court reporter. She should be used to the ugly, sordid stories of the violence and pain humans inflicted on others. She should be immune.

But every now and then some of them got to her. Especially the ones that involved children.

No child should suffer.

And that monster in the courtroom had shown no remorse on the stand today. Instead, he'd graced the jury with a smarmy smile as if he was proud of the child-porn pictures the prosecutor had shown.

Simply typing the vulgar man's testimony had made her feel vile inside.

She flipped on the hot water and scrubbed her hands, but she couldn't scrub the images from her mind.

That sick perv had to pay. So did the others who shared those pictures. The DA was going to cut the man a deal if he revealed the names of the members of the child-porn ring.

That meant they might let him go free.

If they did, he would hurt someone else.

Unless *they* stopped him.

She lifted her head and stared at her reflection in the mirror. Rage seethed inside her. Her eyes looked shell-shocked and wild.

CHAPTER TEN

Gray clouds shrouded the morning sun, adding a dismal feel to the small garden area behind Korine's house as she jogged up the steps and let herself inside. Her five-mile morning run usually relieved stress and helped her focus for the day.

She needed a shower but poured herself a cup of coffee first, then took it to the garden, a peaceful, quiet reprieve from the city.

Except yesterday she had seen someone in the bushes.

Senses on alert, she scanned the area but saw nothing except the shimmering mist rising above the treetops. Morning shadows almost made them appear as spirits lingering and lost.

Like some homes in the area, the owner claimed this one was haunted. A house with a history always drew interest, although those afraid of ghosts tended to shy away from buying. Others bought for the history that was part of Savannah's charm.

She didn't mind the ghost stories. The legends of Savannah added character. Star-crossed lovers had allegedly been murdered in the garden, their killer never caught. Sometimes she thought she saw them lying, entwined, bloody, and weak, their eyes begging her for help, their hearts linked as one for eternity.

She couldn't imagine loving a man with such devotion.

Or a man loving her that way.

Her job and her office with her wall of wanted criminals and articles and pictures of crime scenes usually sent the normal ones running.

Hatcher's strong, square jaw and deep-set dark eyes teased her with longing, though. That night with him had been filled with animalistic passion.

Passion, not love.

He'd lied to her, had said he was single when he was still married.

Because he'd wanted in her pants.

Not going to happen again.

She rolled her aching shoulders and tilted her head from side to side to crack her neck. She had no time for lingering and dwelling on her mistakes.

The first soothing taste of caffeine sent a much-needed jolt through her system. She liked her coffee strong and black.

The nightmare had invaded her sleep again last night. *The music playing, her father's loving voice singing, "You're so pretty, oh, so pretty . . ." as he danced her around his office.*

Then the gunshot. The blood. He was falling. A crash followed.

Her beautiful new doll, her porcelain face shattered . . .

She screamed and slipped in the blood . . . reached out to catch herself and sliced her hand on one of the shards of broken porcelain.

She flexed her left hand and stared at the scar. It had faded somewhat but was still visible. It was the ones on the inside, though, that never faded.

She'd woken from that nightmare, then finally fallen back asleep, but this time she'd dreamed about Tinsley Jensen being locked in her house. A shadow was lurking outside, watching Tinsley. The Skull. He enjoyed tormenting her, thrived on her fear, lived for the game.

A second later, Tinsley screamed . . .

That nightmare bled into another.

The faces of the rape victims pressed against the window, terrified, their tear-filled eyes, their throaty whispers begging her to save them . . .

She stood and paced the garden. She didn't want to interview those victims today. But she had to do it.

Sweaty from her run and determined not to be late and give Hatcher any excuse to get her reassigned, she quickly showered and dressed. She strapped on her holster and weapon, clipped her phone to her belt, and poured another strong coffee to go.

While she waited on Hatcher, she booted up her computer and flipped on the television. Photographs of women's marches across the state and protests against the judge's ruling, as well as marches to raise awareness of spousal abuse, flashed on the screen, then the story about the judge's murder. The lead investigative anchor, Marilyn Ellis, was aggressive and a pain in the Feds' ass.

"Special Agents Hatcher McGee and Korine Davenport are investigating the case," Ellis said. "Speculation has surfaced that the judge's decision to release the alleged River Street Rapist could have been motive for the judge's murder."

Photographs of Wadsworth and his family flashed on the screen, along with images of the judge in court looking very much the staunch authoritative figure he'd been.

The fact that his body had been left on the dock facing Tinsley's bothered Korine. She texted Cat to see whether she had any information on the case yet and immediately received a reply.

Ten years ago, Judge Wadsworth owned the cottage next to Tinsley Jensen's rental. No reports of a crime or disturbance at the house when the judge and his family owned it.

Also, no police reports filed regarding spousal abuse involving the judge.

Wadsworth probably paid the doctor off so he wouldn't report it.

Rita Herron

She accessed Tinsley's blog, *Heart & Soul*, and skimmed an entry Tinsley had written the night before, then another posted this morning.

I am alone again this morning, trapped in this world of darkness. Held hostage by my fears. In a prison I made for myself to protect me from the monster who nearly stole my life.

He's still out there. Perhaps he's a million miles away. Hiding out in another country.

Perhaps he's right next door.

Watching me. Waiting to trap me again. Waiting to take my life.

The pain and fear are like living, breathing beasts inside me. Sometimes I think death is the only answer, the only thing that will make them go away.

But I did survive and I escaped. And I didn't live through his evilness to die at my own hand.

I will fight for myself and for you, and for all the other women in my shoes.

We can't let the monsters win.

Tinsley signed the post—*Taking Control.*

A shudder rippled through Korine. She felt the same way about her father's killer. As if one day he'd come back for her.

Maybe he'd even killed again . . .

Several responses to Tinsley's post followed.

Free124
Hostage No More

> I understand how you feel. I was held prisoner by my own husband. I feared him for years.
>
> But finally he's gone.
>
> Some may wonder why I'm not sad. Why I don't grieve for him. Why there are no tears for the man I vowed to love, honor, and cherish.
>
> Why instead of poring over romantic pictures of us and sobbing at the sight of the empty space beside me in bed, I'm rejoicing in being alone.
>
> He can no longer hurt me.
>
> There is peace in that. And peace in knowing that he suffered in the end.
>
> That I finally got justice.

Korine inhaled sharply. She understood how traumatic memories could hold you prisoner. Could keep you from living and being happy. She'd let her father's death do that to her.

Just as Tinsley couldn't move on or be whole again until her abductor was caught and punished, Korine couldn't imagine a future until her past was resolved and she found the person who'd shot her father in cold blood.

A knock sounded at the door, startling her. Hatcher.

Time to get to work. Find the judge's killer.

Talk to Andi and the other girls the River Street Rapist had victimized.

She just prayed one of them hadn't killed the judge. Not that they didn't have motive.

But locking up a victim wasn't justice.

That last entry on Tinsley's blog disturbed her. The woman had been abused by her husband. Now the husband was dead.

Had the woman killed him?

◆ ◆ ◆

Hatcher kept his eyes trained on the road as he drove to Andi Rosten's parents' house. Cat had emailed him information on all three victims along with their backgrounds and locations.

All three women were in their twenties, attractive, single, and lived alone. At least they had until the attack. Andi currently lived with her mother and father.

He had to force himself not to look at Korine. She looked too damn sexy this morning, with those doelike eyes and ivory skin and pale-pink lips.

His cock twitched. Those lips had teased and tormented his body in ways he'd never forget.

Dammit, he had to stop thinking about her lips.

"I've been looking at Tinsley's *Heart & Soul* blog," Korine said. "One entry I read this morning could have been written by Judge Wadsworth's wife. The woman describes being abused, feeling like a hostage, then being relieved that her husband had died."

"Do you know who she is?"

"The screen name is anonymous."

Hatcher made a clicking sound with his teeth. "Mrs. Wadsworth isn't the only woman who's fallen victim to domestic abuse. And she's certainly smart enough not to put a confession on the Internet."

"I realize that," Korine said. "But since the body was left on the dock outside Tinsley's residence, the killer may feel a connection with Tinsley."

Good point. "If she posts something more concrete, we'll have Cat try to figure out who she is."

He veered onto the street leading to the Rostens'. They lived in Pooler, a small town near Savannah, in a wooded area that backed up to a creek.

The SUV bounced over a rut in the road, and he barreled down the drive, which ended at an outdated brick ranch. Winter had robbed the leaves off the trees, and the grass looked brittle and dry. Swampland backed up to the property. A rusted van sat in the drive, along with a small gray sedan.

"Tell me about Andi Rosten," Hatcher said.

Korine wet her lips with her tongue. "Before the rape, she was a barista at a coffee shop and studying fashion design at SCAD, the Savannah College of Art and Design. Milburn came in for a latte every morning. She thought he was nice. Safe. He flirted with her. She . . . flirted back. She blamed herself for being a victim. Thought she'd invited his attention."

Hatcher cursed. "A facade for the sick fuck inside."

"Exactly."

"Did she finish her degree?"

Korine shook her head. "After the attack, she was so traumatized she moved back with her parents." Korine paused. "Maybe if her rapist was in prison, she'd finally be able to sleep at night. And maybe she could move past the attack and get her life back."

He understood that need. He felt it about his wife's killer.

He could use that to make a connection with Andi and hopefully convince her to talk.

◆ ◆ ◆

Nerves gathered in Korine's stomach as the door opened. Andi's father, a thin, wiry man, answered the door.

"Hello, Mr. Rosten, my name is Special Agent Davenport."

He snapped his fingers. "I know you. You worked Andi's case."

Korine nodded. "I did when I was with the police department." She gestured toward Hatcher. "This is Special Agent McGee."

His brows furrowed. "Are you going to put that son of a bitch who hurt my daughter in jail?"

"I wish I could, but we don't have any new evidence at this point," Korine said. "If you see him, call the police. He's not allowed to come near Andi."

"Fat lot of good a restraining order does," the man grumbled. "I feel like Andi's the one in jail."

"I'm sorry." Korine took a deep breath. "Is Andi here?"

The man pulled at his chin, a wary look in his eyes. "In the kitchen, having coffee with my wife."

He motioned for them to follow him, and they walked through a modest family room to a kitchen that smelled of coffee and cinnamon. Korine bit back a gasp as she spotted Andi.

When Korine had first met the young woman, Andi was slightly plump. Now she looked like an empty shell. Her clothes hung on her skin-and-bones frame, her face was milky white with dark shadows beneath her eyes, and her hand trembled as she self-consciously smoothed tangled hair from her forehead.

Her mother, a chubby woman with short, curly brown hair, sat with her at the oak table. Mr. Rosten introduced his wife to Korine and Hatcher, then offered them coffee, but they both declined.

Korine crossed the room to Andi, leaned over, and greeted her with a warm smile.

Andi's eyes widened. "What are you doing here? Do you have news? Did you catch him?"

The hope in her voice tore at Korine. She wanted to tell her that her rapist was locked up so Andi could feel safe again, but she couldn't. "I'm afraid not."

Hatcher cleared his throat. "Have you seen the morning news?"

The parents exchanged questioning looks, and Andi shook her head.

"There are too many gruesome stories," Mr. Rosten said. "It upsets her."

Korine's throat thickened. "Judge Wadsworth was murdered Monday night."

Andi's eyes darted sideways, then back to Korine. "What happened?"

"We believe he was bludgeoned to death," Hatcher said, intentionally omitting the details.

Mr. Rosten laid a protective hand on his daughter's shoulder. "That's unfortunate," he said, although his voice lacked sincerity. "But what does it have to do with us?"

"We're investigating his murder," Hatcher said. "His ruling on the River Street Rapist case garnered media attention and controversy. We're talking to everyone who knew the judge or had connections to his cases."

Korine slipped into the chair beside Andi. "I understand this is difficult. You were brave to testify against your attacker."

"Yes, she was," Mr. Rosten said. "So were those other women. That damned prosecutor promised it would be worth it, but my daughter suffered through all that for nothing."

"It wasn't for nothing," Mrs. Rosten cut in. "The counselor insisted that standing up to her attacker was cathartic."

"If you want me to say I'm sorry the judge is dead, I can't," Andi said. "Because of him, that sadistic monster who raped me is free to do it to someone else."

Korine gave her a concerned look. "Has Milburn contacted you?"

Andi shook her head. "Not yet, but he will." She shivered. "He always keeps his promises. I learned that the hard way."

"I understand your bitterness toward the judge," Hatcher said. "Last year my wife was murdered by a suspect I was hunting down. I wanted that bastard to pay with his life. I'm sure you felt that way about Milburn. And maybe even Judge Wadsworth."

Andi's eyes flickered with emotions. Then anger and hurt at the implication of Hatcher's statement registered. "My God, you think I had something to do with his death?"

"I can't believe you're treating my daughter like a criminal," Mr. Rosten snapped.

Andi started to speak, but her father squeezed her shoulder to quiet her. "We'd like to see Milburn dead," Mr. Rosten said. "But we didn't murder the judge or anyone else."

"You said it happened Monday night," Mrs. Rosten cut in. "We were all here. I made lasagna, and we watched a movie together."

Mr. Rosten's face hardened. "I think you should leave now. My daughter has suffered enough."

"I'm sorry, Andi," Korine said. "We didn't mean to imply that you did this. But we have to talk to everyone associated with the judge."

Mrs. Rosten stood, hands clasped. "Well, you have. Now leave us alone."

Korine gave Andi a compassionate look, but Andi averted her gaze as if Korine had crossed a line and she'd lost the woman's trust.

Korine couldn't leave things like that. She pressed her hand over her heart. "I wasn't judging you. I told you about my father being murdered when I was a little girl. Not a day has passed that I haven't thought about finding his killer and making him pay." Her pulse hammered. "If you had wanted revenge, I'd understand."

"I told you that we were all here together Monday night," Mrs. Rosten said sharply. "In fact, Andi hasn't been outside this house by herself since the trial. So take your suspicions somewhere else."

Korine bit back a response. She couldn't blame the woman for being upset. Watching her daughter suffer must be excruciating.

"One more question," Hatcher asked. "Do you know Tinsley Jensen?"

A puzzled expression stretched across the parents' faces.

"No," Andi said quickly.

"She was a victim—abducted by the Skull. You may have seen the story on the news," Hatcher said.

"I told you we don't let her watch the news," Mr. Rosten said.

Korine ignored him. "Tinsley started a blog—*Heart & Soul*—where she talks about how she felt during her abduction. She encourages other victims of violence to share their stories. It's as much a support group as anything."

Andi knotted her hands.

A tense second passed.

Korine gave her an imploring look. "You might benefit from reading Ms. Jensen's posts and communicating with some of the other victims."

Mrs. Rosten glared at Korine. "The last thing my daughter needs is to hear more gory stories about women who've been violated. Now please leave. Our family needs time alone."

Korine bit the inside of her cheek as Mr. Rosten escorted them to the door and yelled at them not to come back.

CHAPTER ELEVEN

Hatcher struggled to keep his anger at bay as they left Andi Rosten's house. He understood the Rostens' protective instincts toward their daughter. He'd felt that way toward his wife.

But he'd failed her.

He didn't want to fail Andi. Although his job at the moment wasn't to find her rapist.

His job was to find Judge Wadsworth's killer.

The next stop was to see another rape victim. "Tell me about Renee Wiggins."

"Let me pull up the files to refresh my memory. Cat said she updated them with current information." Korine accessed the information on her iPad. "Renee Wiggins is twenty-three, was studying nursing at College of Coastal Georgia."

"Did she finish?"

Korine scrunched her nose as she skimmed for information. "Not yet. She took a couple of semesters off for counseling. But she's back at school now."

"Good for her. Where does she live?"

Korine recited the street address for a small house in Brunswick.

"She was engaged, but she broke it off," Korine said, a note of sadness to her voice.

Hatcher clamped his mouth shut. The attack had probably wrecked her relationship with the fiancé. Not uncommon in rape cases. The female was traumatized. Her partner suffered from guilt over not keeping her safe. He didn't know how to help her.

She didn't want him touching her.

Five minutes later, he parked in front of a small white clapboard house in a neighborhood that catered to rentals for students. Flags in the Mariners' colors of royal blue and gray swayed in the breeze from several of the homes. He and Korine climbed out and walked up to the door; then he knocked.

Seconds later, a sandy-haired woman in pale-blue scrubs dotted with cartoon characters answered the door.

"Renee Wiggins?" Hatcher asked.

"Who wants to know?" A wariness darkened her eyes.

Korine spoke softly and introduced them. "We need a few minutes of your time."

She crossed her arms. "I know what this is about. Andi called."

Damn, he hadn't realized the women were in contact. "So you heard about Judge Wadsworth's murder?"

"How could I not? It's been all over the news." She opened the screen and shoved a piece of paper in his hand. "I was at the hospital Monday night, working. That's my supervisor's name and phone number so you can verify my story. For the record, I didn't like the judge, and naturally, I was upset that he let that son-of-a-bitch rapist out of jail. But I sure as shit didn't kill him."

Her challenging look suggested they were dismissed. "Excuse me. I have to get to the hospital, or I'll be late for my shift."

"You're finishing your degree?" Korine said. "Good for you."

Renee lifted her chin. "That lowlife jerk took my peace of mind, but I'm a survivor. I don't intend to let him ruin the rest of my life."

Whereas Andi Rosten had seemed broken and afraid of her own shadow, this woman was using her anger to push forward.

♦ ♦ ♦

Natalie Cox, the rapist's third victim, had been strong and had held up well during police interviews and the trial.

Korine skimmed the information Cat had sent for updates, but according to the file, Natalie and her sister still co-owned the gym they'd bought together a few months after the attack. A photo of Natalie and her sister at the grand opening of the gym after they'd renovated it was in the file. The sisters looked proud of their new venture. "Natalie should be at the gym. She opens at five a.m. and leaves round five p.m. The sister works the evening shift."

"A gym? Her way of fighting back?"

"Probably. The center's emphasis is on the whole woman. They teach self-defense classes, yoga, weight training, aerobics, spinning, and Zumba. They also have a running-and-swimming club and a CrossFit boot camp. In addition, they offer seminars to encourage women's empowerment, mental health, and financial planning."

She gave Hatcher the address, and they found the center in a refurbished warehouse near SCAD.

Midday, and the parking lot was full. "What did you think about Renee Wiggins?" she asked as they walked to the door of the center.

"She seems nervous but smart. You?"

"My gut instinct says we can cross her off the suspect list."

Hatcher opened the door, and they entered to the sound of voices and country music. A glass partition designated an area for childcare, another one showcased the lap pool, and other rooms housed various classes.

A slender woman with coffee-colored skin and long, dark braids greeted them. "Welcome to Fab Female. What can we do for you today?"

Korine recognized Natalie from the press coverage of the trial. She flashed her badge and introduced the two of them. "We need to talk to you about Judge Wadsworth."

Natalie's smile faded. "I saw the story about his murder on the news. But what does that have to do with me?"

Hatcher cleared his throat. "We're speaking to everyone connected to trials he presided over."

Natalie narrowed her eyes. "Because you think one of us killed him?" Disbelief edged her voice; then she waved over a shorter version of herself. Her sister. "Tori, tell these federal agents where you and I were Monday night."

Tori adjusted her ponytail. "We spoke at a women's seminar at Georgia Tech University in Atlanta. It was a packed crowd."

Easy enough to check.

"Now we have that out of the way, are you going to retry Milt Milburn?" She leaned over the counter, brows raised. "If you have time to question the women he victimized, surely you have time to get more evidence on that asshole."

Korine didn't blame the woman for being bitter. Milburn's rape victims had suffered emotionally and physically at his hands. Making matters worse, they'd relived their ordeal in court, and the defense attorney had ripped them apart.

Then Judge Wadsworth had let him go on a damned technicality.

"I'm sorry for what you've been through," Korine said. "And sorry that Milburn was released."

The muscles in Natalie's arms bunched as she crossed her arms. "Then do something about it." She gestured around the center, at a group of young women gathered in the corner near the water fountains. "We deserve to be safe. And none of us are until he's locked up for life."

Korine couldn't argue with her on that. She was a trained agent, but she still looked over her shoulder, kept alert for strangers watching her, and slept with her weapon by her side.

CHAPTER TWELVE

Rachel Willis was sick to death of the liars she dealt with every day.

She slammed the door to her office, frustrated that justice didn't always prevail.

News of Judge Wadsworth's death had hit the media first thing that morning. The creep had used his authority to browbeat women into doing what he wanted and talked down to females on the job. He tended to be lenient in cases of violence against women—one of those archaic men who held the belief that the woman had incited the man's rage by the way she dressed or talked or by her makeup.

She wouldn't be surprised if his wife had killed him. Maybe if she did, a good lawyer could get her off.

The picture of her own family, her mother and father, mocked her from the credenza.

At twenty-one, she'd been idealistic and certain that she could make a difference in the world. She knew firsthand that the system didn't always work. Her father had spent ten years in jail for a crime he hadn't committed. Ten years of his life lost because a witness had mistaken him for another man.

Ten years that he'd never been able to recover from. He'd gotten hooked on drugs in the dark corners of Hays State Prison, a maximum-security hellhole where he'd been abused and raped and beaten until he had no fight left.

Her mother had passed away during that time, her heart broken and defeated from trying to convince someone to push through an appeal.

No one had been there to help him when her father was finally freed. By then, the damage was done. He had no work experience, no recommendations from coworkers or employers. No money or savings. No education.

Even though he had been cleared of the charges, people still looked at him as if he were a murderer.

Depressed and defeated, he'd died with a needle in his arm in a dirty alley in some backwoods town where drug dealers were a dime a dozen.

She'd thought by working as a parole officer, she could save others like her father who'd been crapped on by the system. She could help them turn their lives around. Help them find jobs. Places to live. Keep them on the right path.

She was a fool.

She shoved the mountain of paperwork on her desk to the side, then retrieved the list of people she needed to phone. A knock sounded at the door, and she checked her schedule. Her next appointment wasn't due for three hours—Rodney Hornsby, a dog beater who'd tortured his pit bull under the guise of training him to fight.

The man made her want to puke. Anyone who abused or mistreated animals, women, or children should be punished.

The knock sounded again.

She checked to make sure her weapon was in place beneath her desk. The panic button she'd installed went straight to the police to alert them if she was in trouble.

Before she reached the door, it opened, and a tall, broad-shouldered man with a ratty beard and shaggy hair drawn up in a man bun stepped inside. Tattoos snaked up and down his arms and neck, and a jagged scar rippled down his right cheek. She returned behind her desk.

Rachel searched her memory to place him. He looked familiar, but she hadn't met him before. Had she received his file?

It could be in the pile she hadn't yet had time to review. There were dozens to be handled. The work never ended.

Were there any good people left in the world?

"Can I help you?" she asked, careful to remain behind her desk. Keeping distance between herself and the ex-cons was imperative for her own safety, a lesson she'd learned her first day on the job when a supposedly innocent man had jumped her with a knife and nearly slit her throat.

A lecherous grin slid onto her visitor's face, making her skin crawl.

"You're scared of me, aren't you?" he asked in a cocky voice.

The exhilaration in his tone fueled her rage. She'd been taught not to show fear. Predators fed on it.

Slowly and calmly she removed her pistol from beneath the desk, raised it, and aimed it at his chest. "Who are you, and what do you want?"

His eyes landed on the gun, and he held up a scarred hand. "Hey, sweetie, don't shoot."

If he called her "sweetie" again, she might not be able to stop herself. "Answer the question. Who are you?" she asked.

"My lawyer said I was supposed to check in with you."

So he was on her case list. God, she wished the county would hire some help. Her caseload was insane. "Your name?" she asked again, her voice cold.

He shifted and inched toward her, eyes gleaming with amusement. "Sutton Frasier, but you can call me Sly. That's the name my buddies gave me in prison."

She didn't intend to ask how he got the name. "You have paperwork for me?"

He shook his head. "That shithead they assigned me as a lawyer was supposed to contact you."

He'd been assigned a court-appointed attorney. He probably had no money, no friends, no family. If he did, they'd given up on him.

The first year on the job she would have sympathized.

Now she was hardened. Maybe she was burned-out and needed to rethink her career.

She glanced at the files piled on her desk and wanted to review this man's before they went any further. "What is your attorney's name? I'll give him a call, then we'll set up a schedule."

"The lawyer is a her. Gina Weatherby," the man said with another lecherous grin. "Pretty as a peach, but a big-assed dyke."

His comment stirred her anger, but she didn't react. Her parolees were seldom politically correct. Arguing with them, especially correcting them, was futile.

She scribbled the lawyer's name on her notepad. Her cell phone buzzed, and she contemplated answering and asking for help. But she didn't have time.

He moved so quickly and quietly that she didn't see him coming. Then he was beside her, his hand over her gun hand as he pushed down the nose, aiming the .22 at the floor.

The scent of cigarette smoke and sweat wafted around her. No, it was weed. The idiot had probably just smoked a joint before he'd come in.

She mentally reviewed her self-defense training. *Go for his eyes. A knee in the groin . . .*

"Don't point a gun at a man unless you plan to use it." His gruff voice held laughter. "And, honey, we both know you wouldn't do that."

Her blood turned cold.

"You're wrong," she said with a defiant lift to her chin. "I'm just smart enough to choose when to shoot." As far as she could tell, he was unarmed. Timing was important.

He leaned closer, so close his breath bathed her ear. With a low groan, he licked her cheek. "I'll let Gina know we met."

A chuckle rumbled from him, and he released her hand and sauntered toward the exit, his boots clicking on the hard floor. When he reached the door, he paused, one hand on the knob. He lifted the other and blew her a kiss.

"See you soon, baby. And next time, wear something sexy for me."

She gripped the gun with a trembling hand, her lungs squeezing for air as the door closed behind him. She hurried and locked the door, then raced into the bathroom and scrubbed her hands.

Fuck, fuck, fuck. She'd wanted to shoot the asshole. And he was wrong—she could do it. She had, once.

An image of the blood on her hands flashed behind her eyes. That cocksucker had deserved what she'd done to him.

But if she shot Sly today and he wasn't armed, she'd end up in a cell herself.

What justice would there be in that?

None.

She raised her head and stared into the mirror with a smile.

Karma would get him. Just like it had the judge.

She envisioned jabbing a knife in Sly's gut or watching him collapse from the bullet she'd put in his chest, and she instantly felt better.

Just like she did knowing the judge was dead. He would soon be nothing but bones in the ground.

CHAPTER THIRTEEN

Wadsworth's personal assistant didn't seem surprised to see Korine and Hatcher or the warrant. Two file boxes sat on a credenza behind her desk, and a clerk carried another one in and set it with the others.

Gretta Breer gestured toward the boxes. "Director Bellows phoned and asked me to gather the materials you need to review. We've been working all morning, pulling any cases where complaints or threats were made against the judge for his ruling or his behavior during a trial. I've also compiled a folder containing copies of emails, hate mail, and other threats he received." Her face looked grim. "There's a lot to sort through."

Hatcher nodded. The suspect pool was growing fast.

They needed more manpower. Wyatt had been pestering him to stop by, but he'd avoided his former partner. He couldn't stand to see him in pain, struggling to walk, when it was his fault Wyatt had been injured.

A thirtysomething ash-blonde woman wearing a dark-blue pantsuit walked by, muttering beneath her breath, her phone in hand.

"Beverly, come here," Gretta said. "I want to introduce you to these federal agents."

Beverly hung up, then quickly jammed her phone in her jacket pocket. Her expression remained wary as she joined them and Gretta made the introductions.

"Special Agents McGee and Davenport are investigating the judge's death." Gretta indicated the file boxes. "If you have questions about the judge's trial transcripts, ask Bev," she said. "She's one of our court reporters and has worked a lot of the judge's trials."

Bev gave them a nonchalant look. "I just record the proceedings," she said. "That's my job."

"But those recordings are important and imperative when cases come under scrutiny and up for appeals," Hatcher said.

The young woman patted her pocket where she'd stored her phone. She looked impatient, as if she was expecting an important call. Then she pulled a card from her purse and handed it to Korine. "My cell number is on there. I'll be glad to help if I can."

"How did you feel about the judge?" Hatcher asked.

Her eyes flared with unease. "Like I said, I recorded testimony, the lawyers' remarks, the rulings. It wasn't my place to have an opinion."

She was a master at deflecting questions. Maybe she'd learned that from listening to all those lawyers and witnesses.

"Thank you," Korine said diplomatically. "We want to close this case as soon as possible."

"Of course." She lifted her fingers in a tiny wave, then hurried away.

Hatcher stepped to the doorway as she ducked into the hall. She was already on her phone, talking furiously, obviously upset.

Whatever was going on with her could be personal. None of their business.

But she'd seemed nervous about their questions. She gave the impression that she was a robot, recording information without thinking about the cases or people involved.

His gut instinct told him that wasn't true. That her work got to her at times.

She wouldn't be human if it didn't. Counselors, social workers, doctors, nurses, first responders, medics—everyone who dealt with victims of crimes started out wanting to help, sympathizing with people.

Some burned out. Others hardened and became immune. It was the only way to survive.

He didn't think Beverly Grant was immune.

His phone buzzed. Bellows.

Damn.

◆ ◆ ◆

Korine watched the court reporter leave with a tightening in her gut. That young woman intrigued her—she was holding something back.

But what?

Her phone buzzed. Her mother's number.

Good grief. She didn't have time for more family drama. But with her mother's condition, she couldn't ignore a call in case an emergency had arisen.

She held up a finger to Hatcher. "Excuse me, I need to take this."

He gave a quick nod, and she stepped into the ladies' room and connected the call.

"Have you seen Kenny?" Esme sounded panicked. "Is he with you?"

She inhaled a deep breath, willing herself to be calm. "I'm working, and no, I haven't seen him. Why? Did something happen?"

Esme's shaky breath echoed back. "He stopped by, but your mama was playing that song again. Kenny heard it and went into a rage. Then he stormed out of here like a demon was chasing him."

Korine pinched the bridge of her nose. "Was he high?"

Esme hesitated.

"Tell me the truth, Esme. I need to know."

"I think he was on something. His pupils were dilated."

Korine clamped her lip with her teeth. How could Kenny show up and upset their mother like that? Didn't he realize how fragile she'd become? "How is Mom now?"

"I had to give her one of her sedatives, but she finally settled down."

Sometimes Korine thought it was better when her mother got upset than when she just sat and stared into space as if she were a vacant shell. At least a reaction meant she had some life left in her.

"Did Kenny say where he was going?"

"I couldn't understand what he was saying. He was mumbling one minute and shouting obscenities the next."

"If he shows up again, call me. Meanwhile, encourage Mother to rest, and I'll find Kenny."

"Of course, dear."

Korine thanked Esme, then stared at herself in the mirror. The photographs of the rape victims flashed behind her eyes. The painful injuries, the scars on the women's bodies.

She didn't have visible scars. But the reflection of a wounded woman stared back at her.

Nothing could bring her father back, but finding his killer would give her closure. He was a real hero in her book. He'd helped countless children as a child psychologist. And he'd loved her and Kenny with all his heart.

She wouldn't be whole again until she found the person who'd taken him.

A knock sounded at the door. "Korine, are you in there?" Hatcher's voice.

"I'll be right out." She wet a paper towel and blotted the perspiration on her forehead and neck, then opened the door.

Hatcher studied her with hooded eyes. "Everything okay?"

"Just a family thing."

His eyes narrowed in question, but leaning on Hatcher was not an option. Those broad shoulders were too damn tempting.

So were his big strong hands and his body.

"I talked to Bellows," Hatcher said, cutting into her wayward thoughts. "I told him we needed more manpower to review those files." He paused. "My former partner has been asking for an assignment."

Was this an attempt to weed her out? Maybe she needed to step up her game. "I didn't think Wyatt was ready to return to duty."

"He's not, physically." Pain underscored Hatcher's voice. "But he could analyze the files."

"That would save us time," she admitted.

"We'll drop them off when we leave here."

She followed him back to Gretta Breer's office where he solicited help in transporting the boxes to his SUV.

She felt confident they could clear Andi and the other two rape victims, but the judge's family still remained persons of interest.

Once they started digging, they'd probably uncover others. Hopefully forensics would find some evidence to offer a concrete lead.

Although if the murder was premeditated, the unsub was probably smart enough to cover his tracks.

Mentally, she reviewed what she knew about the killer's MO. This killer had bludgeoned the judge to death, possibly with a gavel like Wadsworth used in court when he rendered his decisions. When he wanted to call the court to order. When he wanted to exert his power.

The injuries on the man also seemed violent. As if the unsub was in a rage.

As if he wanted to inflict pain, to make the judge feel the same kind of humiliation and suffering a woman felt when she was overpowered or beaten by a man.

That suggested the crime was personal.

Except there was no sexual element.

Or . . . they might be looking at this case all wrong. Tinsley's blog and the comments she received could be significant. Perhaps the unsub left the judge's body in the cove to gain Tinsley's attention.

Someone who wanted to brag to Tinsley that they'd rid the world of the judge.

The Skull was still at large. What if he'd beaten the judge to death as some kind of sick message to Tinsley that he was watching her?

That he knew where she was and that he could get to her?

♦ ♦ ♦

Hatcher never thought he'd dread seeing Wyatt Camden. They'd been a good fit on the job, had become running buddies, and had bonded over beer and Braves games.

When Wyatt was first hospitalized, he'd been in a lot of pain. Seeing his former partner suffer and then watching the frustration on his face when his leg wouldn't work had been hell and had intensified his guilt.

As he had done a hundred times since the night Wyatt was injured, Hatcher mentally replayed the events. Tinsley and his wife, Felicia, had been friends. Wyatt and Hatcher had been working day and night to find Tinsley.

But he and Felicia had been on the outs. He'd asked for a divorce, packed his bag, and checked into a motel. That night, he'd succumbed to his burning attraction to Korine.

Then Wyatt had gotten a lead on the sadistic maniac holding Tinsley, and they'd chased it down. At the time, they hadn't realized there were two men who called themselves the Skull, two men who worked as a team, sharing their violent rituals with each other, competing for their conquests.

Just as he and Wyatt approached the shanty where the Skull was holding Tinsley hostage, Hatcher had heard a scream in the woods.

Felicia.

He'd raced to find her and left Wyatt alone to save Tinsley. Tinsley's abductor had attacked Wyatt with a hunting knife and sliced his leg to the bone. Wyatt had fired a round and hit the bastard. Bleeding but still standing, the monster had escaped. Even injured, Wyatt had managed to rescue Tinsley and call 9-1-1 before he passed out from blood loss.

Sweat broke out on Hatcher's brow as he drove. He fought the image of Felicia dangling from a tree, her naked body dripping blood. That image would haunt him forever.

He didn't realize he was breathing hard and sweating until Korine's voice jarred him back to reality.

"Hatcher, are you okay?"

He nodded, wiped at his forehead, and slowly exhaled. "Just wondering if Wyatt is really up to this. Last time I saw him he could barely stand."

"Work may be the therapy he needs."

"He needed a partner who wouldn't let him get injured."

He hadn't realized he'd said that aloud and silently cursed himself.

"I read the file. There were two perps. You had to divide up to try and save your wife."

Raw pain sliced through him.

"At least you took one of those psychos off the streets," Korine said. "If you hadn't killed him, he could have taken another victim by now."

True. And that gave him solace.

But Felicia was still dead. Wyatt had nearly lost his leg. Tinsley was holed up in that cottage, terrified her kidnapper was coming back for her.

He should be searching for him instead of looking for the judge's killer.

Korine touched his arm in a sympathetic gesture. He bit back a moan. He'd forgotten how good her touch felt.

How much he wanted those hands on him, assuaging his pain and giving him pleasure.

But his selfishness and weakness had cost his wife her life.

He shrugged off Korine's hand and clenched the steering wheel. He would never let himself care about anyone else again. And he sure as hell wouldn't jump back in bed with Korine.

CHAPTER FOURTEEN

Korine sized up Wyatt while he and Hatcher did the man-hug thing. Wyatt was almost as tall as Hatcher, with broad shoulders and a strong jaw. Even wearing sweats, Wyatt's muscles bunched beneath his black T-shirt and baggy pants.

Shaggy dark-brown hair framed a square face, and his skin was slightly pale, probably from being inside and his injuries. He met them at the door, leaning on a cane.

She offered her hand and introduced herself. "I'm working with Hatcher now."

"It's temporary," Hatcher said bluntly.

He must be counting the days until she was reassigned.

Wyatt gave her a warm smile and his partner a dry look. "Nice to meet you, Korine. You got your work cut out for you with him."

Hatcher grunted. "How's the leg?"

Wyatt lifted his cane to demonstrate that he could stand on his own, but his wince suggested he was still in pain.

"You don't have to show off because there's a woman around," Hatcher said, a mixture of amusement and irritation in his voice.

"I don't want the pretty lady to think I'm helpless," Wyatt said with a wink.

Korine bit back a smile. Had Hatcher told Wyatt about their one-night stand? Was Wyatt flirting with her to see whether he got a reaction from his buddy?

Wyatt leaned on his cane and led them through the entry of his apartment to a den that adjoined an open living area complete with a home gym.

"My torture chamber," Wyatt said as they passed the exercise bike.

Hatcher grunted again. "By the time you come back, you'll be in better shape than me."

"Hell, man, I always was." Wyatt lowered himself in a chair and gestured for them to sit. "You talked to Bellows?"

Hatcher nodded. "He said you've been pushing him for work."

A darkness shadowed Wyatt's eyes. "I'm sick of physical therapy and sitting on my ass."

"He told you about the case we caught?"

Wyatt settled his cane by the chair and murmured that he had. "You found the body near Tinsley Jensen's place?"

"That's right."

"I don't like it," Wyatt said. "That bastard may have done it just to let her know he found out where she lived."

"I thought about that," Hatcher admitted. "We're still looking for him, you know."

"I know. When you stopped calling, I stayed in touch with Bellows."

Hatcher looked down, his expression tortured. "I'm sorry, man."

"I'm going to find him and make him pay," Wyatt said gruffly.

"*We'll* find him," Hatcher said, his tone full of conviction. "We just need a lead."

Korine felt as if she was intruding. These men shared a close bond. And now a cause.

Wyatt rapped his knuckles on the arm of the chair. "How's Tinsley?"

Hatcher glanced at Korine, then his former partner. "Scared. She had no association with the judge, although he once owned a place on Seahawk Island. A cottage near the one Tinsley's renting."

"Where are you on the case?" Wyatt asked.

Korine filled him in on the family dynamics and the rape victims.

"I wouldn't blame those women if they killed him," Wyatt said. "But if I were them, I would have saved my vengeance for Milburn."

Hatcher mumbled agreement. "I'll bring in the file boxes. The sooner we clear this case, the sooner we can get back to tracking down the Skull."

"I'll help." Korine followed Hatcher outside. It took them several trips to haul all the boxes in.

Wyatt whistled. "Wow, he was an unpopular man, wasn't he?"

"That's why we need your manpower."

Wyatt patted his chest. "I'm on it."

Korine's phone buzzed with a text. She quickly checked it. Bellows.

"You two want a drink?" Wyatt asked. "We can get started on those files."

Hatcher licked his lips but declined.

Korine gestured toward her phone. "Bellows just texted. Judge Wadsworth persuaded the parole board to deny parole to a convicted felon last week. That inmate escaped after the transfer bus crashed the morning the judge died."

Hatcher stood. "Let's go."

She said goodbye to Wyatt and headed to the door. Hatcher was on her heels, his expression solemn as they climbed in his SUV.

"Add another suspect to the list," Hatcher muttered as he drove toward Pooler, where the escaped prisoner's brother lived. "No telling how many others Wyatt will find in those files."

Korine sighed. "True."

"Tell me about this inmate."

Korine accessed the police database on her iPad and found Pallo's history. Skimming it made her skin crawl. "Pallo Whiting is a child molester. Started with his niece, then his appetite was whetted. He coached a Little League T-ball team where two of the kids told their parents that he molested them."

"I can see why the judge didn't want to release him," Hatcher said. "Did the brother help him escape?"

"Not sure how the brother felt about Pallo," Korine said. "It was his little girl that Pallo molested."

"Brother could have broken him out to get revenge," Hatcher suggested.

"That's possible, although the record indicates that he didn't visit Pallo." Korine continued studying the file. "Looks like Pallo was targeted in prison for preying on kids."

"Not unusual." Hatcher had zero sympathy for pedophiles. The bastard deserved to suffer for what he'd done to those children.

"Why did the judge speak to the parole board?" Hatcher asked.

"Says here that Pallo stabbed two other inmates to death. He claimed it was retribution because they raped him, but murder charges were added to his other charges. He was being transferred to Hays when he escaped."

Nobody wanted to go to Hays. The maximum-security facility housed the worst of the worst.

Hatcher veered onto a country road leading to swampland. Late-afternoon shadows played across the road, the sea oats waving in the wind, the sky dark with storm clouds. Downed trees from the hurricane had been pushed to the side to clear the road, and blue tarps covered roofs that had sustained damage until insurance settlements ponied up to fund repairs.

He barreled over the ruts in the dirt road until he reached a wooden shack that jutted up to the marsh. Senses alert, he scanned the property in search of the brother or Pallo. The last thing they needed was to walk into a trap.

A rusted black pickup was parked beneath a tin-roofed carport to the side. Hatcher climbed out, hand on his gun, braced for Pallo or his brother to attack.

Korine did the same, her posture alert, her eyes scanning. She'd been sharp in training at Quantico—not the first thing that had caught his eye, but impressive.

They inched toward the house, guns drawn. Seconds ticked by, the wind whistling, gravel crunching beneath their boots as they crept to the front porch. The rotting wooden stairs creaked as Hatcher climbed them, and Korine stepped to the right to peek through the front window.

"Dark inside, no movement," Korine said in a low voice.

Hatcher raised his fist and knocked, then twisted the doorknob. The door screeched open. He peered into a dark entry, then an outdated kitchen/living room. No sounds inside.

He gestured that he'd check the hall and bedrooms, and she moved through the kitchen to the back stoop. A quick sweep through the dingy rooms, and he'd cleared the space. No sign the brother was on the premises. Or that a child lived in the house either.

Korine's shout echoed from the back. "Hatcher! Get out here!"

Adrenaline shot through him, and he gripped his gun at the ready and raced to the back door. A gunshot blasted the air, and his stomach clenched.

He pivoted, searching the yard for Pallo or his brother. Did one of them have Korine? Was he going to have to watch another woman die?

A movement near the swamp caught his eye, and relief spilled through him when he spotted Korine. She was standing upright. No one holding a gun or a knife to her. *Thank God.*

His heart pounded as he inched his way outside. A mangy-looking dog was slumped on the ground. At first he thought it was dead, but it howled and tilted its head toward him. It was alive, and blood dotted its nose.

"Korine?" He moved slowly, eyes tracking the property, gun braced. Korine pivoted slightly. Then Hatcher spotted the reason she'd called his name.

A man lay on the ground, naked, covered in blood. An alligator lay dead beside him.

The gunshot. Korine had killed the gator to prevent it from sinking its teeth into the man's carcass.

Korine's face paled as he drew closer. "It's Pallo Whiting." She stepped aside, giving him a better view.

He halted. Pallo was naked, arms yanked above his head, tied to the tree, eyes wide in shock. Blood was everywhere.

He'd been emasculated. Penis cut off.

Body left for the gators to feast on as if he were nothing but roadkill.

Hatcher quickly phoned for the ERT.

Just like the judge, the killer had painted SS on the man's forehead in blood.

♦ ♦ ♦

The scene disturbed Korine. Not because Pallo Whiting was an innocent who hadn't deserved to die. Because his death had been violent. Sadistic.

It was also fitting to his crimes.

Judging from the fresh blood, she'd estimate he hadn't been dead long. Meaning he could have killed the judge.

So who had murdered him? His brother?

A parent of one of his victims?

She stooped to pet the dog and check it for injuries. It appeared fine. The blood on its nose had come from Whiting.

She led it back to the porch, then tied it to the rail to keep it from contaminating the scene any further. Animal Control could take it to a shelter and find it a home.

After she called Animal Control, she and Hatcher walked the property as they waited on the ERT, studying the layout of the land and looking for forensics.

A few minutes later, it roared up in a blaze of lights and sirens. Hatcher went to greet them. It was Bellamy and Hammond again. They were keeping them busy this week.

Korine snapped photos of the body, the rope, the way Whiting's hands were stretched above his head, and the bruises on his face and torso. They could have come from prison, the bus crash, or his murderer. Pinpointing time of death would help. Hopefully the ERT would find forensics that would lead to the truth.

The investigators fanned out to search the swamp, property, truck, and house.

Hatcher approached, jaw clenched. "I've issued an APB for Pallo's brother, Ernest."

"I can understand why he hated him," Korine said. "But why would he have killed him on his own property and left him here for us to find? That wouldn't be smart. It was like he was pointing the finger at himself." She gestured toward the marsh. "Pallo's body is only a few hundred feet from the swamp. Why didn't he drag him out there and dump him in the water? The gators would have disposed of him, and no one would have ever found him."

"Maybe he figured the blood would draw the gators, and they'd finish him off."

"Leaving no evidence." Korine twisted her mouth in thought. "But still, he could have disposed of him more quickly. His body might never have been found. We would have thought Pallo was still on the run."

Hatcher turned and surveyed the land, then walked to the edge of the swamp. "Maybe he planned to do that, but he was interrupted and decided to run."

Korine considered that theory. "That's possible, I suppose. Although the judge's killer did the same. He could have dumped the judge in the water and let the tides carry him out to sea. We might never have found him."

"Good point."

"Do you see any indication that another car was here?"

Hatcher pointed to footprints at the edge of the swamp. "No, but the unsub could have come via boat and escaped the same way."

"The unsub had to be strong to subdue him, then tie him up out here. Whiting's a big man. We know from his prison file he was a fighter."

"He had bruises," Hatcher said. "The ME should be able to tell us more about the source and timing after the autopsy."

Korine nodded agreement. Speculation did no good. They needed evidence.

"I'll check with the prison warden, dig into the details of the bus crash." The pieces were all connected in some way. And too coincidental not to be important.

A white van bearing the logo for the local news station careened up, and Marilyn Ellis jumped out with a microphone in hand, a cameraman on her heels.

Shit. The press would blast details they didn't want revealed. Create panic.

Drummond snapped a picture of the body. "No one's gonna throw a memorial for that creep."

Korine tensed. Drummond was right.

But something about that seemed odd as well. The judge had a boatload of enemies. And so did Pallo.

Now both were dead.

The reporter made a beeline for Hatcher, and Korine ducked into the shadows. Hatcher could handle the barracuda, Marilyn Ellis.

Right now Korine needed to watch. To think.

If Pallo had killed the judge, one of the judge's family members could have come after him as payback.

But how would they know that Pallo had killed the judge when she and Hatcher had only learned about Pallo's escape a couple of hours ago?

From that crime-watch app Serena had created?

She had to consider all the possibilities. If Pallo hadn't killed the judge, they still had a mountain of suspects.

The same for Pallo.

Unless . . . the same unsub killed both men. The justice symbol on the victims' foreheads indicated that was true.

A chill slithered up Korine's spine as a theory took shape in her mind.

CHAPTER FIFTEEN

As the crime scene investigators combed the yard and house, Hatcher phoned Wyatt and filled him in. Next, he called Cat at the bureau.

"Pallo Whiting's brother, Ernest, is not home. Do you have a work address or cell phone where we could trace him?"

Computer keys clicked in the background. "No job. He was laid off from a construction gig because he was drugging. Oxy. No cell phone either."

Damn. "Is there another house or apartment he might go to?"

Cat sighed. "Not that I have listed."

"What about his daughter and his wife?"

"Wife divorced him and took the daughter away during his brother's trial. She blamed her husband for what happened to the little girl. Denied him visitation or parental rights."

That would have been enough for motive. "Was there any evidence to support her belief that Ernest knew what the brother was doing?"

A tense few seconds passed. He assumed she was skimming for information.

"Ernest was called to the witness stand and testified that he had no idea."

"Did Judge Wadsworth rule in the custody hearing?"

"No, he was strictly criminal trials. This was a family-court judge, Arthur Yale."

Hatcher scratched his head. "What did the judge base his decision on?"

"Give me a minute."

Hatcher scanned the property. Bellamy was taking a cast of the partial footprint by the swamp's edge. It would help if they could find the murder weapon, but most likely the unsub had taken it with him or tossed it into the water.

"Ernest's wife claimed Ernest got hooked on Oxy after he hurt his back. On top of the Oxy, he drank, a bad combination," Cat continued. "He sent her to the hospital with bruises at least twice. Judge Yale ordered Ernest to attend AA and anger management. He was supposed to review the situation in a year."

"My guess is Ernest didn't follow through."

"There's no record that he did," Cat said.

Hatcher made a low sound in his throat. "Maybe he blamed his brother for ruining his marriage and his life and decided it was payback time."

"Sounds plausible."

He ended the call and went to catch up with Korine, but his mind spun with questions.

Two vicious murders, two days apart. Two cases where no one would really mourn the dead. Two cases that might be connected.

A feeling of foreboding engulfed him.

The SS painted in blood on the victims' foreheads indicated they were dealing with one unsub or . . . two, as in the case of the Skull. The symbols could be the unsub's—or unsubs'—signature.

Did they have a vigilante killer on their hands?

◆　◆　◆

An hour later, Hatcher parked at the Porters' house on the outskirts of Savannah. The Porters' daughter, Chelsea, had been molested by Pallo

Whiting when she was seven. In the three years since, the couple had divorced.

The thought of questioning this family gave Korine a bad taste in her mouth. "Apparently Chelsea has suffered from emotional problems since the molestation."

"No surprise there," Hatcher muttered.

"She's in counseling. But the trial was hard on the family and tore the couple apart. Father moved to South Carolina. The mother, Polly, lives here with Chelsea. She's a teacher at the local high school."

"Let's find out if the father was in town," Hatcher said.

Together they walked up to the door on the front stoop of the duplex. Shadows fell across the weathered place, which sat on the edge of the marsh.

A red Ford SUV was parked in the drive, and a low light burned in the front room. Korine knocked, her heart aching for the family.

A thin woman with brown hair in a ponytail answered the door, wearing a sweatshirt and sweat pants. She barely cracked the door. "Who are you?"

Korine and Hatcher quickly identified themselves.

Polly exhaled sharply, then opened the door. Her expression turned wary as she looked at their identification. "This is about that awful man who hurt Chelsea, isn't it?"

"I'm afraid so," Korine said.

"I heard that he escaped." She glanced past them, her gaze darting up and down the road nervously. "I've been scared to death he'd come here."

"Why would you think that?" Hatcher asked. "Have you heard from him?"

The woman rolled her eyes. "No, but we testified against him at the sentencing," Polly said. "I told the judge I thought child molesters should get the death penalty."

"You wanted him dead?" Korine asked.

"Wouldn't you if he'd molested your child?"

Korine couldn't argue with that.

A dark-haired little girl rounded the corner holding a spatula covered in pink icing. "Mommy, we need to finish!"

Polly gave them a warning look, which Korine interpreted as a message to tread carefully in front of her daughter. Korine would do that anyway.

She offered the child a smile. "That icing looks delicious."

"It is." Chelsea swiped her finger along one edge of the spatula, then licked the frosting. "The teacher's birthday's tomorrow, so we're making her a surprise."

"Honey. Go on back in the kitchen," Polly said. "I'll be there in a sec."

Chelsea smiled and skipped back through the doorway to the kitchen.

"She's been through enough," Polly said. "I didn't want to tell her that sicko had escaped, so I kept her home from school today. She's just recently started sleeping without nightmares." Pain etched itself on her face. "I'm terrified that he'll come after her. Please tell me you found him."

"Were you here with Polly last night and this morning?" Hatcher asked.

"I'm always with her when she's home, and I drive her to school so I can keep her safe. Why do you ask?" Polly cut her eyes between them. "Where is he? Is he nearby? Did someone see him in our yard?"

The panic in the woman's voice tore at Korine. This mother and her child had suffered enough. "No one saw him around here. But we did find him."

She heaved a sigh. "So he's locked up where he belongs?"

Korine gave her a sympathetic look. "Don't worry—he can't hurt your daughter or anyone else. Pallo Whiting is dead."

♦ ♦ ♦

Hatcher forced himself not to react as Polly Porter staggered backward and leaned against the wall in the foyer. The color had drained from her face.

Korine gently touched her arm. "Are you okay, ma'am?"

It took Polly a second to respond, but when she did, relief flooded her eyes. "This probably sounds heartless to you, but I'm glad he's dead. I testified because I didn't want him to hurt another little girl the way he did Chelsea."

"No child should have to suffer," Korine agreed softly.

The woman gave her a grateful look, tears blurring her eyes. "It's been awful. But now he's dead, we're finally free, and I can stop looking over our shoulders."

Hatcher couldn't imagine the horror of knowing your child had been abused. If it had been his little girl, he would have tracked down the bastard and made him suffer.

Maybe a family member of one of Whiting's victims had.

But he didn't think it was Polly.

"Mrs. Porter, where's your husband?"

"My ex," Polly said in a voice laced with bitterness. "He couldn't handle Chelsea's nightmares or mine. He left us and moved to South Carolina."

"I'm sorry," Hatcher said. "Do you have a number where you can reach him?"

She shook her head. "I could give you his cell, but he's hard to reach. Howard's an ER doc and in Honduras on a mission trip, giving medical care to the needy," she said. "Ironic, but I think he tries to save others because he couldn't save his own child."

Hatcher bit the inside of his cheek. Noble, but how could a man abandon his daughter when she needed him?

"Besides, if you think Howard killed Pallo Whiting, you're wrong," Polly said. "He was enraged at the creep, but he's devoted to medicine and saving lives. He's also the most passive person I've ever known."

Hatcher remained silent. Maybe she was right. But someone had killed Pallo Whiting, someone who'd wanted him to suffer for what he'd done.

No one had more motive than the parents of the children he abused.

Hatcher thanked her, and he and Korine stepped outside. Dark clouds rumbled above, and lightning streaked the sky. Tree limbs swayed and bobbed in the gusty wind, raindrops pinging off the drive as they hurried to his SUV.

"Who's next on the list?"

"The Green family," Korine said. "Little girl, Lottie Forkner, was abused by Whiting a year ago. She's a foster child. Foster mother, Lynn, works at a women's shelter and took the child in when the birth mother died."

Hatcher gritted his teeth. Foster families got a bad rap. Abuse was a problem.

He had to hold off on forming an opinion, though, until he heard what Lynn Green had to say.

◆ ◆ ◆

Night was setting in as they reached the Green's home in an apartment complex not far from the Porter house.

Pallo Whiting had worked as a janitor at the school both of the girls attended and had apparently watched them for weeks before taking them. The fact that the girls had recognized him from school made it easy for him to lure them outside their homes. Damn man had used a common ploy—he pretended to be hunting for his puppy. A puppy that he'd intentionally put out near the little girls' yards.

Korine swallowed back bile. Polly Porter had been relieved that Whiting was dead, but she wasn't a killer. *Thank God.* The little girl needed her mother.

Korine rang the doorbell, while Hatcher scanned the property surrounding the apartment complex. The buildings were old, desperate for repairs, and catered to residents who needed subsidized housing.

A fortysomething woman with short, black hair answered the door, her eyes narrowed. "I'm not buying anything."

Korine flashed her badge. "We aren't selling anything. We just need to talk about what happened to your foster child."

A frown deepened the grooves beside her eyes. "That guardian ad litem, Laura Austin, convinced them to take Lottie from me, so unless you're here to tell me I can have her back, I ain't got nothing to say."

"You lost Lottie?" Hatcher asked.

A wave of sadness washed over the woman's face. "The state said she needed a family with child-counseling experience. I guess they blamed me for that crazy man abusing her." Pain colored her voice. "As if I didn't blame myself enough."

"Why would you blame yourself?" Korine asked gently.

The woman rubbed her temple. "I had a bad migraine. Lay down for a bit. I thought Lottie was watching TV, but she slipped out." She brushed at a tear. "I couldn't have kids of my own and loved that little girl like she was mine. I'll never forgive myself for that day."

Korine's heart went out to her. "I'm so sorry for both of you. Maybe the court will reconsider."

Lynn blew a breath that lifted her bangs from her forehead. "I don't think so. They won't let me foster kids anymore at all."

Korine's throat closed. She didn't know how to respond to that. The state did have to be cautious. But this woman was hurting and had lost the child she loved because of Whiting.

Was she bitter enough to kill him?

CHAPTER SIXTEEN

The anguish in the woman's voice sounded real. She'd obviously loved the little girl, which meant she had good reason to hate Whiting. "Did you know that Whiting escaped prison during a bus transfer?" Hatcher asked.

Her eyes widened. "Oh my God, that's why you're here? You think he's coming after Lottie?"

"Lottie is safe from him." Hatcher shifted. "Did you know about his escape?"

The woman shook her head no. "Do you think he's coming after me then? Two of the other little girls' parents and I testified against him."

"You didn't hear from the other parents after the prison escape?"

She shook her head, but her eyes darted to the side table where her phone was. He sensed she was lying, that someone had given her a heads-up.

"I haven't heard from them since the sentencing. We all needed space and time to heal."

Korine cleared her throat. "Where were you last night, Lynn?"

Confusion flashed on Lynn's face. "Why do you want to know where I was?"

Hatcher folded his arms. "Please just answer the question, ma'am."

"At the women's shelter," she said. "I'm there most nights, especially now they took Lottie." Her voice trailed off, wistful, sad. "It's just too lonely here by myself."

Hatcher sympathized, but he had a job to do. Emotions had no place in it. Hadn't he learned from prior cases that people could be consummate liars? "Can someone verify that you were at the shelter?"

"You could go by Hope House, but they have a strict rule about not giving out information. They're there to protect women and children in trouble. Sometimes that means keeping secrets."

And not talking to the police.

Hatcher knew the drill and understood.

Anger simmered below the surface of her words. "Now, tell me the truth. If someone saw him lurking around here, I have a right to know."

"He hasn't been lurking around here," Korine said. "He's dead."

Lynn gasped. "What? How? Where?"

"He was murdered," Hatcher said matter-of-factly.

Shock streaked her eyes. Then relief. "Well, good. When you find his killer, let me know. I'd like to shake the hand of the person who rid the world of that monster."

◆ ◆ ◆

"What do you think?" Korine asked as they left the Green apartment.

Hatcher shrugged, his gaze lingering on the place as he backed from the drive. "A tough situation. She had good reason to hate Whiting."

"But you don't think she killed him?"

"My gut says no. And no one at the shelter will give us information."

"That's true," Korine agreed. "Maybe the guardian ad litem can shed some light on Ms. Green. But we should talk to her in person."

Korine called Cat and learned Austin's office was in the courthouse, but she'd gone for the day, so they drove to her townhome. Hatcher rang the bell, and Austin answered a minute later.

Korine introduced them, and Austin invited them into the foyer. Korine quickly explained the situation. "Tell us about Lynn Green."

Austin pursed her lips. "I don't discuss my clients."

"We don't need details, just your impression of her," Hatcher said. "We're trying to clear her of Pallo Whiting's murder."

The young woman hesitated. "All right, but I can't share confidential information."

"Understood," Korine said.

"Lynn Green is a loving, caring person," Laura said. "But she was caught in a bad situation."

"Did she do anything to suggest she was responsible for what happened to Lottie?" Korine asked.

"Absolutely not. She loved that child more than anything. It broke my heart to separate them."

"But you did. Why?"

Austin cleared her throat. "My job is to look out for the child's best interest. I spoke with the child psychologist and forensic interviewer, who agreed that Lottie needed a safe haven and stable environment. Returning to the place where she had been lured by Whiting triggered nightmares. Lynn was devastated by what happened to Lottie and was emotional herself. That wasn't helping Lottie."

"You said Lynn was emotional. Do you think she would go after Whiting for what he did?"

Austin shook her head. "Lynn is protective of children and she hated Whiting, but she's a tender heart and wouldn't hurt a fly. She suffered her own hard knocks—grew up with an alcoholic father and ran away when she was a teenager. When she isn't volunteering at that shelter, she volunteers at the animal-rescue center."

"Please call me if you think of anything that might help," Korine said.

The young woman agreed, and Korine and Hatcher said goodbye and left.

"Where next?" Korine asked.

Hatcher cleared his throat. "I want to talk to a man named Ned Banning. Whiting killed his son in prison."

"That would be motive."

Hatcher pulled into traffic, drove several blocks, then veered down a side street and stopped at a fish market located at the pier. The area looked almost deserted, although a low light burned in a covered shed at the end. The pier housed stalls for shrimpers and fishermen to sell their products during the summer and was overrun with tourists and locals, buying the fresh catches. Except for a heavyset guy in a bloody apron hosing down the end stall, the booths were empty.

The scent of fish and the marsh enveloped Korine as they parked.

Hatcher opened his car door. "You can stay here."

She squared her shoulders. She might have allowed him to take the lead in bed, and he had more experience than her in the field, but he wouldn't shut her out. "I'm here for backup, Hatcher, not to sit on the sidelines."

He shrugged. "Suit yourself. I thought you might call Cat and track down the family of the other prisoner Whiting killed."

Korine gritted her teeth. "I can do that, but I'll be watching in case you need me."

"I won't." In spite of his cold tone, his gaze met hers, dark eyes raking over her. Heat flickered in the depths, a sensual, hungry look that turned her stomach upside down.

Damn him. The chemistry that had made them tear each other's clothes off in a hasty frenzy of lust a few months ago still simmered between them.

But they couldn't act on it.

Irritation flashed in his dark eyes as if he felt it, too, and didn't like it, but he didn't comment. He stalked down the dock to see the man.

She punched Cat's number and explained what she needed.

"Whiting killed two men. The first is twenty-seven-year-old Gerard Banning. His father works at the fish market. The second is fifty-one-year-old Tyrone Hubbard, a lifer, in for a gang-related shooting. Whiting stabbed him in the mess hall."

"What about Hubbard's family?"

"He had one daughter, but I doubt she's your killer. According to his file, she hadn't spoken to him in years. Didn't attend his trial, never visited, sent mail, or called. She lives in Seattle with two sons. Never met their grandfather."

Korine massaged her temple where a headache was starting to pulse. So far, everyone they'd talked to had motive, but they also had alibis.

A movement caught her eye. Hatcher flashed his badge as he approached the fisherman. Suddenly the man shoved a cart toward Hatcher, then jumped into his boat, which was tied to the dock. The man fired at Hatcher.

Hatcher ducked to avoid the bullet; then the boat sped away.

Korine slipped her weapon from her holster, threw open the car door, and took off running.

◆ ◆ ◆

Hatcher cursed as he dove behind a barrel, then fired at Ned Banning. Footsteps pounded on the dock, and Korine's voice echoed behind him. "Hatcher?"

"I'm here." But Banning was getting away.

Hatcher jumped up and ran to the edge of the dock. A wave crashed against the shore from Banning's boat. Hatcher quickly searched for another boat to give chase.

Korine must have had the same idea and ran to the opposite side. "Come on!" She jumped into a small fishing boat tied near another stand and fired up the engine as he raced toward her. Seconds later, she grabbed the wheel and sped after Banning.

Hatcher kept his eyes and gun trained on Banning as Korine steered the boat around the cove into open water and raced up behind Banning. Banning swung around and fired at them.

He and Korine both ducked to dodge the bullet as she closed in. The boat bounced over the choppy waves, but Banning accelerated and added distance between them. A second later, he was going so fast he skimmed a dock and nearly lost control.

Korine punched the gas and swerved around a buoy. Banning looked panicked as he glanced back at them. He released another round and sped up. Hatcher fired at him, and Banning jerked the wheel to the right, but in his haste, misjudged and slammed into the embankment. The impact sent Banning over the wheel and into the water.

Korine guided their boat to the right and coasted to the shore. Banning flailed in the water, but his jerky movements suggested he didn't know how to swim. He shouted, gurgling water as he fought to stay above the surface. The current dragged him under.

Hatcher cursed, shucked his gun and jacket, then jumped in to save the man. Cold water seeped into his pores as he dove beneath the surface.

Banning panicked and fought, kicking and clawing for the surface.

Hatcher grabbed his arm and tried to pull him toward the shore, but Banning struggled to get away from him. Furious, Hatcher dragged him above the surface, then punched the man in the jaw.

Banning went limp, his head lolling to the side. Hatcher slid one arm around his upper torso, then paddled to the edge.

Korine guided the boat to the dock, cut the engine, and climbed out. She rushed to the edge just as he crawled onto the shore with Banning, then she grabbed Banning's arm and helped haul him onto the embankment.

Banning stirred, sputtering water, his eyes wild. Panic flashed onto his face, and he shoved at Hatcher to escape, but Korine pressed her gun to the man's cheek. "Move and I'll shoot."

Banning froze, face contorted with fear.

Korine tossed Hatcher her cuffs.

"You're under arrest for attempted murder," Hatcher growled.

He shoved Banning to his side, jerked his arms behind him, and handcuffed him.

CHAPTER SEVENTEEN

Laura Austin's hand trembled as she punched the number of her best friend, Liz. The two of them met on the swim team in college and had been close friends since. Laura traced her finger over the photograph of her baby boy and five-year-old daughter, her heart squeezing.

She'd do anything to protect her children. *Anything.*

Although Liz didn't have children yet, she would one day, and she would be an awesome mother. Just as she was a fierce advocate for the victims she worked with—some were abused women, others children. Domestic violence ran rampant in every city, and Liz had devoted herself to counseling victims as well as helping them maneuver the legal system and reroute their lives. She held their hands through trials, arranged for court orders, and aided in the victims' recovery on multiple levels.

The phone rang three times; then Liz finally answered.

"It's Laura, Liz. The FBI just stopped by, asking about Lynn Green and her foster daughter, Lottie."

"What's wrong? Are they okay?"

"Pallo Whiting was murdered last night."

A strained heartbeat stretched between them.

"What did you tell them?" Liz asked.

"Nothing, just that Lynn loved Lottie and wouldn't hurt anyone."

Another heartbeat passed. "Let's meet in the chat room."

"That's what I was thinking. I'll let Rachel know."

"I'll call Bev. We all need to talk."

Laura hung up, her nerves on edge. She ran her finger over her baby's face in the photograph. Her children deserved to grow up in a safe world.

When she, Liz, Rachel, Bev, and Kendall had first met, they'd been young and trusting. Innocent.

None of them was innocent anymore.

CHAPTER EIGHTEEN

Hatcher gripped Banning by the collar and shook him. "You don't get to pass out after that stunt. I know you hated Pallo Whiting for killing your son. Then he escaped and you murdered him." Although the MO of the crime—cutting the man's penis off—seemed more personal, a crime of passion, something the parent of one of the child victims would do.

Then again, the signature SS could have been a ploy to throw off the police.

Although they hadn't divulged details of the justice symbol, so how would Banning have known about that?

Banning's eyelids flickered open, then closed, and he moaned.

"Did you help him escape so you could murder him?" Hatcher barked.

The big man moved his head from side to side. "You got it wrong. Didn't kill him."

"Sure you did," Hatcher muttered. "Really, I don't blame you. He killed your son, so you had to pay him back."

"No," the man mumbled again. "Wish I had, but I didn't."

Hatcher's breath hissed between clenched teeth, and he exchanged a questioning look with Korine. "Then why the hell did you run?"

Banning coughed, his thick lips curled into a snarl. "Because I knew you Feebies would try to pin it on me the way you pinned that crime on my son."

Hatcher released the man's shirt collar. "Do you know how many men in prison claim they've been framed?"

Banning's breath rattled out. "Probably thousands, but my son *was* innocent. His ex-wife wanted to get back at him because he left her, so she came up with a plan—"

"That doesn't give you the right to kill Whiting," Hatcher said.

"I told you I didn't, but you're probably no better lawman than the one who arrested my son. That lazy jackass got Gerard killed."

Hatcher bit back an argument. Banning could be right about the lawyer. He could have someone look into Gerard's case, but it was too late to save Gerard.

But now that his father had shot at him and Korine, he couldn't just release him.

He jerked the man to his feet and shoved him toward the dock. "Maybe you didn't have anything to do with Whiting's death, maybe you did. But a few days in lockup will give you time to cool down."

"I want an attorney," Banning bellowed.

"I thought you didn't trust lawyers," Hatcher said with an eyebrow raised.

Banning gave him a go-to-hell look.

Korine jumped into the boat, Hatcher shoved Banning down inside it, and then she started the engine and guided the boat back to the fishing dock. Together they escorted Banning to Hatcher's SUV and stowed him inside.

"Why don't you do some real police work and protect the innocents instead of locking up people who've been hurt by the likes of Whiting?" Banning shouted as Hatcher pulled from the parking lot.

Hatcher silently cursed. Banning had a point.

He had taken justice into his own hands when he'd killed the man who'd murdered his wife. And he hadn't regretted it for one second since.

But he couldn't condone others doing the same by looking the other way.

Could he?

♦ ♦ ♦

Korine's hopes of quickly finding Whiting's killer died as she and Hatcher parked at the field office in Savannah.

Hatcher climbed out and retrieved Banning from the back seat. Banning had clammed up, his body rigid, his eyes stony. He was probably regretting firing at them. If he hadn't, they wouldn't have had reason to bring him in.

Was he right about his son being framed? If so, the system had failed his family . . .

Her phone buzzed. She clenched her jaw—a text, her mother's number. The instinct to ignore it hit her, but how could she when her mother's condition was frail?

"The case?" Hatcher asked.

She shook her head. "Family. I'm sorry. I need to check in." Motioning for him to take care of booking Banning, she stopped inside the doorway and read the message.

Kenny was arrested on a DUI charge—he called looking for you to bail him out. Your mother overheard and is upset. Come ASAP.

Korine's breath stalled in her chest, and she punched in her mother's number. The phone rang a half dozen times, ratcheting up her nerves. No answer.

She ended the call and tried again, tapping her foot as she waited, but no one responded.

Hatcher returned, his expression grim. "A night in jail will do Banning good."

"You think?" Korine wasn't so sure. "Or it could antagonize him. He already thinks his son got a bum deal. And now we're arresting him."

"He shot at us," Hatcher said.

Korine nodded. She shouldn't be sympathetic to the man. The law was the law. When people took it into their own hands, anarchy would prevail.

"I need to go." She gestured to her phone. "Family emergency."

His eyes darkened, and he jangled his keys. "All right. Where to?"

Her heart stuttered. Except for their one night of indiscretion, they'd kept their personal lives separate. The last thing she wanted was for Hatcher to witness her family drama. He'd see how screwed up her life was.

"Just drop me at my place, and I'll drive from there."

He narrowed his eyes, tension stretching between them. "If it's an emergency, I'm driving you." He didn't wait for a response. He strode out the door.

She chased him to his SUV, and he opened the back, grabbed a shirt from inside a duffel bag, then yanked off his wet one.

Heat flared inside her at the sight of his bare chest. God, she wanted to touch him.

Oblivious to her turmoil, he climbed in the front seat. Shoot, she wanted to see him take off his pants.

But Hatcher was right. She didn't need to take the time to go by her house. And she sure as heck didn't need to think about Hatcher without his pants.

She had to get to her mother.

♦ ♦ ♦

Hatcher pulled from the parking lot and followed the GPS to Korine's mother's house. She had virtually shut down. Not that she'd talked much about herself when he'd known her at Quantico, but her demeanor indicated she didn't want him to ask questions.

He had a right to know what was going on with his partner. For fuck's sake, she might have a boyfriend or husband or crazed, jealous lover.

He didn't like the idea of any of those possibilities.

"Talk to me, Korine."

She simply glared at him. "It's nothing that concerns you."

"If we're going to have each other's backs, we have to be honest with each other. I need to know what I'm dealing with."

Her jaw tightened. "Honest? Like you were when you told me you weren't married?"

Anger flickered in his eyes. "I didn't lie."

"You were still married."

"Legally, maybe," he said in a gruff tone. "But we'd had problems for a long time and were separated. I had asked for a divorce. That's . . . the reason I didn't answer her phone call that night."

"You didn't answer it because we were in bed," Korine snapped.

He shot her a look of contempt. "That was obviously a mistake on my part."

"On both our parts," Korine said.

Their gazes locked, the heat once again flaming between them. Memories of her hands and mouth touching him intimately seared him, stirring his arousal.

He had to stop thinking about her that way. Focus on the case. On whatever secret she was hiding.

Something had upset her about that phone call, and he damn well wanted to know what it was.

He should have researched her in depth before he started working with her. Found out about her past, her family, *her* weaknesses.

But Bellows hadn't given him time.

The deputy director had probably planned it that way.

Korine fidgeted, her teeth worrying her bottom lip. She did that when she was thinking.

"Is this about your father?"

She jerked her gaze to his, surprise and wariness mingling. "What do you know about my father?"

He shrugged. "Not much, just that he was shot to death when you were five."

Her heavy sigh punctuated the air.

"His shooter was never found?"

She shook her head. "This isn't about my father." She shifted in the seat. "My mother is suffering from severe depression," she said, her voice brittle with anguish. "She's digressed to a catatonic state most of the time. Her caretaker, Esme, just texted that I needed to come over. And she's not answering the phone, so something is wrong."

She pointed to a long drive lined with live oaks and pecan trees. A small pond lay to the right of the house, a stately-looking antebellum mansion.

Hmm . . . So Korine came from money.

Funny, but he never would have guessed that from her clothes or her attitude.

She tensed as he parked, and he touched her arm. "Tell me how I can help."

"Stay here," she said sharply. "There's no need for you to get involved in my family drama." She climbed out, slammed the door, and hurried toward the columned porch.

He pushed the automatic window button to lower it, then tilted his head to listen. She wanted him to stay in the car because she was a private person.

Either that, or she was hiding something.

If it was the latter, he'd find out.

Partners couldn't have secrets between them and keep each other safe.

A gusty breeze fluttered the trees and sent dry leaves raining down on the lawn. He imagined the grass was a lush green in spring, flowers blooming in the beds in front and the garden to the side of the house.

Now everything was brown and dead.

His gaze tracked a lone bird soaring over the pond, then dipping down in search of food. Loud voices floated to him on the wind.

Then a shrill scream pierced the air.

He threw open his car door and ran toward the house.

◆ ◆ ◆

Korine bit her tongue, forcing a calm to her voice as she soothed her mother.

The melody "I Feel Pretty" echoed in the background, making matters worse.

Her mother's shrill screams ripped into Korine's thoughts. Her eyes were wild, frantic as she rocked herself back and forth in the wheelchair.

"Shh, Mom, it's okay," Korine said softly.

Her mother looked at her with teary eyes, eyes void of hope as if she was lost in grief and despair.

"I know that Kenny was arrested, Mother, and that he called here looking for me." She stroked her mother's arms, trying to soothe her.

"Kenny needs rehab," Korine continued, striving for an even tone. "When I bail him out of jail, that's where he's going."

Her mother's sobs quieted, then she looked down at her hands. She stared at her fingers as if they were foreign objects and then disappeared into that shell again.

Footsteps sounded behind her, and Korine tensed as Hatcher stormed toward them.

Humiliation washed over her. She hadn't wanted him to witness this. But it was too late.

He halted at the doorway, fists by his side. "Everything okay?"

Korine gave a quick nod. "I told you to wait in the car."

"I heard screams and thought someone might be hurt."

She shot him a lethal look. "I have things under control." She faced her mother again, heart breaking at the sight of her tormented eyes. Grief and . . . fear?

What was she afraid of?

Korine squeezed her mother's hands. "This isn't the first time he got a DUI. If he hurts himself or someone else, then he'll serve time."

Her mother's lips compressed into a thin line, but she remained silent and didn't seem to realize Hatcher was even present.

Esme darted toward her with a glass of water and one of her mother's pills. "Here, time for your medicine."

Her mother shoved the pill away, then turned and wheeled herself out the back door.

A gust of cool air filled the kitchen, the silence deafening.

Esme trembled. "I'm sorry, Ms. Korine."

"It's not your fault," Korine said. "I'm just glad you're here with her." The doctor had suggested an inpatient facility, but her mother loved this house. She'd paid it off with her father's life insurance money and made Korine promise to keep it in the family.

Esme went to the house phone and made a call to the doctor.

Hatcher cleared his throat, sympathy in his dark eyes. "What can I do?" he asked gruffly.

"Meet the doctor at the door," Korine said. "I'll go outside and make sure she's okay."

Hatcher nodded, and Korine dashed through the back door. The low lights that she'd strung around the garden glittered against the night sky. In summer the garden was vibrant, full of colors.

Now it looked desolate.

Bushes rustled, and she spotted her mother wandering through the garden. She paused by what used to be her biggest rosebush. The look on her face was so sad that tears pricked Korine's eyes.

A second later, a memory tickled Korine's mind: she was eight years old. She'd come outside to pick flowers for the dinner table.

Then she saw him. Kenny. He was by the biggest rosebush, on his knees, digging . . . no, he wasn't digging. He was burying something.

She tiptoed toward him, careful to be quiet. Kenny was nice sometimes, but other times he was mean to her. And he didn't like to talk about Daddy.

But she had to talk about him, or she might forget . . .

Leaves crunched beneath her shoes. Kenny heard her and looked up. Dirt covered his shirt and jeans. His hands, too.

Something was in his hand. One of her dolls. Jasmine, the one with the gold ringlets.

Kenny was putting her in the ground.

"No, stop it!" She ran toward him and tried to grab her doll from him. But Kenny was so mad. He shoved her backward. She fell into the dirt and jabbed her palm on a sharp rock.

Then Kenny threw the doll into the hole and began to dump dirt on top of her.

Tears flooded her eyes, and she screamed for her mother.

But when her mother came out, she told her to hush. Then she went over and hugged Kenny . . .

Her mother made a low mewling sound, jerking Korine from the memory. She was kneeling on the ground by the rosebush. The one where Kenny had buried Jasmine.

Her mother was digging the dirt with her hands.

Korine hurried to her, then dropped down beside her. "Mother, what are you doing?"

The woman who looked back at her was a stranger.

The one who'd lost her mind to depression.

"The doll isn't there anymore," Korine whispered. "I dug her up, remember?" Of course, Jasmine had been filthy, her dress was torn, and one of her eyes had been cracked. Her mother had forced her to give the doll to charity.

It had been years since that had happened. Why was her mother thinking about the doll today?

CHAPTER NINETEEN

Korine thanked the doctor for sedating her mother, then kissed her mother on the cheek. "I'll take care of Kenny. Don't worry."

Her mother might not be happy with how she intended to handle the situation, but Kenny needed tough love, not coddling. She wasn't his parent, but she was the only one left to fill that role.

Hatcher had faded into the woodwork, but he'd witnessed enough to understand the gist of their dysfunctional family.

And the fact that she had no control over the situation.

The CD was still playing "I Feel Pretty" as she descended the steps, as if her mother had put it on auto repeat.

Esme looked shaken but was cleaning the kitchen and greeted her with a tentative smile. "Do you want dinner? I made shrimp and grits for your mother, but the doctor said she'll probably sleep all night."

"I couldn't eat right now." Korine's stomach was churning. "Put it in the fridge for later. Maybe Mom will wake up and feel better tomorrow."

Esme covered the casserole dish with foil. "I'm sorry I had to call, but when Kenny phoned, she became hysterical."

Korine gave the little woman a hug. "You don't have to apologize for calling me, Esme. She's my mother. I appreciate everything you do for her. You're a godsend."

Esme wiped at her eyes. "I wish I could do more."

Korine's chest clenched. "You're there for her and me. I can't thank you enough for that."

Esme nodded, and Korine clicked off the CD. "She seems to be playing that a lot."

"I know." Esme frowned. "It's like she's obsessed with it. It must bring back good memories for her."

And sad ones for Korine. Every time she heard the music, she had a flashback of that horrible night, of the door squeaking open and the glint of metal. Then the sound of the gunshots and blood splattering across her father's shirt as he began to stagger . . .

"Korine?" Hatcher's gruff voice jerked her from the troubling thoughts. "Do you need to stay here tonight?"

Korine shook her head. Her mother found the house comforting, but it was the opposite for Korine. She hadn't slept here in years.

Esme squeezed her hand. "Go home and get some rest. I'll call you if we need anything."

Relief filled Korine. As much as she hated leaving Esme, she needed to escape. Being in the house, listening to that song, and hearing her mother's screams resurrected her childhood trauma.

Guilt followed the relief, but she shoved it aside. She had to stay strong. Survive. So she could take care of everyone else.

"Thanks, Esme." She turned to Hatcher. "You can drive me home if you don't mind."

Like a seasoned agent, he was watching her, dissecting her. She felt vulnerable. And she didn't like it.

She averted her gaze as they walked to his SUV.

◆ ◆ ◆

The few minutes alone with Esme while Korine sat by her mother's side with the doctor offered Hatcher insight into Korine's family situation.

Esme had filled him in on the brother. He was nine when their father was murdered. Korine had been five.

After that, Kenny had become sullen, angry, and developed emotional problems that led to drinking and drug use.

Sympathy for Korine filled him. She'd acted tough, but he'd seen the pain in her eyes.

Although Esme hadn't worked for the family at the time of Mr. Davenport's murder, she claimed that Mrs. Davenport had always raved about how close Korine and her father had been.

His stomach growled, a reminder that they'd worked nonstop all day and hadn't eaten. "Let's grab dinner."

"No, thanks. I'm not hungry."

"You have to eat, Korine," he said as he maneuvered through Savannah.

"I just want to go home," she said, her tone short. "I'll look over the case notes and figure out our next move."

For some reason, he didn't want to leave her alone.

A dangerous thought, but he could no more help it than he could have resisted sleeping with her that night after training.

"We can pick up takeout, carry it to your place, and hash over the case together." Work would deter any sexual activity.

She glanced at him, then out the window. "Let's go our own way tonight, then meet up tomorrow and compare notes."

He gripped the steering wheel with clammy hands. She was right not to invite him inside, but he still wanted to be near her. Make sure she really was okay. Hold her and comfort her and take away her pain . . .

Hell, he could not do that. One touch and he'd kiss her senseless and beg her to let him stay.

Not a good idea.

Storm clouds hovered in the sky, casting a gray blanket over the dark night. He pulled in front of her house and parked, then let the engine idle, hoping she'd change her mind.

Instead, she climbed from the SUV.

He couldn't help himself. He followed her to the door.

"Thanks for the ride," she said as she fumbled with her keys.

She really wanted to get away from him. Which, dammit, made his urge to stay even stronger.

She dropped the keys, and he stooped and snatched them, then jammed them in the lock.

"I can do it myself," she snapped as she shoved his hand away.

He held up his hands in submission, then saw tears blurring her eyes, and emotions sucker punched him.

He didn't want to get involved. Didn't want to care.

But he couldn't stop himself. He gently touched her arm.

"You don't have to be so tough," he murmured.

Her body quivered. "People depend on me."

"Your mother's depression sucks, but she has no right to expect you to save your brother."

"They're my family, Hatcher," she said in a strained voice. "I owe them."

He wrapped his arms around her and drew her to him. Anxiety tightened every cell in her body. He rubbed her back to relax her. "I'm sorry," he said in a low voice. "I could stay or . . . you could call a friend."

She released a cynical laugh. "I've been too busy training and with Mother to have a social life."

That sounded like his story. "Well, we're partners now. I'll do whatever you want to help."

She leaned her head against him for a fraction of a second. Her body felt hot, shaky, needy. Or maybe that was his imagination.

His own responded anyway, aching to be closer to her. He closed his eyes, and images of her naked and panting below him teased his mind, her luscious red hair spilled across the pillow.

He lifted a strand of hair and swept it from her face, then she looked into his eyes. A blush stained her cheeks. Her eyes sparkled with tears and something else . . . need? Desire?

His body hardened, his cock twitching.

Shit. He could not go there again.

He was just about to push away, but she did it first. "We'll talk about the case tomorrow."

A second later, she slammed the door, shutting him out.

He stood on the front stoop for a moment, drinking in the night air, wallowing in the lavender scent of her hair and the strength and vulnerability in her voice and body.

Korine Davenport was an interesting woman. Hardheaded and tough. A woman with problems. Baggage.

He had his own.

But the memory of her body against his taunted him as he drove home. He wanted her. Again. And again . . .

♦ ♦ ♦

Korine locked the door, desperate to escape Hatcher.

The sound of music wafted to her, and she froze. Her music box . . .

I feel pretty, oh, so pretty, so pretty and witty and bright . . .

Senses alert, she went very still. She'd left her music box on the mantel, but the music was coming from the back of the house . . .

Fear whispered against her neck, and she reached for her gun. Was someone inside?

She scanned the living room and kitchen, then eased into the hallway. The wood floor creaked as she walked, and she paused every few inches, listening for sounds of an intruder.

Nothing except the music.

She peered inside her bedroom first, then her bath. Nothing.

Breathing a little steadier, she stepped into her office. The music box sat on her desk, the ballerina twirling, the melody drowning out her own breathing.

She hadn't left the music box in her office. And she certainly hadn't left it open and playing.

Someone *had* been there.

She made a quick visual sweep but didn't see anything else that was disturbed.

What the hell was going on? Why would someone come in and play the music box? And why leave it in her office?

Had someone been interested in her files?

She crossed the room and studied the wall. Snippets of cold cases covered a section, while another featured her father's case.

She focused on the notes from the sheriff who'd investigated her father's murder. Her mother's statement. Kenny's. Hers, although at five and having fallen in her father's blood after watching him get shot, she'd been too traumatized to talk.

All the notes and pictures and files appeared to be intact.

For a brief second she considered filing a report about a break-in, but there was no threat here. No damage.

She'd look like a fool if she claimed someone had come in and messed with her childhood music box.

She rubbed her temple, then went to the kitchen, poured herself a glass of wine, and sipped it while she fixed a grilled cheese sandwich and carried it to her desk.

But she couldn't shake the sadness from being with her mother. It was almost as if she'd lost both of her parents the day her father died.

A memory floated into her consciousness: a summer day—hot, humid, the sun relentless. Fourth of July.

Her mother had packed a picnic lunch with fried chicken, home-made buttermilk biscuits, fried peach pies, and fruit cups. Kenny had been so excited he'd grabbed his fishing rod and hat, eager to spend the day fishing off the pontoon boat their father had rented.

They swam in the river, floated on inner tubes, and picnicked beneath a giant oak tree. Her mother had fallen asleep on the picnic blanket, reading a book.

The wind stirred again, launching her back to that scene.

Kenny baited his hook. "I'm gonna catch our dinner."

She laughed. "Mama brought chicken just in case."

Kenny stuck his tongue out at her, then cast the line.

"Look, Daddy!" Kenny yelled.

Her daddy patted Kenny's shoulder. "Do you want to fish, princess?"

She shivered. She didn't like the squiggly worms. "No, I wanna swim."

Her father laughed, then scooped her up and tossed her in the river. She squealed, and he dove under the water. She climbed on his shoulder. Time after time, he tossed her in the water. She made big splashes, then went under. Each time he ducked below to catch her.

They laughed and played, and she squealed and pumped her arms and legs, determined to learn to swim.

Finally, her arms and legs grew tired. They climbed out, and he carried her to the blanket, and she snuggled beside her mother.

Then he turned to look for Kenny.

But Kenny was gone. His fishing rod lay on the riverbank.

"Kenny!" Her father's shout scared her. She sat up and scanned the area. No Kenny.

"Kenny, come here!" her daddy yelled.

Tears blurred her eyes. What if something had happened to Kenny? He was a good swimmer, but he could have fallen in, gotten swept up by the current, and dragged downstream.

If he'd hit his head, he could be dead.

Korine blinked, focusing again and trying to blot out the fear she'd felt that day. After an hour of searching, her father had found Kenny by the bait shop at the pier. He was furious with Kenny and grounded him for a week.

Kenny had been sullen and moody for weeks afterward.

Looking back, she realized Kenny had been jealous because he'd wanted his father to fish with him. Instead, he'd ignored Kenny and spent the day with her.

Kenny's resentment of her grew from that day on. Whenever her father spent time with her, Kenny had done something to get his attention. He'd acted out. He'd snuck away from the house. He'd turned to friends who rebelled against their parents and upbringing.

Her father had become increasingly impatient with Kenny, while her mother defended and coddled him.

He was adult now, though—she couldn't coddle him.

"I'm bailing you out one last time, Kenny," she whispered. "But tomorrow you're going to rehab."

Decision made, she turned back to the two murder cases she and Hatcher were working. Tinsley Jensen had called in the first crime.

Whoever had left the judge near her cottage was making a point—that finally, justice was served. Not to the man who'd hurt Tinsley, but to the judge's victims because he'd released a rapist.

Tinsley's blog had drawn hundreds of comments. Maybe the killer had left her a message hidden among the posts.

Adrenaline surging through her, she Googled the blog and began to read. The first entry made the hair on the back of her neck prickle.

I clawed the wall to mark the days I had been held hostage here.

Seven so far.

At first I was strong and I fought him. I even challenged and goaded him. Called him less than a man.

135

He punished me for that. My skin was still raw from the cleansing. My body hurt from the beatings. My back burned from the whip.

I finally learned to keep my mouth shut.

Except for when I screamed.

He liked that sound. He laughed and taunted me. I tried to hold it in.

But as he drove whatever object he'd chosen to shove inside me to my core, I felt like I was splitting in two.

And the sobs and screams came. But even they could not drown out his breathing and his laughter . . .

CHAPTER TWENTY

Anxious to get off his wet jeans and rid himself of the river-water smell, Hatcher showered and yanked on sweats and a T-shirt. His stomach growled, and he heated a frozen pizza and reached for a beer, then decided to get a bottle of water instead. Too wired to sleep, though, he went to work.

He accessed records of the Davenport murder case and skimmed the file. The sheriff had identified no real suspects or leads. The fact that Dr. Davenport was a child psychologist was interesting, especially in light of the cases Hatcher and Korine had been working lately, but his murder had occurred twenty-five years ago. There was no connection.

The sheriff had questioned the families of Davenport's clients, his secretary, and colleagues, but no one raised suspicions. He'd found no motive for murder and finally speculated that it was a robbery gone awry.

The problem with that theory was that even though it was Christmas Eve and mounds of presents were under the tree, and even though the Davenports had expensive silver and Mrs. Davenport's jewelry box was full of gemstones, nothing had been stolen.

Of course, the intruder could have thought the family was out for the night, then panicked when he discovered they were home.

Still . . . if he'd seen lights on inside the house, why not come back a different night?

According to the sheriff, Korine's mother loved her husband. He was a brilliant child psychologist, adored his kids, and provided for the family. He was faithful to her, and they had a good marriage. No complaints from patients or their families either.

Davenport had held seminars on children's behavior and psychological issues, including schizophrenia, bipolar disorder, borderline personality disorder, and obsessive-compulsive disorder. He'd also treated children who'd suffered trauma from loss of a parent or sibling and had earned awards for innovative therapy techniques in forensic interviewing.

Hatcher scratched his head. Now to the details of the night he was murdered.

The family had attended church, then had a celebratory dinner at the country club. When they returned, Mrs. Davenport went to bed with a migraine. Korine's brother had been moody all night.

When they arrived home, Kenny retreated to his room.

Korine's mother had left Korine and her father in his study. According to Mrs. Davenport, Korine's father had let Korine stand on his feet while they danced.

"I Feel Pretty" had been playing the night of the murder. The same song had been playing when they'd stopped at the Davenports earlier.

Mrs. Davenport had just been drifting off to sleep when a noise jarred her. The gunshots. She raced down the steps and found her husband lying on the floor, soaked in blood.

Apparently, he'd collapsed with Korine in his arms. She was screaming and had blood on her pink satin dress and hands.

The porcelain doll her father had given her had fallen from the piano. Korine had cut her hand on a shard of the doll's shattered face.

The photo of Dr. Davenport's body lying on the floor in shock with blood pooling around him matched the description of the murder scene.

But it was the picture of Korine at age five, her eyes wide in horror, blood splattered on her dress and hands, that made his chest clench.

He'd seen death too many times to count. The most personal one: his wife's.

But Korine had been five years old when she'd witnessed a bloody shooting. An innocent little girl, dancing with her father on Christmas Eve . . .

He forced himself to look at his wife's picture on the desk. Their marriage had been a mess, but he shouldn't have ignored her call.

He flexed his fingers and stared at his hand where his wedding ring had once been. That band had symbolized his love for his wife, his commitment and devotion.

But he never wore it on the job. In fact, he'd taken it off weeks before he'd asked Felicia for a divorce.

The memory of Korine in his arms taunted him, and he closed her file, then stood. When they finished their current assignment, he'd help her investigate her father's murder.

Meanwhile, he'd keep his hands to himself.

♦ ♦ ♦

Once Korine started reading, she couldn't stop. The women's stories made her skin crawl. But like a rubbernecker watching a car accident, she couldn't tear her eyes away.

He called me Sprite.

I hated it, but he said he only gave pet names to special little girls, and I was special. He chose Sprite for my name because I giggled when the bubbly drink tickled my nose.

I stopped giggling a long time ago.

At first I wanted to please him. He told Mommy I had nightmares because my daddy died, and he would help me.

He said he loved me like Daddy did. That he would teach me about love.

But I didn't like his lessons.

They were icky.

When he took me on his lap and rubbed me all over, I closed my eyes and pretended I was somewhere else. Like in a magic castle. But I felt the wind blowing through the castle against my bare skin, and suddenly I was freezing. Then my dress was gone.

And he was heavy on top of me.

"This is our special time," he whispered. "And you're my girl."

Only I didn't feel special. I felt cold and dirty, and I hurt all over.

He wiped my tears with his fingers and told me not to cry. That he'd never leave me like Daddy.

That we had to keep our special time a secret.

Korine pinched the bridge of her nose. *God. The poor little girl.* How long had she suffered before an adult discovered what was going on? Or had an adult found out? Had she kept the man's dirty little secret? Was that man still free to hurt more children?

Shivering from revulsion, she moved to the next entry.

It was a Friday night. The night my little sister died.

She was a virgin. Only fourteen years old.

But that monster changed everything.

She liked basketball and pizza and country music. She had a crush on a guitar player who played in a country band named Boot Stompers. She snuck out to see him play that night, but some creep jumped her in the parking lot of the teen center before she went in.

He dragged her into an alley, tore off her clothes, raped her, then beat her until she was unconscious.

Now she's in a coma, where she lies in silence.

She's not technically dead, but the girl who looked at life with rose-colored glasses is dead. Gone forever.

The bruises on her face and body are healing. The bones were put back together.

But she won't open her eyes. I don't know if she hears me when I sit by her side and talk to her.

I want her to wake up and tell us who did this to her.

I want him to pay.

I want to make him suffer for hurting her. Because when she opens her eyes, I know she'll have to relive the horror of his attack again.

Maybe she'll play basketball once more. Maybe she'll still like pizza.

But she'll never smile that innocent virgin smile again.

The monster who did that to her needs to die.

Hatcher couldn't sleep. That image of Korine at age five in her pink satin dress covered in blood kept flashing behind his eyes.

Frustrated, he finally tossed the covers aside, threw on sweats, and went for an early-morning run. The fresh air, woods, and a trip along the river helped to clear his head. Unfortunately, even jogging couldn't completely stamp out his lust for his new partner.

He phoned Korine as he returned to the house and left a voice mail relaying that he'd set up a briefing with everyone involved in the case. Next, he texted all the parties involved with the time and location.

He showered and dressed quickly, anxious to steer his mind back to the job. Last night he'd dreamed about Felicia. As usual, she'd screamed his name and begged him to save her.

But instead of going to her, he'd pulled Korine into his arms. Driven by passion, he'd stripped her clothes and touched every inch of her.

Then Korine was panting below him. Her lips parted in a moan of pleasure. She cried out his name and begged him to take her again . . .

He'd woken up shaking and craving Korine so badly he'd reached for Jack Daniels.

He'd gone as far as to pour himself a shot. But when he'd lifted it to his lips and sniffed, he'd seen Wyatt's face. Wyatt, who'd been severely injured but was fighting back.

He'd tossed the bottle aside and gone for a run.

Eager to get to work, he brewed a pot of coffee. Then he polished off a piece of toast and poured to-go mugs, one for himself and one for Korine. He had to get out of the house. Away from the photo of Felicia staring at him, blaming him for her death. Calling him a cheater for thinking about how good Korine felt, naked and writhing in his arms, when his wife lay in the cold ground.

Rain clouds hovered outside, obliterating the sun and casting a dismal gray over the river and marsh. For a brief second, a hazy figure floated above the water. A woman. Her hair swirled around the slender heart-shaped face.

Felicia. She was reaching toward him. Her mouth open in a plea. Tears streamed down her cheeks.

She was in pain, in limbo, and she couldn't move on. He didn't know how to help her . . .

♦ ♦ ♦

Anger mounted inside Korine as morning dawned. She needed to stop reading and get some sleep. But she'd been too intrigued by the heart-wrenching posts to close her eyes.

I didn't mean to kill him . . . it just happened.

I lifted my hands and stared at the blood dripping down my fingers. It splattered the floor and my feet with its vibrant color.

Panic seized me. I had to wash it off. Clean up. Call the police.

Instead, I stared at my bloody fingers in awe. That blood had come from a monster.

He was gone because of me. I could finally sleep without the terror clawing at me every night.

Although even with my eyes open, those creepy doll eyes stared back at me. Glowing in the dark like they were possessed by the devil.

Except this time they were staring at his dead body. And they were smiling as he lay limp and helpless.

Korine rubbed her eyes.

The stories could have been written by the victims from the cases she was investigating.

Could one of them be connected?

CHAPTER
TWENTY-ONE

Morning joggers, commuters, and tourists were already filling the Savannah streets as Hatcher drove toward Korine's.

He flipped on the radio to hear what the media had to say.

"Downtown Savannah is expected to be flooded today with women from all walks of life as they take part in the Women's Protest Movement spreading across the country. Although purported to be a nonviolent march, police will be out in full force."

The reporter continued. "In addition to women's rights, the groups today are protesting the release of over fifty prisoners statewide. The governor, with the consent of the president, cited overcrowding and poor prison conditions as the reason for the decision. However, many of the inmates were in prison on domestic violence charges, creating fear in the minds of the victims and their families."

Hatcher parked in front of Korine's just as a flash of dark-red hair caught his eye.

That luscious hair was enough to drive a man insane.

He struggled to rein in his lust as she jogged down her stairs to meet him. Her skin glowed in the dim morning light, her dark-blue jacket accentuating her vibrant eye color. She wore her hair, which still looked wet from a shower, in a long braid draped over one shoulder.

Except for dark smudges beneath her eyes, she looked fresh and young and . . . sexy.

He glanced down at his finger where his wedding band used to be. The tan line had faded, the passage of time erasing any sign that he'd been married.

Korine opened the door and leaned inside, adjusting her holster.

He gestured toward the coffee in his cup holders. "Hot coffee if you want."

The wariness in her eyes made him wonder at her thoughts.

"You don't like coffee?" he asked with a twitch of a smile. Or was it that she just didn't like him?

Maybe it was better she didn't. He had no business doing extra favors for her, bringing her coffee . . .

"I do, thanks."

"There's sugar and creamer—"

"Black is good." She accepted the mug, but she still didn't get in. "I'll meet you at the station."

He leaned forward, eyes narrowed. "Anything I can do?"

She shook her head, a grim expression on her face. "I'm driving my brother to rehab this morning. I've already made arrangements."

"Will he go willingly?" Hatcher asked.

"I doubt it. But if he doesn't, I'm done with him. I'll leave him in jail."

He didn't blame her. "If you need support, I'm here." Now why the hell had he offered that?

"Stay out of it," she said tersely.

An awkward moment passed between them. "Everyone has stuff," he said, wishing he were better with words. "Considering what your family went through with your father's murder, it's not a surprise."

Her mouth flattened. "I don't want to discuss my family with you."

Shit. He'd overstepped. "Don't get defensive, Korine. I'm a detective. We solve crimes. Don't tell me you didn't research me."

Her face blanched then, and she hissed a breath between her teeth. "I didn't have to. You're legendary at the bureau."

He arched a brow. That almost sounded like a compliment.

"We're both screwed up," she said, shattering any semblance that she actually might admire him.

"True."

She jangled her keys. "I'll meet you at the station in an hour."

He nodded. "I'll check on Banning in lockup, see if he's decided to talk."

She started to close the door, then gestured to the coffee. "Thanks. I needed this."

Her soft admission did something to his insides, made his gut twist and sweat bead on his forehead. He couldn't drag his gaze from the sway of her hips in those tight jeans as she hurried to her car.

He didn't want to want her. Or to like her.

But he did.

Agitated, he glanced at his ring finger again, then at the seat beside him, searching for Felicia's image.

But the seat was empty.

Determined to beg her forgiveness so she could move on, he drove toward the cemetery. A flower shop on the street caught his eye, and he swung in and parked, then jumped out and bought a bouquet of roses.

He put them on the seat beside him, then drove to the graveyard, parked, and carried the roses to her grave.

Felicia's image appeared, hovering above the marker, but it was thin and papery, and he couldn't make out her face.

He dropped to his knees in front of her grave, wiped away twigs and leaves that had fallen on her marker, then lay the flowers on top as an offering.

Then he closed his eyes and willed her to come back to him.

A light touch settled on his shoulder. His breath caught, and he opened his eyes, then looked up.

She was there. Bathed in a soft white light. Her image was paler today, almost transparent as if she was disappearing.

"I'm so sorry," he whispered. "I should have taken your call . . . I should have been there."

But her cold gaze pinned him to the spot, and the blood dripping from her neck mocked him.

◆ ◆ ◆

Korine didn't have time for her brother's bullshit. She had more important matters to deal with, murders to solve.

She rubbed her tired eyes as she entered the jail. Sometime soon she had to get a decent night's sleep. But those blog posts had kept her awake most of the night.

She flashed her badge and went through security, then an officer led her to the holding cell. Kenny was passed out on one cot, while a homeless man lay snoring on another.

Disgust and worry fueled her anger, and she banged on the bars. "Kenny, wake up."

He didn't stir.

She banged again. "Kenny, get your butt up. We have to talk."

The homeless man stirred, looked up at her, then leaned over and shook Kenny's arm. "Someone's here for you, boy."

Kenny roused and grumbled as he rolled toward the door and opened his eyes. He blinked a few times, obviously struggling to focus.

"Come on, I don't have all day," Korine said. "Get over here."

Bleary-eyed, he scraped a hand through his shaggy hair, then stood and staggered toward her. His jeans were holey, his flannel shirt tattered and dirty, and he hadn't shaved in days.

The stench of sweat and booze wafted toward her. "God, you reek."

He squeezed the bridge of his nose with two fingers, then growled. "Did you come to jump down my throat or bail me out?"

"Both." Korine clenched the bars of the cell in a white-knuckled grip. "I'm going to post bond, but there's a price."

He kicked at the floor. "What the hell? I don't have money—"

All because their mother had wisely put restrictions on when and how they could access their inheritance. "I'm not talking about money," she said in disgust. "I've made arrangements for you to enter a rehab program. It's not too far from here—"

"I don't need a goddamned rehab program," he muttered. "Those places are for losers."

Korine folded her arms and glared at him. "Take a look in the mirror. What do you think you are?"

He kicked the floor again. "I just had a bad night—"

"You've had a lot of those," Korine said. "Too many. I won't keep enabling you while you drink yourself to death or hurt someone else." Her voice cracked, the pain and anger so strong that her chest was going to explode with it. "For heaven's sake, think of someone besides yourself. Esme had to call me because Mother was so upset. You were her favorite, so why are you breaking her heart now?"

"You're just mad because we're an inconvenience to you and your job."

His antagonistic tone made her grip the cell bars tighter. "You really hate me, don't you?"

He closed his eyes and leaned his head into his hands. For several tense moments, she watched as he wrestled with emotions she didn't understand.

"Well, go ahead and hate me," she said quietly. "But I won't post bail unless you agree to go to rehab. It's time you figured out the reason you drink, big brother."

He mumbled an obscenity, then stared up at her, his eyes clouded with turmoil. For a moment, he looked like a lost child, as confused and hurt and angry as he had the night their father was murdered. Not that she really remembered his reactions that night.

They'd both been in shock.

But it was time for him to get help. "Shall I leave, or do you agree to go?"

He cursed again, then clamped his mouth tight but nodded.

She just prayed he'd stay when she left him instead of sneaking out like he'd done before.

◆ ◆ ◆

Hatcher tried to put Korine out of his mind as he asked to speak to Banning. She was a big girl. She could take care of herself. And her brother.

So why did he wish he'd gone with her?

The lean young officer behind the desk cleared his throat. "Sorry, Special Agent McGee, but Banning lawyered up. Attorney's bailing him out now."

Muttering a curse, he strode down the hall toward the clerk's office and found Banning looking haggard as he sat slumped in a chair. A young blonde woman in a gray pantsuit stood at the clerk's window.

"Thank you so much," she said. "We'll be going now." She turned toward Banning, then spotted Hatcher as he approached. Banning's eyes widened in panic, but he dug his hands in his pockets and bent his head back down.

Hatcher stopped in front of the man's big feet. "Banning?"

The woman's heels clicked as she stared at Hatcher. "May I ask who you are?"

Hatcher gritted his teeth, but flashed his badge. "Special Agent Hatcher McGee."

"Kendall James." She extended her hand and Hatcher reluctantly shook it. "I'm Mr. Banning's attorney. I've advised my client not to answer any more questions without my presence."

Of course she had. "You realize that we found Pallo Whiting murdered?"

Her eyes sparkled with an odd look. She seemed . . . pleased. "Yes, I'd like to say that was a tragedy, but under the circumstances . . ." She let the sentence trail off.

Unfortunately, Hatcher couldn't argue.

She shifted her briefcase to her other hand. "As far as I know, you have nothing to hold Mr. Banning on—"

"He fired a gun at me and my partner, so actually I do have something to hold him on."

She lifted her chin. "I meant no evidence that he committed a crime against Whiting. That said, I believe we can strike a deal regarding those other charges. Mr. Banning was distraught and frightened when you approached, and he panicked."

Banning lifted his head slightly. "I'm sorry, but I don't much trust the cops. Not after what happened with my boy."

James rubbed Banning's back sympathetically. "That's understandable, and we'll stress the reason for that in court." Her gaze met Hatcher's. "By the way, there is new evidence to support Mr. Banning's statement about his son being framed. Gerard Banning was a victim of a faulty justice system. He spent years incarcerated for a crime he didn't commit, during which he was physically and mentally abused. Then the poor man was murdered by Whiting. If the system had worked and Mr. Banning's son had been free, he would be alive today. And you wouldn't be questioning his father regarding Whiting's death."

"That may be true, but—"

"But nothing." The lawyer gave him a challenging look. "Go ahead, Agent McGee, take my client to court, and I'll prove just how much a victim he and his son have been in this situation. The jury will be sobbing when I'm finished. Not only will they acquit my client, but they'll be ready to give whoever killed Whiting a medal."

CHAPTER
TWENTY-TWO

The dolls sat like beautiful little princesses on the white scalloped book-case. Their bright hand-painted faces and eyes were a result of an artist's touch.

Their hair looked human—gold, brown, red, black; it draped their shoulders, some long and silky straight, others curled into ringlets that spiraled along the doll's back.

Rosy cheeks glowed above pink lips that smiled back at her. Tiny delicate ears were adorned with shimmering earrings that matched the doll's dress.

All chosen carefully to create the perfect image a little girl would dream about and treasure forever.

Especially when that doll came as a gift.

Like the ones Korine's father had given her. She had a collection. Ones she'd gotten from her loving, doting daddy.

The Keeper had wanted a daddy like that. Had wanted to be special like Korine was to her father.

But she wasn't special. She was ugly and empty.

So she'd started her own doll collection. A sick weakness, an obses-sion that she couldn't control.

She had twenty-six now. Her shelf was full.

The dolls watched her suffer at night, watched her toss and turn as she fought the demons. They listened silently to her screams and her cries.

They whispered that she should just say goodbye.

She wanted to oblige.

But each time she tried, each time she stuck the blade tip to her wrist and watched the first droplet of blood seep down her arm and drip onto the floor, she stopped. The pain gave her life. Gave her purpose.

She didn't know how to live without it.

You miss him, don't you, one of the dolls whispered. *You want him back. To touch you. To love you.*

To make you feel something other than the hollow, ugly emptiness you have inside.

No one will ever want you again.

Tears slipped down her cheeks, and she tasted blood as she bit down hard on her lip.

No one can ever love you. They'll smell his touch on your skin. They'll know he's been inside you. That you have no place for anyone but him.

Rage burned through her, and she picked up the knife, took one doll from the shelf, and slashed its head off.

The porcelain head fell to the floor, its eyes staring vacantly, its body limp and headless on the cold stone. Yet the doll's scream echoed in the room and bounced off the walls.

Laughter bubbled inside her, and she carefully removed another doll from the shelf. She straightened its perfect green dress, then raised the knife and slashed its neck, sending the head flying against the bedpost.

A surge of excitement spiked her adrenaline. Yet one of the dolls was laughing at her.

The doll with the ivory gown.

"Shut up!" She waved the knife in front of the doll's face, but the doll sneered at her. One quick swipe of the knife, and its head flew through the air and landed against the floor.

The other dolls screamed in protest.

Filled with exhilaration, she took the dolls one by one and slashed their necks, pummeling the room with the doll heads.

Their beautiful eyes and rosy cheeks and lips didn't look so pretty now.

Their whispers that she was unlovable died as their own pain took root and they screamed for their lives.

She showed no mercy. They hadn't shown her any.

Instead, she laughed at the sight of the doll heads scattered across the floor, their cries blending with the wind as the ocean outside stirred the tides.

Then the last one—the one with the pink satin dress.

She kissed its precious cheek, then brought the blade down quickly and added its body to the pile of porcelain carcasses and its head to the mass on her floor.

The screams continued, loud and shrill. The choked last breaths. The pleas for help.

She raised her foot and stomped on the heads, shattering the eyes and then the mouths.

Slowly the cries and screams died. The whimpers lingered longer, but eventually they faded, too.

Then finally . . . finally everything was quiet as it should be.

CHAPTER TWENTY-THREE

Korine's heart ached as she signed the admission forms for Kenny's rehab. He shot her venomous looks, then scribbled his name on the consent form with a low curse.

"You may not believe it right now, but you're making the best decision of your life," E. L. Foote, the addiction counselor, said with a welcoming smile. "Our staff has had great success in helping patients in the recovery process."

Kenny slumped forward and stared at his hands, twisting his fingers around and around, a nervous gesture he'd developed after their father's murder. Korine remembered fixating on his hands the day the sheriff had questioned them.

Except then his fingers hadn't been shaking from withdrawal.

Two years later, Kenny had discovered their dad's liquor stash. He'd dived in and never looked back.

"I'll give you a few minutes to say goodbye," the counselor said. "Then I'll show you to your room, Mr. Davenport."

Kenny shoved the chair back so hard it toppled over. The counselor didn't seem surprised or upset at all by his moodiness.

"I don't need time," he said, swinging toward Korine. "Just throw me away so you don't have to bother with me anymore. Here I am, sis. Happy now?"

Korine blinked back tears. "I am anything but happy, so don't put this on me. You made the choices that landed you here. I love you, or I wouldn't have brought you for help."

"Love?" he barked. "You have no idea what love is."

She ignored the hateful barb. He was always belligerent when he was hungover. And judging from his shaky hands and dark eyes, he needed a drink bad.

"I do love you," she said softly. "But this is it, Kenny. If you sneak out or leave this time, you're on your own. I want you to stick it out so you can get healthy and happy again. So you can have a future that's not at the bottom of a bottle."

She didn't bother to wait for a response. She spun around and strode out the door. His curse words echoed behind her.

Korine sympathized with the counselors and staff. They had their work cut out for them. Then again, their work was their calling, just as tracking down murderers and rapists was hers.

Guilt gnawed at her. How could she help her brother when she was partly the source of his rage?

There had to be something deeper bothering him, something besides sibling rivalry or the fact that he'd thought their father favored her.

He'd had a bike wreck when he was ten; maybe the concussion had caused damage. Or he might have some kind of psychological disorder that triggered his need to self-medicate.

The counselors would figure that out.

Her phone buzzed. Hatcher.

A longing stirred inside her, one that made her ache for him.

She rolled her eyes. Lord help her, she was weak. Kenny craved the bottle. She craved Hatcher's physical touch.

Maybe she needed therapy.

She quickly connected the call. "Agent Davenport."

"Banning lawyered up and is out on bond. I set up a briefing with the ME, local sheriff, and Cat to discuss both cases, but first I want to talk to the warden at Coastal State Prison. Maybe he can shed some light on how Whiting escaped."

"Good. I'll meet you there."

She rushed out the door, grateful to breathe in the fresh salty air. But emotions clogged her throat, and she turned one more time to glance at the facility, Serenity.

Instead of a cold sterile hospital, the rustic structure had been built to resemble a retreat center with warm blue tones, a wraparound porch complete with rocking chairs, and hiking and biking trails that covered the twenty-five-acre spread. Set against the marsh with the sea oats swaying in the wind and the Spanish moss draping the ground like giant spider webs, it epitomized a tranquil atmosphere for healing and self-discovery.

Hopefully, here Kenny would uncover the demons that fueled his self-destructive behavior and learn techniques to deal with it and find peace.

If he didn't get help, he might end up in a cell like the criminals she locked away.

Or in the graveyard with her father.

Hatcher met Korine at the entrance to the Coastal State Prison. The medium-security facility housed over eighteen hundred beds, provided mental-health services, and also offered a program for reentering the workforce.

Whiting had been targeted because he was a pedophile and was being transferred to Hays when he escaped.

Damn bastard had learned what it felt like to have a man twice your size force himself on you.

Korine looked exhausted, but she squared her shoulders as she approached him. "Banning didn't confess?" she asked.

He shook his head and opened the door to the facility. "His lawyer made it clear she'll paint him and his son as victims of the justice system. We'll probably have to cut a deal with him and let him go."

Korine shrugged as they approached security. "If his son was innocent, I can understand the man's bitterness. But taking the law into his own hands isn't right."

Hatcher balled his hands into fists. Was she making a statement about what he'd done?

He didn't care. He didn't regret killing his wife's murderer.

"We have no proof that he did that," Hatcher said. He wasn't sure he wanted to dig for it either.

Korine folded her arms. "We have to do our jobs."

He glared at her. "You don't need to lecture me. I've been in law enforcement a lot longer than you."

His comment seemed to strike a nerve. She shot him a cold look, then stepped up to security. They put the topic on hold as they were escorted to the warden's office.

Warden Johnson was a big man, tall with an imposing physique. Thick black brows framed a solemn face and a no-nonsense look.

Hatcher and Korine flashed their credentials and introduced themselves. "You're here because of Whiting's escape, aren't you?" Warden Johnson asked.

"Yes, as it may pertain to his murder," Korine filled in.

The warden gestured for them to sit, and they claimed two chairs facing the man's massive desk. Framed documents attesting to his military service and professional qualifications hung on the wall behind him, while security cameras in the corners of the room logged everything that happened inside his office. He pressed an intercom button, then made a request to an assistant.

"I want mental health in here while we talk," he said. "Whiting's counselor may have insight that I don't."

Five minutes later, an attractive brunette with funky blue glasses appeared and introduced herself as Reba Boles.

"Tell us about Whiting," Hatcher said. "What kind of prisoner was he?"

The warden clicked some keys on his computer and glanced at the file. "He kept to himself, but word spreads quickly when a pedophile comes in."

"Did he brag about what he'd done?" Korine asked.

Boles crossed her legs, her expression neutral. "Mental health records are confidential—"

"He's dead," Korine cut in. "We have reason to believe that someone assisted in his escape in order to get revenge on him."

"I'm not sure I can help."

"He made enemies in here?" Korine asked. "Did he discuss them with you?"

"We talked about his conviction and his urges," she said, her tone controlled, void of judgment. "He knew the other inmates hated him."

"Did he express remorse for what he'd done?" Hatcher asked.

Boles adjusted her glasses. "Not exactly. He said he would agree to medication to control his urges in exchange for his release."

Korine made a small sound in her throat. "You believed him?"

"I did, but not because he was sorry for his behavior," Ms. Boles said. "He was terrified of the other inmates. He knew they would destroy him. Transferring to Hays is usually an inmate's worst fear, but Mr. Whiting thought he'd be safer there because he'd be in a private cell."

"Did he have visitors while he was here?" Hatcher asked.

The warden consulted his computer. "One visit shortly after he was brought in."

"His brother Ernest?" Hatcher asked.

The warden shook his head no. "The brother's wife. Donna Whiting."

Hatcher narrowed his eyes. "And the nature of that visit?"

"I think she needed to make sure he was locked up," the warden answered.

"Can you add anything, Ms. Boles?" Korine asked.

The therapist consulted her notepad. "According to him, his sister-in-law threatened to kill him if he was released and came near her daughter again."

Hatcher shifted. "Who could blame her?"

Boles pursed her lips and refrained from comment.

"Did she have any further communication with him?" Korine asked. "Letters? Phone calls?"

The warden shook his head no. "We log in all mail and communication. They had none."

"Did he mention any other threats?" Hatcher asked the counselor.

"Just the typical gang activity. Usually inmates make alliances. No one wanted to be Whiting's ally."

Korine leaned forward, hands on her knees. "Do you think his sister-in-law hated him enough to arrange his escape so she could kill him?"

The counselor and warden exchanged looks. "I can't say," Ms. Boles replied. "I never talked to the woman myself. But you have to understand that it's not uncommon for families and friends of victims to make threats in the heat of the moment. Emotions are running high. In situations like this, parents deal with guilt, anger, fear, shame, and the feeling that they've failed their child. Carrying out those threats is a different story."

"You're right," Korine said. "Helping to break Whiting out of jail would require planning. Whoever did it would need help. She would need to know timing of the transfer and the route of the prison van."

"We take every precaution necessary," the warden said. "Transfers are kept quiet until shortly before they occur. The inmates aren't even told. When it's time, the guards go in and give them only minutes to pack their belongings and prepare to leave." He rubbed his forehead. "Besides, why would a woman go to the trouble of breaking him out when he was locked up and would probably die in prison anyway?"

"We'll check her alibi," Hatcher said. "Warden, anything else you can tell us about Whiting?"

The warden folded his hands on the desk. "He killed Banning to prove he was tough. He thought the inmates would leave him alone after that, but it didn't work."

"That's the reason he was being transferred?" Korine asked.

The warden nodded. "Hays is more secure."

"What happened during the transfer?" Hatcher asked.

The warden leaned back in his chair and shrugged. "According to the driver, who gave a statement seconds before he died, a dark truck rammed into the front of the prison van. He tried to right the van, but it spun and rolled. Chaos, then. The windows shattered, his legs were trapped, and the prisoners inside took advantage. One grabbed his keys while the second stabbed him in the chest. Whiting unlocked their cuffs, then he disappeared with the truck."

Korine turned to the warden. "What about the guards or another employee? Would one of them have helped him escape?"

The warden stiffened. "There have been times when we've caught staff members sneaking contraband to inmates, and four years ago, a female nurse fell in love with an inmate and aided in his escape, but we've tightened our security and staff since. And like I said, no one wanted to help Whiting."

"If the guard knew whoever was going to break out Whiting planned to kill him, he might have taken a bribe to leak information about the transfer," Hatcher suggested.

Once again the warden and counselor exchanged looks. "I don't think so," the warden said. "But I'll look into it and talk to the other staff members."

Korine thanked them, and Hatcher followed her into the hallway. A guard escorted them to security.

As soon as they stepped outside, Hatcher texted Cat and asked her to check Donna Whiting's alibi.

"Cat's on it," he said a minute later when they reached the parking lot.

"Good. There's still the issue of the justice symbol," Korine said. "Unless someone from the bureau or ME's office leaked that information, this Whiting woman couldn't have known."

"That's been bothering me, too," Hatcher commented.

"I want to talk to Tinsley Jensen again."

Hatcher narrowed his eyes. "Why?"

"Just a hunch," Korine said. "Last night I read through some posts on her blog." Korine reached inside her pocket for her keys. "Some of the comments are disturbing."

"I imagine so," Hatcher said.

"I'm worried there's more going on than just venting," Korine said.

He touched her arm, but she stiffened and drew away from him.

"What are you saying?" he asked, irritated that he'd forgotten his own rules by touching her again.

Worry creased her face. "A couple of comments sounded like confessions of murder."

CHAPTER TWENTY-FOUR

Liz Roberts forced herself to give Latoya Clinton a smile of encouragement as she gently closed the hospital room door and stepped into the hall.

Anger and sadness engulfed Liz. She'd worked as a victim's advocate for domestic violence for four years. Some thought you grew accustomed, even hardened, to the women's and children's stories.

So not true.

She struggled to not carry the victims' problems home with her at night, to keep them from tainting her own relationships and trust, but that took work. She wanted desperately to believe in the good of others.

But it was difficult when animals like Germaine Stokes took a hammer to his girlfriend's face like Stokes had done this morning.

The poor woman hadn't seen it coming. She'd broken off their relationship the week before.

When Latoya had gotten home from work last night, he'd been hiding in her bedroom closet. He'd beaten her so badly the bones in her face were crushed, her eyes were swollen shut, her lips bloody and cracked, her jaw wired. She'd lost partial vision in one eye and would never be able to have children after the damage the man had inflicted by repeated kicks to her abdomen, and she would need months of therapy to be able to speak again.

Those were only the physical injuries. The emotional scars would be even more difficult to overcome. On top of that would be a financial burden—medical bills, counseling, attorneys, and lost wages . . .

Money Latoya didn't have. Money she'd never see from Germaine if he accepted a plea and served time.

And if he didn't, there would be the long, drawn-out trial, the ruthless interrogation by the defense attorney, the fear that he'd come after her again.

Convincing Latoya to testify against Germaine Stokes wasn't difficult at the moment.

Unfortunately, with time, victims often changed their minds.

And if Germaine managed to get near enough to threaten her . . .

Liz couldn't let her mind go there yet. She'd covered the bases.

Just as she'd done with the teenage girls who'd reported their driver's ed teacher, Louie Hortman, for sexual harassment. They'd almost gone to trial; then something happened to change the girls' minds . . .

Hortman had gone free. Sure, he'd lost his job, but he was already working at a private driving school and most likely back to his demented ways. Someone needed to stop him, but . . . her hands were tied.

Her phone buzzed with a text just as she stepped outside the hospital. She scanned the area, looked for stalkers and strays, anyone who didn't belong.

Satisfied for the moment, she checked the text.

Laura sending a 9-1-1 call to the Keepers.

Gripping her key with the attached mace in one hand, she kept alert as she sprinted to her car. When she climbed in, she instantly locked the doors and searched the parking lot.

Paranoia about safety came with the job.

Her phone exploded with return texts from the others. Everyone was anxious.

A list was also circulating—people who needed punishing.

The police and federal agents were asking questions.

Questions none of them wanted to answer.

CHAPTER
TWENTY-FIVE

Hatcher's keys dug into the palm of his hand as he gripped them. "You think you read a confession of murder?"

"I'm not sure," Korine said. "The posts are anonymous. No names mentioned, and no specifics. But a couple of entries really disturbed me. I thought Tinsley might have some insight."

He didn't want to have to face Tinsley again, but if she had answers, he had to. "You want to drop your car at the precinct?"

"The women's march is taking place now," Korine said. "Traffic will be a nightmare. Let's leave my car here and come back afterward and pick it up."

She was right. They needed to stay clear of the downtown for a couple of hours, especially the area near the courthouse.

Korine climbed in the passenger seat of his SUV, and he started the engine. "How did it go with your brother?" he asked.

She stared out the window as he drove. "He's mad. Sullen. I just hope he stays this time."

"He's been in rehab before?"

She nodded. "Under duress. He left, twice. I told him this is it. If he doesn't stick it out, I'm done."

Rita Herron

He didn't blame her. But cutting off a family member would be difficult. Not that he knew. He'd lost his family when he was young. A tractor trailer had run into them head-on.

The temptation to reach out and comfort Korine hit him, but he fought it off.

Her family wasn't his problem.

He had his own ghosts to deal with.

Rain fell as he parked at Tinsley's cottage. Dark clouds hovered just above the horizon, the dull gray bleeding into the tides as the waves crashed angrily against the shore. Sea oats swayed in the gusty breeze, the wind howling as if warning that something bad was about to happen.

The beach was deserted—rain pinging onto the sand and creating wading pools along the seashell-lined shore where birds soared and dipped down, scrounging for food.

Korine climbed out as soon as Hatcher parked, tugging her jacket hood up to ward off the rain. He didn't bother with a jacket. He ran for the porch and the cover of the awning. Korine joined him, shaking the rain off as he knocked.

A light burned through the kitchen window, another in the den. Seconds later, Tinsley peeked through the peephole in the door, her eyes flaring with worry when she spotted them.

"Please open up, Tinsley," Korine said. "We have to talk."

A tense second passed, then the sound of the locks turning, and Tinsley opened the door.

"Did you find the person who killed Judge Wadsworth?" Tinsley asked.

"Not yet." Hatcher clenched his jaw at her pale face. This woman needed sunshine and fresh air, not to be locked away like a terrified animal.

"That's why we're here," Korine said. "We think you may have connected with the killer."

Tinsley gasped. "I don't know what you're talking about."

She gestured toward the door as if to ask them to leave, but Korine took a step closer to her. "It's possible that the killer may have commented on your blog."

Tinsley clenched the door edge with a white-knuckled grip. "Are you accusing me of something? Because if you are, maybe I need a lawyer."

Korine raised a brow in question. "*Do* you need a lawyer, Tinsley?"

The uneasiness in Tinsley's reaction made Korine take a deep breath. The last thing she wanted to do was to put this poor young woman through any more pain.

But if she knew who'd killed the judge and was keeping silent, she could be considered an accomplice.

Hatcher gave Korine a dark look. "Take it easy, Agent Davenport."

She glared at him. He was sympathetic where Tinsley was concerned, but she couldn't allow his personal involvement to keep her from doing her job. Bellows had assigned her to Hatcher to make sure he still had game, and she intended to follow orders.

"Do you want a lawyer?" she asked Tinsley again, although this time she softened her tone.

Tinsley clasped her hands together, her wary gaze darting between the two of them. "I haven't done anything wrong. For goodness sake, I haven't left this house since I moved in."

"I'm not accusing you of anything," Korine said. "But there was another murder case that we caught, a pedophile named Pallo Whiting."

Tinsley's face blanched.

"Do you know him?" Hatcher asked.

Tinsley swallowed hard. "Not personally, but I heard the news story about him. It was horrible what he did to those children."

"Yes, it was," Korine said. "He was serving time but escaped during a prison transfer." She waited for Tinsley's reaction, but the young woman simply breathed deeply, then turned and walked into the living area. She and Hatcher followed.

"Someone cut his penis off and let him bleed to death," Korine stated bluntly.

Tinsley made a strangled sound in her throat. "That's horrible. But . . . I'm sure the mothers of the children he hurt will sleep better now he's gone."

"Probably," Korine said. "Unless one of them killed him."

Tinsley sank onto the sofa. "I didn't know any of those children or their families. And I certainly didn't kill that depraved man."

"Maybe not, but let's talk about your *Heart & Soul* blog, specifically responses from individuals," Korine said.

"I want victims and their families to share their stories," Tinsley said. "My therapist suggested it would be good for me, and it has been. I hope it's cathartic for others."

"It's a form of group therapy, isn't it?" Korine asked.

"In a manner of speaking," Tinsley said. "Except there isn't a counselor to lead the group. Everyone is free to speak their minds. No judgment, just honest feelings."

"It's all anonymous?"

Tinsley nodded. "If someone wants to post their real name, they're free to, but most people choose to remain anonymous or use fake names. The only rule I have is that everyone refrain from criticizing others. Feelings and emotions aren't right or wrong. Everyone reacts differently to situations and trauma. Speaking those feelings or writing them down is a healthier way to purge dark emotions than acting upon them."

Korine slid onto the sofa beside her. "I know you want to protect the individuals posting, but a couple of the comments read as if they're murder confessions."

Tinsley chewed her bottom lip, then looked up at Hatcher. "Some of us have fantasized about killing the person who hurt us," she said in a choked voice. "You understand that—don't you, Hatcher?"

Hatcher muttered yes.

"But that doesn't mean we acted on those fantasies," Tinsley said.

Korine's gaze met Hatcher's. "But it's possible that one of them did."

Hatcher's eyes glittered with anger, then he gestured toward Tinsley's computer. "Show us what you're talking about."

Korine gave him an icy look, then crossed the room to Tinsley's desk. Tinsley quickly joined her, accessed the blog, then allowed Korine to scroll through the posts.

◆ ◆ ◆

Hatcher hoped to hell Korine was wrong. But if someone had written a confession to Tinsley, he couldn't ignore it.

It didn't mean that Tinsley knew a crime had been committed.

Hell, she'd reported the judge's murder.

Still, Korine might have found a lead.

His stomach rolled as he began to read:

> He had hurt too many young girls. Stripped them of their innocence and scarred them for life. Not just physical scars. But mental ones.
>
> The emotional ones were easier to hide. At least on the surface.
>
> But they are the hardest to overcome.
>
> I tried to make him pay before. The legal way.
>
> But he escaped justice.

I knew he'd come for me. I lay in the dark with a knife gripped in my hand.

The floor creaked. Then his voice.

"I love them. You can't take them away from me."

He liked to taunt his victims. To watch their faces contort with fear.

To hear them scream.

He lunged at me and reached for my throat.

Channeling rage and pain into my will to live, I lifted my hand and rammed the knife into him.

Blood gushed from his heartless chest and flooded my hand. I dug the knife deeper.

His body jerked and spasmed, a guttural, choked sound filling the air as he realized he was going to die.

That he would never touch another young girl again.

He collapsed on top of me, and I gasped for air. That vile smell, his blood, the stench . . . I had to get away from him.

His blood soaked my gown, my sheets, my arms and legs.

I choked back a scream and shoved him off me. His head hit the floor with a whack. The rest of his body followed.

Tears blurred my eyes. I had killed someone. Taken a human life.

Only he hadn't been human.

I smiled. At least one monster was gone.

But there would always be another.

CHAPTER
TWENTY-SIX

Hatcher shifted uncomfortably as he finished the comment. He understood Korine's suspicions.

But these responses were anonymous, so Tinsley couldn't know who'd written them. The author of that post hadn't mentioned names either, not the name of her attacker or his alleged victims. And it didn't fit specifically with the details of the crimes they were investigating.

Tinsley bit down on her bottom lip. "This account could be of a dream or a nightmare. Sometimes victims are plagued by their experiences, and their fears and anger present themselves in dreams."

He could attest to that. For God's sake, he was seeing his wife's ghost.

"That could be true," Korine agreed.

"There's nothing specific that indicates anything about the judge or Whiting," Hatcher added.

"There are others." Korine scrolled through and paused on another entry.

Hatcher's pulse clamored as he read:

A MOTHER'S VENGEANCE

My baby is seven years old now. Seven but I still call her my baby.

I listen to her cries at night, and it tears me up inside. She no longer runs and plays with the innocence of a child.

Instead, she has retreated into a silent world all her own. A world that holds her prisoner to the past and the day that awful man stole her youth.

I should have seen it coming.

I should have known.

But I trusted him.

I was wrong.

A scream rips through the walls, and I race to her bedside. She's tossing and turning, thrashing at the covers, fighting off the monster in her sleep.

Except that he is very real.

Rage boils inside me and possesses me like a live breathing animal.

He walks free now while my little girl suffers.

I won't let him do this to another child. I have to get payback for my daughter.

I close my eyes as I wrap my arms around her and rock her back to sleep. She's stiff and tense at first as if she can't stand me to touch her. Me, her own mother.

That's what he did to her.

Made her afraid to be loved or held, afraid of affection. Afraid of her own shadow.

I can do this, I think. I can take him out of this world.

A plan takes shape in my mind. I will follow him. I will make him suffer. And one day my baby will know that I fought for her.

And that I made him pay in the end for robbing her of her childhood.

Hatcher scraped his hand through his hair. "These are disturbing, but they aren't proof of anything."

"Do you read all the comments on your blog?" Korine asked.

Tinsley drummed her fingers on her thigh. "I do. But remember, I set this up so people could share their feelings. Posting them online doesn't mean they acted on any of these fantasies."

"But if you thought one of them had, would you tell us, Tinsley?" Hatcher held his breath while he waited for her response.

◆ ◆ ◆

The more entries Korine read, the more she sensed an underlying theme behind the scenes of Tinsley's *Heart & Soul*.

"Tinsley?" Korine asked. "Would you tell us if you thought someone on your blog had acted out their violent thoughts?"

Tinsley pressed the backs of her hands against her eyes, drawing Korine's attention to the scars on her hands. How could she possibly judge this woman after the way she'd suffered?

"I don't know," Tinsley finally answered in a strained voice. "I'd like to think I would, but . . . reading these personal accounts is gut-wrenching. I know how I feel about my attacker. I used to think I couldn't take a life, but if he came after me again, I would kill him and not blink twice." She rose and went to stare out the window, her tone far away. "He changed me. I don't like it, but he did."

Korine forced herself not to react. Hatcher gave her a cutting look, then eased up behind Tinsley. "It's normal for you to feel that, but he hasn't changed you as much as you think."

She spun on him, tears in her eyes. "How can you say that? I used to be active. I jogged, I had friends, I was social, I liked people." Her voice cracked. "Now, I hide like a coward."

"You're not a coward," Korine said firmly. "You have reason to be afraid."

Tinsley gave a self-deprecating laugh. "Afraid? It's more than that. I'm terrified of going outside, much less socializing. Last week two of my girlfriends wanted to visit, but I told them no. I can't see them and talk about what happened, about Felicia. But I can't see them and not talk about it." Tears trickled down her cheeks. "He took her because of me. She's dead because of *me*."

"That's not true." Hatcher reached out to touch her arms to comfort her, but she jerked away.

"Don't, Hatcher. I told you, I can't stand to be touched."

"I'm sorry." He dropped his hands. "I understand more than you realize," he said gruffly. "I blame myself for Felicia's death. Wyatt and I both blame ourselves for not finding you sooner. If we had, that monster wouldn't have gotten Felicia, and you wouldn't have suffered so long."

"You didn't know there were two of them," Tinsley said.

"We should have figured it out sooner. We let you both down."

Korine felt like an outsider, a voyeur to this private, heartfelt moment. But she couldn't tear herself from the room.

She had a job to do, and Hatcher was too personally involved to be objective. That meant she had to play bad cop to his good cop.

Rain drizzled down the windowpane like tear tracks, the fog thickening over the inlet. The dreary mood inside the house mirrored the gray overcast sky and cloudy horizon.

The vivid sunset well-known on the island would be missing tonight. It had been missing now for months for Tinsley.

Hatcher was obviously not over his wife either.

How could she possibly compete with her?

The thought disturbed her—she wasn't competing for Hatcher. She didn't want him.

Did she?

Hatcher stepped away from Tinsley. He looked confused, lost.

"Hatcher is right, Tinsley," Korine said, eager to console the woman. "None of this was your fault. But if you know something, if someone tells you they're going to commit a crime or have already done so, you have an obligation to tell us."

Tinsley's tear-filled eyes turned to Korine. "What if I think they did the right thing?"

Korine breathed out. "It doesn't matter what we think," Korine said softly. "If everyone took justice into their own hands, the world would be pure chaos. That's why we have police and detectives and courts."

"They don't always work," Tinsley said.

"She's right," Hatcher said in a low growl. "We failed her, just like the system failed the rape victims when Judge Wadsworth released the River Street Rapist."

"I admit that it doesn't always work, but it's the best we have," Korine said. "And if we abandon it, who's to say worse mistakes won't be made?

Look at that safety app and the chaos it caused. It was supposed to help keep the public safe. But instead it caused panic, and innocents were hurt."

Hatcher heaved a weary sigh. "In theory, you're correct. But—"

"There is no 'but,'" Korine cut in. "Tinsley, promise me that if you learn something, you'll call us."

Tinsley traced her fingers over a spot on the fog-coated window.

"Promise me," Korine said firmly.

"I promise," Tinsley said in a voice so low it was almost lost in the whir of the rumbling furnace.

"Thanks for talking to us," Hatcher said. "We'll get out of your hair now."

Tinsley didn't respond. She simply remained by the window as they walked to the door and let themselves out.

Korine tried to squash her internal voice of suspicion. She wasn't sure she trusted Tinsley to call.

She'd ask Cat to analyze the blog posts and see whether she could locate the origin of the suspicious comments.

Guilt nagged at her, though. She was invading these women's private lives and thoughts. A therapist would argue that their comments were confidential.

But they were on the Internet, and nothing there was sacred.

◆ ◆ ◆

Hatcher drove Korine to the prison to pick up her car, then followed her to her house so they could ride together to the briefing meeting.

He understood Korine was doing her job. He should have been asking the same questions as she was. But . . .

There was no way he could accuse Tinsley of anything. Not when her captor was still at large.

The bastard was probably biding his time until he had the opportunity to come back for Tinsley.

He'd stalked his victims before abducting them. He might be watching her now.

Concerned for her safety, he phoned Wyatt. The phone rang three times before he answered, enough time for Hatcher to question his decision to call him.

Wyatt sounded winded when he answered. "I was just getting ready to leave for the meeting."

Rain slashed the window in a steady rhythm as Hatcher drove across the causeway. "You're coming?"

Wyatt sighed. "I'm sick of these four walls. I told you I'm ready to get back to work."

An image of Wyatt lying bloody and helpless flashed in Hatcher's mind. Wyatt connected to dozens of tubes while he lay in a medically induced coma for weeks. Wyatt struggling to walk . . .

"Are you sure? I thought you were going to work on those files from home."

"Don't start," Wyatt said. "Now, is there a reason you called? Cause it'll take me a few minutes to shower before I come."

"I just talked to Tinsley."

An awkward silence followed.

"How is she?" Wyatt finally asked.

"Struggling," Hatcher said. "She blames herself for Felicia's death."

"Shit, that's not right."

"I know, but she's alone and scared and probably not sleeping."

"What can I do?"

"Actually, I called to fill you in before the meeting." Hatcher explained about the blog and Korine's suspicions.

"Do you think Tinsley knows who murdered the judge?"

Another awkward silence. "She says she doesn't, but . . . I'm not sure. Have you seen her or talked to her?"

Wyatt muttered something beneath his breath. "I'm probably the last person she wants to have contact with."

"She might open up to you," Hatcher said.

Wyatt cursed. "Don't ask me to use Tinsley, not for anything." Wyatt's breath hissed out. "I'll see you at the meeting."

The phone went silent. Hatcher felt like a heel for his suggestion. But if Tinsley opened up to Wyatt, they could control the situation.

Keep her name out of it.

Irritated, he punched the accelerator as he followed Korine to Savannah. Traffic thickened as they drove past the square, then onto Korine's street.

He pulled in Korine's drive behind her. She climbed out, then motioned that she was going inside for a moment. He cut the engine and decided to wait in the car.

Thunder boomed above. Storm clouds rolled across the sky, the fog thick, the streets cast in an ominous gray. It was too early for a tropical depression, but tornado season was upon them. The sky looked fitting for a funnel cloud.

Korine swung the front door open, but instead of walking toward his vehicle, she motioned for him to join her.

Something wasn't right.

His heartbeat picked up, and he threw the door open and jogged up the drive. "What's wrong?"

"Someone's been inside," she said, her voice cracking. "Come in and take a look."

Tension knotted his shoulders, and he pulled his gun, holding it at the ready as he entered. She quickly regained composure and joined him, her face stricken as she halted in the living area, facing the fireplace.

His pulse clamored as he realized what had upset her.

Three porcelain doll heads sat on the mantel, their eyes glowing yellow against the darkness, their bodies missing as if the heads had been severed.

CHAPTER TWENTY-SEVEN

Louie Hortman had to pay.

The son of a bitch acted like he was a good man, but she knew different.

He was a deacon in his church, never missed one of his son's basketball games, and regularly donated money to charities.

Looks could be deceiving. He was also a smarmy teacher who'd taken advantage of the teenage girls he taught in driver's education.

The girls had been afraid to come forward. They were embarrassed. Ashamed. Thought they'd done something to invite his touch.

He needed his vile hands cut off.

The Keeper smiled as she removed the duffel bag from the trunk of her car. She'd been watching him for weeks. Knew his routine. Had been waiting for the right time.

Today he had an opening in his schedule.

She'd arranged for a private lesson. The son of a bitch thought he was meeting teenage Zoe.

Zoe wasn't coming.

But she deserved justice for what he'd planned for her.

The sick pervert preyed on the fact that peer pressure would prevent the girls from spilling his dirty little secret.

Tears blurred her eyes as she stepped into the shadows of the nearby oak. The park was a perfect place to meet. It was secluded. Vacant this time of day.

Funny that Hortman hadn't even questioned her choice when any reputable, nice man would have insisted on meeting at the driving school where he worked.

Because he wanted the privacy.

She'd bet he hadn't even listed this lesson on his schedule. He'd told her that he offered discounts on his day off.

Idiot. He was so caught up in his evil fantasies and behavior that he'd been easy to trap.

She watched him park a few spaces from where she'd left her car. Rain clouds darkened the sky, casting shadows on the man's face as he climbed from the driver's seat. He jingled the change in his pockets, searching the parking lot. He seemed to have a little spring in his step.

He was excited. Looking forward to meeting Zoe and getting her alone.

Rage ate at her, and she stowed the duffel bag between two trees, then removed the pistol from the bag.

A smile tugged at her mouth as she inched to the edge of the live oak and called his name. He pivoted, scanning the area.

She remained hidden beneath the shade of the Spanish moss, but gave a little wave.

Just as she'd hoped, he sauntered toward her. Thinking with his dick, that was what drove him.

That would be his downfall, too.

She gripped the pistol behind her, her blood heating with adrenaline.

This man was finally going to get what was coming to him.

Then no other teenage girl would have to put up with his nasty hands again.

He noticed her then. Surprise and confusion mingled on his face. But he didn't rush away. He was too curious.

Asswipe.

"I thought I was meeting Zoe here for a driving lesson," he said with a smile.

"How about a mother-daughter?" She blinked flirtatiously.

A grin split his face. "You're talking about driving, aren't you?"

"Of course." She raised the gun and waved it toward him, and fear widened his eyes.

"Get in."

He shook his head, the brave face gone. "I think there's been a misunderstanding."

"No misunderstanding at all." She pointed the gun at his forehead. "I said get in."

He trembled like a kid caught stealing gum from a store but slid into the interior. "Please don't hurt me," he pleaded.

"You force yourself on young girls, you pervert. You don't deserve to call yourself a man."

"I won't do it again," he cried. "I swear. I'll never touch another girl."

"No, you won't."

When he reached for the keys to escape, she pressed the gun to his temple and he went still. She snatched the keys and tossed them into the bushes.

"Put your hands on the steering wheel."

He slapped them up there with a whiny grunt. She laughed. Weasel.

Then she snagged the rope at her belt. He tried to shove the door closed, but she caught it with her boot and shot at his crotch.

He screamed like a baby as the bullet hit home, then went ashen-faced and pressed his hand over his bloody cock. Satisfied he wouldn't fight back anymore, she jerked his hands up one by one and tied them to the steering wheel.

Once she had them secure, she retrieved the hatchet from behind the tree and brought it toward him. He was crying now, his face shriveled up as he sobbed, blood oozing from his lap.

"This is for Zoe and all the others." With one quick swing of the hatchet, she chopped his right hand off. He bellowed in pain.

She raised the hatchet to cut off the other.

CHAPTER
TWENTY-EIGHT

A wave of dizziness washed over Korine. The dolls . . . looked exactly like the ones in her collection at her mother's.

Except someone had turned them into night-lights, making them look spooky. The brightly lit eyes pierced the darkness as if they were watching her every move.

Hatcher cleared his throat. "Korine?"

"My father gave me porcelain dolls for my birthdays and Christmas," she said in a raw whisper. "I left all but one of them at my mother's." With the memories and her childhood.

Hatcher examined the doll heads, then returned to the front door and studied the lock. "I don't see signs of a break-in. Is there another entrance?"

Korine pointed toward the hall. "There's a patio with a garden in back."

"I'll check it and the windows."

A memory tickled the back of Korine's mind, launching her back in time.

Her father's smile as he placed a beautifully wrapped box in her lap. Excitement made her giddy as she touched the shiny pink bow.

"Happy birthday, my pretty girl," her father said. "Go ahead, open it."

She giggled as she tore into the wrapping. The white, sparkly paper hit the floor, and she lifted the lid on the box.

A beautiful porcelain doll with hand-painted green eyes and freckles dotting her cheeks lay on a bed of ivory satin. Korine traced a finger over the delicate lace hem of the green velvet dress.

"She's beautiful," she whispered as she lifted her from the box. "I love her, Daddy."

She threw her arms around him, and he picked her up and swung her around, dancing with her and the doll.

Later that night, though, as she started to place the doll on her bed with her others, she realized one of them was missing. The doll with the golden hair and Christmas dress, the one she'd received the year before.

She slipped from bed and tiptoed down the hall. A crashing sound came from Kenny's room. She froze. Kenny was cursing and stomping around inside.

She cracked the door and peeked into the room.

The model planes he'd put together with their father were scattered on the floor, broken to smithereens.

Kenny kicked at a broken wing, his hands in fists.

Then he set her Christmas doll on his desk, raised the hammer, and smashed the doll's face.

"No!" she screamed.

He turned toward the door, his face angry. Then he took a menacing step toward her.

Terrified, she ran to her room and slammed the door. She quickly locked it and leaned against the door, her chest heaving for a breath.

She wiped at tears, afraid he'd break in.

But finally he stomped away, and his bedroom door slammed with a bang.

Trembling, she crawled in bed with her new doll and hugged it to her.

Hatcher's footsteps pounded on the floor as he returned from the rear of the house. "The back door doesn't look like it was jimmied. Does anyone else have a key to your place?"

Her mind raced. "My mother." Which meant that Kenny could have access to it.

He was furious with her for forcing him into rehab. And he'd hated the dolls her father had given her.

Had he snuck away from rehab and left those doll heads to frighten her?

◆ ◆ ◆

"Have you seen these doll heads before?" Hatcher asked.

"No." She examined the doll heads but didn't touch them. She had never seen these dolls before, although they reminded her of the ones her father had given her. "It looks like someone decapitated the dolls, then inserted the lights."

Korine was right. The heads had been severed with a sharp knife or instrument of some kind, but the method was crude, the edges rough, not smooth or as if created by an artist.

"Have you had trouble with break-ins before?"

She shook her head with a frown.

He couldn't help himself. He pulled her up against him. She surprised him by leaning her head against his chest. Her breath rushed out, a quiver rippling through her.

God, she acted so tough. She *was* tough.

But she was shaken, and she was his partner, and dammit, he knew what it felt like to be alone.

He also knew what it felt like to have her naked in his arms, passion exploding between them.

His fingers itched to stroke her bare skin again. To press his lips on her body and hear her moan his name.

She flattened one hand against his chest and lifted her head. Storm clouds outside obliterated the sun, and shadows streaked the room. Thunder clapped, almost in time with the furnace rumbling and his heart pounding.

He rubbed her back. "Korine?"

She sighed and pushed away, her breathing shaky. Probably from fear, although something dark and needy flashed in her eyes before she glanced back at the mantel.

"It's probably nothing. But yesterday when I came in, my music box was playing. It wasn't where I'd left it, so I thought someone might have been inside."

Skepticism ate at Hatcher, thankfully forcing his hunger for Korine to take a back seat. "Why would someone move your music box?"

"I don't know." She shrugged. "Maybe I moved it and forgot about it."

Her story reminded him of the lies Felicia had told. Little things that she'd notice were missing or moved.

He hadn't believed her at the time. Had thought she'd just wanted attention because she had exaggerated before, called to say someone was looking in her window or following her, all to scare him into rushing to her.

Then one day someone really had been following her. Only he'd thought she was crying wolf again.

He couldn't ignore Korine. "Is there anything significant about the dolls?"

She sighed wearily. "My brother hated them," she said. "One night I saw him smashing one of the dolls' faces with a hammer. Another time he buried one of them in our backyard."

"Isn't he at the rehab center now?" Hatcher asked.

"He's supposed to be." She gestured toward her phone. "Call ERT while I check with the center."

He stepped into the foyer to make the call, but he couldn't keep from staring at the doll heads and wondering what kind of twisted person had thought of inserting lights into them. They looked like something out of a horror movie.

◆ ◆ ◆

Korine made a quick call to the rehab facility. Kenny was still there, so he couldn't have been in her house.

She scrutinized the doll heads again looking for a clue as to who'd left them. No message or note. Nothing.

She walked through the living room, scanning the bookshelves and coffee table for anything out of place, then did the same in the kitchen. From there, she moved to her bedroom, but her bed was still made, throw pillows exactly as she'd left them, closet in order, her discarded boots in front of the chair in the corner.

She checked her bathroom—toiletries just as she stored them, hairbrush on the vanity, towel hanging on the hook.

She hurried into her office. She wondered what Hatcher thought of her wall of crime photos and notes on unsolved cases.

She quickly glanced at the files and board, but everything seemed in place. Except . . . the picture of her and her father.

Instead of being displayed prominently, it was lying facedown.

She started to pick it up but reminded herself not to touch it. If her intruder had touched it, he—or she—might have left a print.

Korine called her mother's home number. Esme answered on the second ring. "Davenport residence."

"It's me, Esme. How's my mother today?"

"She's been calmer," Esme said.

"That's a relief."

"What happened with your brother?" Esme asked.

"I took him to rehab and gave him an ultimatum," Korine said. "If he doesn't stay, I'm finished with him."

"I'm sure that was painful for you."

Emotions welled in Korine's throat. Esme was like a second mother to her. "It was, but he needs to figure out the reason he drinks. A therapist can help him with that. I can't."

An awkward silence followed.

"There's something else. Does Mom still have that key to my house?"

"Just a minute and I'll check." Esme hummed beneath her breath as she walked, a habit she'd had ever since she'd started to work at the Davenport house ten years ago. "It's in the drawer."

"How about the dolls in the curio? Are all of them still inside?"

"The dolls?"

Korine pictured the way Esme's nose wrinkled when she frowned. "I know it's a strange question, but it's important. There were six in the case."

"They're still there, just as you left them."

Still mystified but grateful her intruder hadn't stolen the dolls from her mother's, Korine thanked Esme and ended the call.

By the time she returned to the living room, Hatcher was escorting the evidence team inside. Tammy Drummond and Trace Bellamy again.

Tammy raised a brow in question at the eerie doll heads on the mantel. "What the hell?"

"That is downright creepy," Bellamy muttered.

"Check the doors and windows for prints along with the mantel and doll heads," Hatcher said.

Korine sighed. "I also need you to dust in my office."

"What happened in there?" Hatcher asked.

It seemed silly to mention, but working a case meant every detail mattered, so she told him about the photograph.

Had her father's killer come after her? If so, why now?

CHAPTER TWENTY-NINE

Tinsley startled at the sound of the rain pounding the roof and windows. The wind tossed leaves and twigs across the sand, the high tides bringing in shells and seaweed.

Her nerves were raw from the visit with Hatcher and that other agent. Korine Davenport. She was tough.

It would be nice to have her on your side if you were in trouble.

But she could also be a formidable enemy.

Though Mr. Jingles's cage door remained open, he hadn't ventured any farther than his post, where he remained perched with his head cocked, tiny eyes following her as if expecting her to run screaming like a banshee any minute.

She pressed her hand against the glass, the cool, slick pane thick with fog. Thunder clapped, the wind roaring. She searched the gloomy outdoors, praying the Skull hadn't found her.

Although it was just a matter of time.

The image of the judge's body on her dock surfaced in the mist. Agent Davenport's questions echoed in her head.

Shivering with the cold and fear, she brewed a cup of tea and carried it to her desk. She logged on and skimmed some of the comments to her blog post, each one tearing her heart out.

The two Agent Davenport had pointed out did sound damning.

There were followers she worried about. She'd done some digging and learned they had a private chat room. One of them had even reached out to her.

They called themselves the Keepers.

Her lungs tightened as she clicked to skim new entries.

If one of them had murdered the judge, or that monster child molester, they might have shared it here.

Did she really want to know? Or was it better that she remain in the dark?

Then she wouldn't have to lie if the police questioned her again.

She paced the room, torn. The Keepers wanted justice, to right wrongs done to innocents, to make up for the law when it failed . . .

She padded back to the desk, then drummed her fingers on her laptop. She could simply avoid looking.

She paced to the window again. But the image of that dead body wouldn't leave her alone. She'd come to this cove for peace and solitude, to escape the violence that had tainted her life.

But violence had found her again.

She couldn't sleep at night unless she knew the truth. Then she would decide what to do.

Bracing herself for whatever she found, she clicked and entered the Keepers' message board.

The first three posts seemed like personal stories, heartbreaking, but not violent accounts.

The fourth entry sent a sliver of unease through her.

Rita Herron

KeepersHand
Out for Blood

Strike three off the list.

One less predator on the streets tonight.

But there are others out there.

We have to stop them.

The police are asking questions. Instead, they should be thanking us.

We are the Keepers, and we won't let anything—or anybody—stop us now.

Whoever tries will have to die.

Next we go after him.

I can't wait to feel his blood on my hands and watch it drain from his body.

But death can't come too easily. He has to suffer first.

Just as he made his victims suffer . . .

CHAPTER THIRTY

As the evidence team processed Korine's house, Hatcher had a bad feeling they wouldn't find anything. With the popularity of crime shows, most perpetrators were smart enough to wear gloves. But, hey, the team could get lucky, especially if this person was an amateur.

Korine's brows were knitted into a deep frown as she stepped onto her back patio. He snapped a few pictures of the doll heads for his own reference, then joined her.

"Are you okay?"

She nodded. "I checked. Kenny's still at the center."

Her back was to him, her face lifted toward the dark clouds. The rain was slacking off, the wind shaking droplets from the branches and adding a cold chill to the gloomy atmosphere.

She pivoted, her expression tormented. "How bad is that, that I suspected my own brother of this?"

He shrugged. "It's understandable. From what you've told me, he's had problems for a while. It sounds like he's jealous of you and the fact that you have your life together."

"I have my life together?" A sarcastic laugh rumbled from her. "You saw the wall in my office. I'm obsessed with murder and old cases to the point of excluding people. I live alone, never had a pet or a serious boyfriend. My mother is mentally ill. I have very little decor because I don't want to get attached to anyplace. I can't even put up a Christmas tree because it reminds me of the night my father was murdered."

Hatcher inched closer to her. "You suffered a terrible shock and loss at a young age. That would affect anyone." Just as losing his wife affected him. "At least you turned your loss into motivation to help others by solving crimes. That's far more healthy than indulging in alcohol or drugs."

She rubbed her hands up and down her arms to warm herself.

Even as he told himself to resist, he couldn't help but reach out and place his hands over hers. "You had every right to question your brother," he said. "You're trained to analyze all angles of a crime, which means starting with the most obvious suspects. Unfortunately, that's usually family." He paused. "But if your brother didn't do this, who did? Who else knew about the dolls?"

Korine closed her eyes as if struggling to remember, then opened them and bit down on her lower lip. "No one except my mother and Esme. That's what's so puzzling."

Hatcher rubbed his chin. "No old boyfriend or a neighbor who might be stalking you? Perhaps someone you pissed off on the job?"

She shook her head no. "Even if I had a stalker and somehow he'd gained access to my house, I don't keep my dolls here. They're at my mother's. Esme said they haven't been disturbed."

Hatcher scratched his head. "Were the dolls mentioned in the media coverage about your father's murder?"

Korine twisted her mouth in thought. "I think the press talked about it. And the broken doll would have shown up in the crime photos."

They both fell silent, contemplating the idea that her father's killer might have put the dolls in her house.

"But I haven't uncovered any leads about Dad's case, so why would his killer taunt me with the dolls now?"

Hatcher made a low sound in his throat. "Good question."

"Maybe it's our unsub, trying to scare me away from this investigation," Korine suggested.

"That's a possibility," Hatcher agreed.

Bellamy appeared in the doorway. "We're finished."

Hatcher checked his watch. "Thanks, keep us posted on the results of your analysis." He touched Korine's arm. "I need to make that briefing. If you want to stay here, you can."

She stiffened. "No way. I refuse to let anyone keep me from my job."

She strode back inside, her courage stirring his admiration for her even more.

But worry nagged at him as he passed those damn doll heads. "Take those to the lab," he told Drummond. He didn't want Korine coming back home to see them again.

He'd also make sure she had new locks installed. And a security system. If this creep broke in again, they'd capture his face on camera.

Then they could put a stop to whatever else he had planned.

As she and Hatcher entered the meeting room at the Savannah field office, Korine tried to shake off her anxiety over the fact that she had an intruder—or possibly that her father's killer had resurfaced.

Hushed voices sounded from the room, which was filling up fast. A thirtysomething detective named Ryker Brockett introduced himself and said he was coordinating information between the FBI and local police. Wyatt entered, his shoulders squared as he gripped his cane and limped to a seat at the table.

Korine sympathized. Wyatt was obviously still in pain and needed physical therapy, but he wanted to work, not be replaced by her or anyone else.

Introductions were made; then Bellows cleared his throat. "Let's have a recap of what we have so far."

Hatcher stood in front of the whiteboard. "Our first murder victim, Judge Lester Wadsworth. He recently released the River Street Rapist. Body found on the dock by Tinsley Jensen's cottage." Hatcher attached photos of the judge and crime scene to the board, then gestured to the ME. "Official cause of death?"

"Blunt force trauma to the head. After studying his injuries and the shape of the blow, we believe Judge Wadsworth was struck several times by a heavy wooden object, which caused bleeding to his brain. The size and shape of the murder weapon is consistent with a gavel."

"Time of death?" Hatcher asked.

"Monday night between the hours of nine and eleven p.m."

"The man was dead when he was dragged to the dock the next day," Hatcher said. "The question is how was he subdued? Where did the unsub keep him for those hours? Were there any forensics on his body?"

"Nothing noteworthy," Dr. Patton said, then verified the info with the evidence team leader, who nodded in confirmation. "Tox screen showed Rohypnol in his system as well as alcohol. My guess is the killer spiked the judge's drink."

"Which suggests the judge knew the unsub well enough to get close to him."

Drummond held up a finger, indicating she wanted to speak. "We searched the judge's home and his chambers for drugs that could have been used to sedate him but didn't find anything. We'll get warrants to pick up any alcohol in the house and analyze it."

"Thanks, keep us posted," Hatcher said as he gathered more photos and displayed them on the board. "Now, let's talk suspects.

"First, the family. Daughter confirmed that the judge abused his wife, giving both of them and the son motive. But the housekeeper claimed the wife was at home. Son alibied out. The daughter's alibi is weaker, but she seems too smart to kill her father. She pointed us toward the judge's old cases, which we'll get to in a minute. We also questioned the victims of the River Street Rapist."

He listed their names and added photos. "At this point, I don't consider any of them persons of interest."

He turned to Wyatt. "Anything on the judge's past cases or threats made to him?"

"There were dozens of threats made in writing and others at trials," Wyatt said. "I've cleared about half of them. I'll let you know if something pans out."

Hatcher nodded and stepped to the second board, then attached Pallo Whiting's photograph. "This is our second victim," he said, although it galled him to call the man a victim. "Pallo Whiting was a convicted child molester. We interviewed and cleared the direct family members of Whiting's victims, although Whiting's brother, Ernest, is missing. He had motive—Whiting molested Ernest's daughter. Ernest's wife divorced him and took the child away, but we cleared her as well."

"We have an APB out for him," Roger Cummings interjected.

Hatcher placed photos of the child victims on the board and groans sounded through the room.

"Bastard deserved what he got," Cat muttered.

Drummond mumbled agreement, and so did Cummings.

"Whiting also murdered two inmates for abusing him. One—Tyrone Hubbard. He had a daughter, although they were estranged, so we cleared her. The more viable suspect was Ned Banning, whose son Gerard was stabbed to death by Whiting." He paused. "Banning insists his son was falsely imprisoned. His lawyer concurred that new evidence had surfaced that would have exonerated the son. Although Banning openly admitted he hated Whiting, he denies the murder."

"What do you think?" Detective Brockett asked.

Korine and Hatcher exchanged looks. "I tend to believe him. The fact that the unsub cut off Whiting's penis suggests that the crime was more personal."

Korine cleared her throat. "Actually, both MOs appear to be tailored specifically to the victims. The judge was murdered with an object that we suspect was a gavel. Whiting molested little girls, so the killer cut off his penis." She stood and pointed to the double SS on the judge's and Whiting's foreheads. "Both victims bore the symbol of justice on their forehead." She paused for effect. "This is the unsub's signature."

Director Bellows cursed. "Jesus. You think we're dealing with a serial killer, don't you?"

Korine nodded. "Not just a serial killer, a vigilante."

◆ ◆ ◆

The phrases *vigilante killer* and *serial killer* spiked Hatcher's adrenaline.

He let Korine take the floor to discuss the blog posts.

The possibility made sense that they were dealing with one killer or a group who had a beef against the system and had murdered both the judge and Whiting.

Unfortunately, it opened up a wide range of suspects, and without concrete forensics, investigating them would be challenging.

"Do you have any leads?" Brockett asked.

Korine added a screenshot of Tinsley's *Heart & Soul* blog to the board, then connected her computer to the screen so everyone could see. "At this point, we haven't narrowed down a suspect. However, the fact that the first body was left on a dock in clear sight of Tinsley Jensen, a victim of the Skull, led me to look at Tinsley more closely to see if there was a connection. She started *Heart & Soul* as therapy for herself and to offer a support group for other victims of crimes. She regularly posts about her experience and journey to recovery. Others respond to her experience or share their own. Most of the posts are anonymous, although some use names. Whether they're real names or not we don't know yet.

"I started reading to see if the judge's killer had sent Tinsley a personal message," she continued. "So far, I haven't found a specific entry regarding his death, but some of the comments are very disturbing."

"I can imagine," Drummond said. "Those women were writing about their personal abuse or rape, or even worse, about their children's."

"That's true," Korine said. "It's not illegal to imagine or fantasize about destroying the source of one's trauma, but at least two posts sound like murder confessions."

She clicked to display them on the screen, and silence descended as everyone skimmed the entries.

"These are disturbing but not conclusive," Brockett said.

"I realize that, but at this point it's something we should explore." She glanced at Cat. "I need you to find the names and addresses of the people who posted these so we can run background checks and question them personally."

Hatcher threw up a finger. "I agree we should explore this, but something else occurred to me. Vigilante killers are often people in the community who have an elevated sense of community and society. These murders might not be personal at all, but the result of a citizen concerned about the nature of our society and the justice system."

Korine nodded, obviously contemplating his point.

"We should look at people in law enforcement, employees of the legal system, members of the local government, anyone who has rallied or spoken out against the court system."

"What about the woman who created that safety app? It's been all over the news," Bellamy said.

"The judge's daughter," Korine replied. "We've talked to her. I don't think she's our killer, but we'll keep her in mind."

Hatcher's mind raced. "This person may also have inserted himself into the investigation."

"You think one of our own had something to do with this?" Cummings asked defensively.

"I'm not pointing fingers at anyone," Hatcher said. "But take a look at your officers. Notice if anyone is vocal against the system's failures. It could be someone who has been let down by the system himself or knows someone who has, or simply someone dedicated to making the world safer and a better place."

"Look at lawyers and clerks as well. Men and women who applied to the police academy and were turned down or failed out for some reason. A lawyer who lost a big case and watched his client be incarcerated because of it," Korine said. "On the other hand, what if a lawyer knew his client was guilty and got him off? Even though he did his job, if he knows he freed a killer, he might want to make things right." She paused. "If this person works in the system, he knows how to cover his tracks."

"You're talking about dozens and dozens of possibilities," Brockett said. "We could be talking about a crime scene cleaner, a cop, a Fed even."

Hatcher let the comment stand as unease settled through the room. "All the more reason we keep our eyes open." He gestured toward Cat. "Get someone to help you look at the women who marched in the protest. Isn't there a specific group advocating against domestic violence?"

Cat nodded. "I'll get right on it."

A knock sounded at the door, and another agent appeared. "Excuse me, but I thought you'd want to know. We've got another one."

"You think it's related to our current cases?" Hatcher asked.

The agent nodded. "Nine-one-one caller said the victim has double SS painted in blood on his forehead."

CHAPTER
THIRTY-ONE

Hatcher grimaced. Another murder. "Come in and give us the details," Hatcher said as he waved the agent inside.

"Jogger found the man dead in his car in a vacant lot by the park where he runs. I'll text you the address."

"Cause of death?" Hatcher asked.

"He was shot, and his hands were severed," the agent said bluntly.

"ID?" Hatcher asked.

"Louie Hortman. Still had his driver's license on him."

"Any witnesses?"

"No. Officer just got to the scene. When he saw the justice symbol on the man's forehead, he thought we should know."

Korine was already standing, ready to go. Hatcher tilted his head toward Cat. "Send us everything you can dig up on Hortman."

Hatcher spoke to the group. "Keep us updated on what you find. This unsub is going to kill again unless we stop him. Or her."

Detective Brockett cleared his throat. "I'm with you two."

Hatcher started to argue, but the body count was rising. They could use all the hands they could get.

He and Korine and the detective rushed outside. The wind hurled leaves across the parking lot, raindrops splattering the ground as the trees trembled.

Hatcher sped from the parking lot with the detective following in his own car.

"I don't want to think that someone in law enforcement is doing this, but cops and lawyers and detectives get frustrated." No one understood that more than him.

"Maybe this time the unsub made a mistake and we can catch him." Korine settled her iPad on her lap and began to work.

"Damn."

"What?" Hatcher asked.

"Hortman taught driver's ed at the local high school until last year. He was fired after a student accused him of sexual harassment during a session."

Hatcher tensed. "What came of it?"

"Two other girls came forward and admitted that he'd done the same thing to them. Charges were filed, and he was dismissed from the school. But when it came time for trial, two girls backed out and the other one's family moved away. Rumors surfaced that the victims received threats."

"So he got off?" Hatcher asked.

Korine nodded. "His lawyer got the charges dropped. A month ago, he hired on at a private driving school."

"The man had enemies," Hatcher said. "Just like the judge and Whiting." Hatcher parked in the lot, which had been roped off by the officer first on the scene. Detective Brockett pulled in behind them, and they parked.

An older dark-gray sedan sat sideways near a cluster of trees. They climbed out, pulling on latex gloves as they walked toward the car.

Crime scene tape stretched across the area and extended to the trees on the edge of the parking lot.

The officer identified himself as Phil Pritchard.

Korine winced as they peered inside the car. The man's arms were tied to the steering wheel, his hands missing. Blood was everywhere, splattered on the seats, floor, windshield, steering wheel, and the man.

The officer was looking over their shoulder. "Looks like he was shot at fairly close range in the crotch." He indicated the bloody ropes dangling from the steering wheel. "The killer tied his hands to the steering wheel before chopping them off."

"To keep him from fighting back," Korine said.

"Did you find the murder weapons? A gun? Ax? Hatchet?" Hatcher asked.

The officer shook his head. "I haven't searched yet. Didn't want to leave the witness and vic."

"Evidence team will search," Korine said. "Although so far our unsub hasn't left any forensics behind."

"They need to check the swamp, too." Hatcher shined his flashlight inside the vehicle and studied the floor and the seats. "Where are the hands?"

The officer's face paled as he gestured toward a marshy area close by. "Haven't had time to look for them either. Killer could have thrown them in the swamp."

Yet the unsub left the man's ID, so he hadn't discarded the hands to slow down identification.

The severing was a message, just as the justice symbol was.

Hatcher pressed two fingers to the man's neck. No pulse, but the body didn't appear to be in full rigor either.

"He hasn't been dead long," he said.

Korine's gaze met his. They were still too late, though.

Hatcher walked over to the swamp edge and shined the light on the area. He combed the bank in search of footprints or signs that the unsub came in on a boat.

Something caught his eye in the marsh. He approached slowly, aiming the flashlight beam on the mud and dead grass.

Good God. There were the man's hands.

The unsub had tossed them into the muddy water as if they were food for the alligators.

♦ ♦ ♦

Korine took deep breaths to calm her queasy stomach as she studied the bloody crime scene.

The area was virtually isolated, not a park people frequented this time of year. It backed up to marshland and offered running trails as well as trails leading to an inlet used for crabbing by locals and tourists.

The unsub had probably figured no one would be nearby, meaning no witnesses or interference while he or she perpetrated the crime.

Hatcher had found the man's hands and pointed them out to the ERT as soon as they arrived.

She checked beneath the seats in the car for the murder weapon, then popped the trunk, but found no gun, hatchet, or ax.

Detective Brockett and Hatcher both began snapping photographs, and Drummond and Bellamy fanned out to work.

Dr. Patton knelt beside the open car door to examine the victim.

A slim man in running gear sat hunched on the curb drinking from a water bottle, his run forgotten as he absorbed the shock of his discovery.

"That guy called it in?" Korine asked Officer Pritchard as Hatcher joined them.

"Yeah." He consulted his notepad. "Runner's name is Ian Hammerstein. Lives in Savannah, manages a restaurant on the river named Fresh Catch. He's training for a marathon and runs here a couple of times a week. He parked on the other side of the marsh and ran the trail, then spotted the car and thought someone might be stranded. Jogged over and discovered the body."

"Did he touch anything?" Hatcher asked.

"Said he didn't. He got close enough to see that the man was beyond help, then called nine-one-one."

"Did he see anyone around? Another car? A runner or anyone leaving the scene?"

The officer shook his head. "He was pretty shook up. Apparently he's squeamish around blood. Threw up in the bushes over there."

At least he hadn't contaminated the crime scene.

"Did he know the vic?" Detective Brockett asked.

The officer shook his head again. "Said he'd never seen him before. I got his contact information. Should I let him go?"

"I want to speak to him first," Hatcher said.

Korine stooped down to study the victim's face. He was midforties, a square jaw, pudgy belly. His wavy dark hair was combed back with some kind of gel. His white golf shirt was soaked in blood, as were the thick ropes holding his arms to the steering wheel.

Same kind of rope that was used to tie Whiting down.

"Victim probably bled out from the amputation and gunshot wound, although I can be more specific once I get him on the table," Dr. Patton said. "Of course, I'll run a tox screen to see if he was drugged or had alcohol in his system."

"The hands were severed while he was still alive?" Korine asked.

Dr. Patton nodded.

"He's a big man, probably two fifty," Korine said. "The unsub probably held the gun on him and made him get in the car. My guess is he was shot trying to escape. Once he was injured he couldn't fight back, so the unsub tied his hands to the steering wheel, then cut them off."

Korine addressed Cummings. "Look for signs that another vehicle was here," Korine said. "Tire tracks, an oil leak, anything that might point to the unsub."

The evidence team fanned out to run a grid search. Detective Brockett had been surveying the parking lot, then veered to the right toward a pavilion for picnickers and recreational activities. Korine wasn't sure whether he'd seen something, but they needed to keep their eyes open for anything unusual. A hair, a button, discarded drink bottles—anything could help.

A white van roared up, and Hatcher strode toward it, a frown marring his face. Korine tensed as the passenger door opened, and Marilyn Ellis, clad in a pristine gray pantsuit, vaulted from the vehicle. A cameraman followed, his microphone ready, as he raced to keep up with Marilyn.

She was sharp as a tack, and a shark when she wanted a story.

"Special Agents Davenport and McGee, you have a third murder here?" she called.

How had she heard so quickly?

Hatcher held out a warning hand to stop her from ducking under the crime scene tape. "Stay back and do not photograph the victim."

She tucked her hair behind her ear and motioned for the cameraman to focus on the car. "Is this murder connected to Judge Wadsworth's death and the murder of escaped prisoner Pallo Whiting?"

Korine went still, her pulse hammering.

"Where did you get that idea?" Hatcher asked, his expression neutral.

"It's true, isn't it?" Marilyn pressed. "It's also true that you suspect a vigilante killer committed both crimes. One who has now murdered three men. One who's cleaning up after the cops when they fail to do their jobs."

Irritation crawled through Korine. "We can't comment on an active investigation and you know it."

"You can't run that either," Hatcher said in a cold voice.

The woman didn't give up easily. "The public deserves to know the truth. And if there is a vigilante killer, a *serial* vigilante killer, they should be warned."

Maybe they did deserve to know. But flashing that story all over the media would create panic and possibly cause the killer to bolt.

Korine didn't want any more murders. But if the unsub decided to lie low or move to another area, they might lose their chance at catching him and putting him away.

CHAPTER THIRTY-TWO

Louie Hortman had deserved to die. No one would be crying at his funeral. Even his wife had gotten sick of his smarmy ways years ago and left.

He'd screamed like a baby when he was shot. He'd begged and pleaded for his life. Promised not to touch another girl ever again.

But he'd lied. If he'd lived, he would have gone right back to his piglike ways. Pressuring girls into sex for a passing grade.

Exposing himself to shock the innocent young virgins, then promising that he'd teach them the right way to please a man so they'd be popular.

His dick would never see another girl again. And no other female would have to look at it or touch it or be mauled by his filthy hands.

Those fucking Feds were asking too many questions, though. Getting too close.

She was the Keeper—she had to let the others know. She was doing their work. Exacting justice.

Those nosy agents had to be stopped before they exposed the truth.

Sometimes sacrifices had to be made for the greater good. Collateral damage.

Korine Davenport had been spoiled by her daddy. Spoiled with those damn dolls and that music box.

It was time for the truth to come out.

Korine was nothing but a two-faced liar. She deserved to die . . .

CHAPTER
THIRTY-THREE

Hatcher shoved the microphone away. "Listen to me, I don't know where you got your information, but no one has said anything about a vigilante killer, and if you announce that, I'll have you arrested for interfering with a criminal investigation and reporting false information."

The reporter lifted her chin. "Those charges will never stick and you know it."

"Maybe not, but I can keep you locked up until we solve this case."

She glanced at Korine as if she thought she would be softer, but Korine gave her a cold look. "Let us do our jobs, and when we make an arrest, you can have the story."

A tense minute stretched between them. "All right," Marilyn said. "But at least tell me what you have here."

"We can't release the victim's name until we contact next of kin," Hatcher said.

"Understood," Marilyn said. "But you are investigating Judge Wadsworth's murder and believe it's related to Pallo Whiting's death." She pushed the microphone in front of Hatcher. "What about this murder? Do you think it's related to the other two cases you're working?"

He did, because of that justice symbol on the man's forehead. But he didn't intend to share that information with this media maniac. "It's too early to tell at this point. But, as Special Agent Davenport said, when we have information available, we'll contact you."

Hatcher motioned toward the crime scene tape. "Now, stay back and keep that camera off our victim."

Hatcher strode back to the car where Drummond was searching the interior. "Find anything?"

She lifted a Baggie. "A strand of black hair. Short. Looks unnatural, but the lab will have to analyze it."

Adrenaline surged through Hatcher. If they could get the DNA, they could hopefully find a match and identify the hair. Although if Hortman used his personal car in the driving school, the hair could belong to a student. Another question for the school. He punched Cat's number and filled her in. "Send us info on the girls who reported Hortman for sexual harassment. Also, contact the private driving school where he worked and see if there have been any complaints about him. We need to know if he scheduled a lesson for today and if so, who it was with. Also, ask if he used his personal car to give driving lessons."

"On it. I'll get back to you as soon as possible," Cat said. "By the way, I got a warrant to search for IP addresses of people posting on that blog. There are a couple who have interesting connections to our victims."

"Send me the information and copy Agent Davenport, and we'll follow up."

◆ ◆ ◆

Korine studied the information Cat had sent.

"This is odd," Korine said as she and Hatcher climbed in his SUV for privacy. "The first two names on the list, Liz Roberts and Laura Austin, help other women and children through their jobs. It's hard to imagine either one of them taking a life, especially in the brutal ways we've seen."

"Maybe they've heard enough horror stories that one of then snapped," Hatcher suggested.

"Hmmm, I don't know." Although when she'd first seen Andi after the rape, she'd wanted to find the son of a bitch who'd attacked her and kill him.

But she hadn't.

These women might not have done anything but express that same feeling, and they'd done so on a blog they thought was a safe haven.

"We know Austin worked with Lynn Green and her foster daughter, Lottie. What about Roberts?" Hatcher asked.

"Liz Roberts counseled two of the girls who claimed Hortman sexually harassed them."

"There's motive. How about the last two names?"

"Rachel Willis is a parole officer. No doubt she's seen the dregs of society and probably been threatened herself. Same with Beverly Grant, the court reporter. We met her at the judge's office that day we picked up the files."

"She acted suspicious to me," Hatcher said. "Like she didn't want to talk to us."

Korine logged on to the police and federal databases, then ran a search on each of the women's names.

"Liz Roberts has a master's in counseling, worked two years with children in at-risk homes through the county school system before joining the court system. She currently works as a victims' advocate and counseled two of Hortman's victims."

"Domestic violence cases are frustrating," Hatcher said. "Hard to get vics to testify. Even harder to break that cycle of abuse."

As evidenced by the fact that Hortman's victims had dropped the case against him.

"I'm sure she's seen the system fail," Korine said, as she continued to skim for information. "This is interesting. Two of her cases were in Judge Wadsworth's court. One of them was dismissed when the judge badgered the victim. The victim ran from the courtroom in tears. Committed suicide the next day."

"Holy shit," Hatcher said.

"Laura Austin, the guardian ad litem who worked with Lynn Green and Lottie, had another troubling case. Against her advice, a child was returned to an abusive father, who left the child in a hot car a week later. The child died."

"Reasons to be bitter," Hatcher said.

"Not as bitter as the mother." Korine sighed. "She shot and killed the husband the day they found the child dead. She's sitting in prison now." Which seemed totally unfair.

"Still, it's hard to imagine these good women risking their careers and lives to take another." Korine searched for information on Beverly Grant but found nothing incriminating. Still, she'd worked on numerous cases Judge Wadsworth presided over so had seen his rulings firsthand.

"What about Willis?" Hatcher asked.

"Rachel Willis's father was falsely imprisoned for years." Just as Banning's son had. "Father got hooked on drugs in the pen. After finally being exonerated and released, he had trouble acclimating. Without an education, he couldn't get a job. Died of an overdose."

"So we have four women who've seen justice fail, but none have any kind of record or history of violence?"

"Not that I've found." Korine's phone buzzed. Cat.

She quickly connected. "Someone just posted a cryptic message on that *Heart & Soul* blog."

"What did it say?"

"To meet in the KR?"

"What is that?"

Cat sighed. "I followed the link to a private message board called the Keepers."

"Jesus," Korine muttered. "The Keepers—Keepers of Justice?"

"Exactly. I'm forwarding the link to the page to you."

"Did you trace those four women from Tinsley's blog to this group?" Korine asked.

"I'm working on it, but it's complicated. For anonymity and privacy, people use fake names and identities, secondary email addresses, or reroute their entries to make it difficult for them to be traced."

She would find it, though. Cat was an expert hacker. "Keep us posted. Meanwhile I'll look at the message board." She ended the call and relayed the information to Hatcher.

Hatcher scrubbed his hand through his hair. "I'll get officers to pick up those four women for questioning. And I'll have Hortman's family notified."

He stepped from the car to make the calls just as the transport team from the morgue arrived.

Marilyn Ellis and her cameraman were still lurking around, hoping for the scoop. Korine frowned as the woman raced toward the ME. She'd seen the way the reporter handled the Skull case and didn't trust her.

Dr. Patton deftly avoided her as he veered toward the transport team.

Korine clicked on the link that Cat had sent. Her eyes widened as she encountered a black door and logo with double SS, the lines blurred and smudged as if they'd been painted in blood.

She clicked on the door, and it opened, revealing the name the Keepers, also in red.

Her pulse jumped. Someone in this group might be the unsub.

◆ ◆ ◆

Hatcher phoned the station and requested officers pick up the four women Cat had identified from the blog comments.

When he ended the call, he got back in the car, started the engine, and headed toward the Savannah Police Department. Korine had grown quiet, her expression troubled. "What are you looking at?"

She exhaled sharply. "Cat discovered a private message board where a group who call themselves the Keepers gather." She angled the iPad for him to see, and he glanced at the web page. His heart pounded at the image of the bloody SS.

"The justice symbol is identical to the one on our victims," Korine said.

He nodded, teeth grinding. The Keepers of Justice—no doubt a group who thought the system had failed.

"Cat is still working on analyzing the page and locating the individuals who posted. Listen to this," Korine said.

> The moment I saw her face, battered and bruised, and her eyes swollen shut, her jaw wired, burn marks on her torso from where he'd held a cigarette to her, I decided he had to die.
>
> I knew she wouldn't testify against him. She was too weak to stand up to him. Too terrified that he'd kill her.
>
> Too full of self-deprecation. She thought it was her fault he hit her.
>
> I vowed to help people. To save the women and children. The innocents.
>
> I used to be innocent, too.
>
> But now my heart is filled with agony from the brutal images of the victims. And my hands are covered in blood.

He used his fists to beat her. And a hunting knife to carve his name on her belly. The slash mark he drew on her neck took thirty-five stitches and almost severed her carotid artery.

She begged me to let her die when I found her.

He has to die instead.

Hatcher's pulse clamored as his gaze met Korine's. "If whoever posted that is planning on murder and Cat can get us an address, maybe we can stop him or her before it happens."

CHAPTER
THIRTY-FOUR

An hour later, Hatcher asked the deputy to get coffee for the four women they'd brought in for questioning.

He wanted them to be comfortable and relaxed so they would talk.

And he wanted that damn news anchor's head on a platter. She'd already blasted the story about Hortman's death.

"I took screenshots of the conversations in the Keepers' chat room," Korine told him as they stood outside one of the interrogation rooms. "*If* they are collaborating, it means they're organized and know enough about crime scenes not to leave evidence behind."

The deputy returned with coffee, and Korine took a cup for herself and one for Liz Roberts inside room one. As they entered, the thirty-something blonde looked up at them from behind the table, her sparkling blue eyes assessing them as they approached. She was not only a professional but also a drop-dead gorgeous woman who looked so sweet she couldn't possibly have a violent streak inside her.

"Miss Roberts," Hatcher said. "I'm Special Agent Hatcher McGee, and this is my partner, Special Agent Korine Davenport."

She nodded, acknowledging them.

Korine set the coffee in front of the woman, and she immediately reached for it.

"Do you know why you're here?" Hatcher asked.

"Not exactly," Roberts said. "Did something happen to one of my clients?"

"Why would you ask that?"

"Because I'm worried about one of the women I work with. She was beaten nearly to death by her ex and was released from the hospital today. Her ex made bail and threatened to come after her if she testified against him."

Hatcher fought a reaction. "I'm sorry. I can check and verify that she's all right if you want."

"Thank you," Roberts said. "I've phoned her several times and left messages, but she hasn't returned my calls."

"What's her name?" Korine asked.

"Latoya Clinton. I can give you her phone number and address."

They paused a second for her to write down the information, then Hatcher stepped outside and asked the deputy to check on the woman.

"You're really worried about her, aren't you?" Korine asked.

The counselor shrugged. "If you'd seen what this man did to her, you would be, too."

Hatcher stepped back into the room. "The deputy is going to check on her."

"I appreciate that." She glanced at Korine, then folded her arms and stared at him. "All right, if this isn't about Latoya, it must be about that driver's ed teacher who was murdered. I'm sure you're aware that I counseled two of the teenagers who accused him of sexual harassment."

Hatcher raised a brow. She was direct. He liked that. "That's true."

"You have a difficult job," Korine said. "Counseling victims. It must get to you sometimes."

Roberts sipped her coffee. "If you mean some of the cases upset me, of course they do. I'm passionate about advocating for victims. But I'm a professional, and just like your job, it's my job to be objective and not allow personal feelings to interfere with my work."

Hatcher exchanged a look with Korine, then claimed the chair across from the young woman. "Where were you midday today?"

She traced a finger around the rim of the disposable cup, then looked directly at him. "In my office." She leaned forward. "You can't possibly think that I killed Louie Hortman."

Korine tapped her nails on the table. "You must have hated that he got off without being tried, that he was free to hurt other young girls."

Roberts released a wary sigh. "Of course I was angry, but his case was minor compared to some I've worked. Women who've been beaten, tortured. Last month a victim's ex-boyfriend came to her office, tossed lighter fluid on her, then threw a match down. She suffered third-degree burns over most of her body and is still in the burn ward." Pain underscored her tone. "I've seen children who were molested, ones whose parent burned them with cigarettes, one whose father locked her in a closet for days on end without food. Another teenager I treated was tied to a post out in the backyard like an animal." She met his gaze head-on. "Do I detest those people? Yes. Would I like to see them suffer? Absolutely." She took another sip of the coffee. "Would I ruin my reputation and life to get back at them? No. I believe in letting you guys handle that part of the job while I counsel the victims through recovery."

Admirable.

Hatcher placed a photograph of the judge, then Pallo Whiting on the table. "You're aware that these two men were also murdered this week?"

Emotions flashed in her eyes as she glanced at the pictures of the judge lying dead on the dock and Whiting covered in blood.

"I saw the news," she said, her voice wavering.

"Where were you the night the judge was murdered?" Hatcher asked.

She picked at a hangnail. "Having dinner with friends."

Hatcher narrowed his eyes. "I assume they can corroborate that?"

She nodded. "So can the waiter at the restaurant. We were celebrating a birthday, so we had cake and champagne."

Easy enough to check.

He tapped a finger on the picture of Pallo Whiting. "How about when Whiting was killed?"

A restless sigh escaped her. "At the gym. I work out most days after I finish with the job." She gave him a pointed look. "That's how I relieve my stress."

She took the pencil and pad and scribbled names and numbers before he could ask.

Korine placed her iPad on the table. "Do you follow Tinsley Jensen's blog?"

Roberts's eyes widened slightly. "Sometimes. I saw the story about her in the news and was glad she found a way to deal with her feelings. I also suggest my clients journal as a form of therapy."

Korine angled the tablet toward the counselor and pointed to the screen. "You've posted on the blog yourself."

Hatcher shifted. Not a question but a statement.

Roberts hesitated. "First of all, let me say I take my victims' rights seriously and would do anything to protect them. That means honoring their privacy and the confidentiality agreement I have with them. I would never write anything about a patient or client or the cases I'm working in a public forum. And I certainly wouldn't disclose information about one of them."

A tense second paused. "Secondly, I respect those who do post. Writing about one's feelings doesn't mean that the person acts upon them. The purpose of journaling is to purge the dark emotions trauma evokes in a healthy way so the victim doesn't implode and do something horrific like take her own life. Or take justice into his or her own hands."

"What about this private chat room, the Keepers?" Korine said.

Roberts adjusted her jacket, buttoning it as she squared her shoulders. "As I said, cataloguing one's inner emotions doesn't mean that the person who posted it has committed a crime." She clenched the coffee cup in one hand, then stood. "Now, am I free to go?"

Hatcher stared at Roberts with mixed feelings. She was a caring woman who devoted her life to helping others. She was also smart, strong, capable, and savvy.

His gut told him she wasn't a killer. But he'd been fooled before . . .

"We aren't holding you at this time," Hatcher said. "But if you know or learn anything about these murders, you need to tell us, or we will charge you with accessory."

She squared her shoulders. "You know that I can't discuss information about any of my clients. I took an oath—"

"We're aware of that," Hatcher said. "But you also know that if you perceive that one of your clients poses a danger to himself or to others, you are required by law to divulge that to the police."

She gave a quick nod and averted her eyes. Just enough of a reaction to make Hatcher wonder whether she was hiding something. Or covering for someone else.

Maybe not a client or patient but a friend . . .

He needed a warrant for her home and office files. But he didn't have enough to justify it yet.

Maybe one of the other women would shed some light on the situation. If they had conspired to exact their own brand of justice, sooner or later one of them would slip up and talk—or make a mistake.

◆ ◆ ◆

"Naturally, I was upset about Pallo Whiting's escape." Laura Austin ran her fingers through her wavy brown hair. "Every parent of every child he touched was terrified. But that doesn't mean I killed him."

Korine chewed the inside of her cheek. For time's sake, she and Hatcher had decided to split the interviews. Hatcher was questioning Rachel Willis.

Worse, on paper and in the eyes of the public and their coworkers, the four they'd brought in not only were model citizens but also gave selflessly to help others and looked like modern-day heroes.

The press would have a field day with the police if they filed charges without proper proof.

"I really don't understand why you brought me in," Austin said.

Korine swallowed hard. "You are friends with Liz Roberts, aren't you?"

"We swam together in college."

"And Rachel Willis and Beverly Grant?"

Austin frowned. "We were all on the swim team together. But you must know that or you wouldn't be asking."

Korine nodded, then angled her iPad to display Tinsley's blog. "All of you frequent this page, *Heart & Soul*."

Austin shrugged. "It's interesting, a place to vent."

"True," Korine said, unable to argue. "But in light of the three murders that have occurred in the past few days, some of the posts sound like murder confessions."

Austin shrugged. "People fantasize about getting revenge or justice for loved ones. That doesn't mean they act upon it."

"No, but considering the fact that there have been three murders in the past week, these posts do seem suspicious."

Austin stood. "Listen, Agent Davenport, if there's nothing else, I need to get back to work. I have an appointment in half an hour, then I need to prepare a statement for family court."

Korine clenched her jaw. She had nothing to hold this woman or any of the others on. They were good-hearted. Caring. Helped others.

If they were conspiring to exact justice, they were smart enough not to include details online.

In fact, if they had killed the judge, Whiting, and Hortman, deep in her heart, she was tempted to applaud them instead of lock them up.

But . . . if they found evidence proving the women were guilty, she'd have to do just that, whether she liked it or not.

♦ ♦ ♦

This interview was going just as it had with Liz Roberts. Not enough evidence to nail any one of the women.

Hatcher studied Rachel Willis. As a parole officer, Willis had seen some of the worst.

"Your father died after finally being released from prison, didn't he?"

Willis slid her rectangular glasses on top of her head. "He certainly did. And before you ask, yes, I blamed the system and the lawyer who should have done a better job defending him. But most of all, I blame the man who framed him."

"And that man was?"

"His business partner," Willis said.

"Where is he now?"

Willis folded her arms. "He died of heart failure while he was awaiting trial."

"So you became a parole officer even though your family was wronged by the system."

Willis nodded. "I thought I could help others in my father's shoes acclimate and rebuild their lives." A bitter chuckle escaped her. "Boy, was I naive."

Hatcher bit back a comment. With her family history and job, she might have reached the breaking point.

"Why are we all here, Agent McGee?"

Hatcher folded his arms. "There have been three murders this week. We think they're connected."

Her brows furrowed. "Do you suspect one of my parolees?"

"Not at this point." He hesitated. "We discovered a chat room called the Keepers. Are you part of this group?"

Her brown eyes flashed with some emotion he didn't quite understand, but she didn't comment. Instead, she stood. "I'd like to call a lawyer."

She tapped her heel on the floor, and Hatcher rocked his chair back. "Listen, Miss Willis. We're prepared to offer a deal to the first person who gives us information regarding the case. Think about that."

She locked gazes with him for a moment. "If I had information regarding the murders, I would tell you. But I don't."

She strode from the room, shoulders rigid.

She was a cool cookie, but beneath that cool facade lived rage.

She had just learned to cover it up over the years.

Had that rage driven her to kill?

◆ ◆ ◆

Korine was quickly growing frustrated. Beverly Grant had deftly avoided her questions and been just as vague as Liz Roberts.

A knock sounded at the door; then Hatcher poked his head inside.

"Agent Davenport, we have to stop. Kendall James is here."

The lawyer who'd come to Banning's defense.

"Apparently one of the ladies phoned her," Hatcher said. "She's representing all four of them."

Korine glanced at Beverly Grant. "Is Ms. James your lawyer?"

Grant nodded. "Yes, although I haven't done anything wrong."

Hatcher stepped inside. "I'm going to tell you the same thing I told your friend. Whoever talks first gets a deal."

The young woman looked back and forth between them. "What kind of deal?"

"There are three counts of murder. We'll take the death penalty off the table," he said bluntly. "Parole is also a possibility."

Another knock, and the door cracked open again. Kendall James appeared, her briefcase in one hand, an air of authority about her. "We're finished here."

She motioned to Beverly Grant, and the young woman hurried to the door. Hatcher and Korine followed them and watched the lawyer usher the four women down the hall.

"What now?" Korine asked.

Hatcher's phone buzzed. Bellows. He answered. "Yes? . . . Dammit."

Korine wrinkled her brow. "What?"

Hatcher strode into the deputy's office and flipped on the TV. Korine's eyes widened as a headline scrolled across the screen and Marilyn Ellis appeared. Shots of the murder scene of Hortman, then Whiting, then the judge appeared.

Ellis smiled into the camera. "The FBI have been investigating a connection between these three murders and now believe a vigilante killer is loose in the Savannah area."

Hatcher cursed. "She wasn't supposed to air that."

"This vigilante killer paints a justice symbol on each of his victim's foreheads." Ellis continued. "If you have any information regarding these murders or the vigilante killer, please phone the FBI."

Korine twisted her hands together. They had asked Marilyn Ellis to hold the story. In a murder investigation, it was important to keep information from the public in case they needed to use it to coerce a suspect into talking. Or to weed out false confessions.

The reporter had just ruined that strategy.

CHAPTER
THIRTY-FIVE

The River Street Rapist had to be dealt with. Stopped. Punished.

He was next on the list.

But first she had to take care of another problem.

She'd been stalking her target for days. Knew where he parked his car, where he ate. Thai was his favorite. He liked curry.

He drank vodka on a hot night at the beachside bar. He preferred his women young and pretty.

He slept in the nude.

He was damn smart, too.

But she was smarter.

She was the Keeper, at least she was one of the Keepers' hands.

She watched through binoculars and spied him through open blinds. He never closed them, as if he knew someone was watching.

As if he wanted the world to see his naked glory.

Muscles bunched in his arms and shoulders. His thighs were solid, his abs washboard flat.

He worked out. He had to in order to maintain that body. He knew the girls liked it. Used it to his advantage, to lure them to his bed.

He padded naked to the bathroom. His dick was thick, long. He'd wanted to put it inside her.

That would never happen.

He stepped into the shower and lifted his head. For a moment, he simply seemed to enjoy the stream of water trailing down his face and chest.

He soaped his hands and began to scrub himself vigorously.

Then his hand slipped lower and curled around his sex.

Revulsion washed over her as he began to stroke his cock. His erection grew more bold as he stroked from his balls to the tip.

Finally he threw his head back and leaned against the shower wall, his body jerking as he came.

Bile rose to her throat as his semen sprayed the shower walls. Yet her body felt hot. Needy.

She hated that feeling.

Anger seized her, and she lowered her binoculars, then slipped back to her car. Inside, she glanced down at the photos of Tinsley Jensen, the ones taken shortly after she'd been rescued. She'd been bloody. Bruised. Traumatized.

Because of a man who called himself the Skull.

Her plan made her smile.

Ten minutes later, she entered the room she'd arranged for him and tacked the pictures of Tinsley all over the wall. She set up her camera. Positioned the chair where he would sit.

Soon all the world would watch as she exposed him as the Skull.

Then he would die.

And the Keepers could continue their work.

CHAPTER
THIRTY-SIX

Another night, and no answers about the murders. They were getting closer, though—Korine could feel it.

"I don't know where Ellis got those details, but there may be a leak somewhere," Hatcher said as he parked at a pub for dinner. "I have a good mind to throw her in jail and make her tell us."

"She won't talk," Korine said as they went inside and claimed a booth. "She's too determined to make her story."

A waitress appeared, and they quickly ordered. Korine mentally reviewed the theory about the conspiracy as the waitress left to get their food and drinks. Hatcher excused himself to make a call, and she washed up in the ladies room. By the time they made it back to the table, the waitress had returned with their orders.

Hatcher dug into a burger while she forked up a bite of shrimp scampi.

"We have to consider the fact that we might be wrong about the conspiracy," Korine said. "But I do believe we're dealing with a vigilante killer."

"Maybe Cat or Wyatt will find some discrepancies in the alibis or narrow down a suspect from the chat room or blog comments."

Korine nodded, ate another bite, then started to take a sip of her wine when her phone buzzed. She checked the number.

The rehab center.

Dread tightened her neck muscles as she connected the call. "Ms. Davenport?"

"This is she."

"It's E. L. Foote from Serenity. I'm calling about your brother."

She rubbed her temple. "What's wrong?"

"I'm sorry, but Kenny somehow snuck out this afternoon. He became agitated during a group therapy session. One of our nurses escorted him to his room to rest. But he didn't show up for dinner, so we searched the facility and his room and realized he was gone."

Korine laid her fork down, her appetite vanishing. "What upset him?" Not that he needed anything specific.

"I'm sorry, but I can't divulge the details of the session," Foote said.

Korine bit her lower lip. But knowing what upset him might give her insight into the reason he was agitated enough to leave.

Then again, he was an addict. He couldn't handle even the slightest bit of stress and self-medicated with alcohol or drugs when things got tough.

"Thanks for calling," Korine said. "If you hear from him, or if he returns, please let me know."

"We will. And Ms. Davenport, we want to help him. The counselor thought she was making progress. Let us know if you convince him to check himself back in."

Korine thanked her, ended the call, then dialed her mother's home number. Hatcher was watching her.

The worry in his eyes twisted her insides. She wasn't accustomed to sharing her problems. She was the one who took care of people—her mother, her brother. Herself.

Esme finally answered on the third ring.

"The counselor from Serenity just phoned. Kenny got upset and left. Is he there?"

"I haven't seen him."

Korine's pulse pounded. "How's Mom?"

A slight hesitation. "She's having a fair day. She spent some time sitting in the garden."

A wave of nostalgia washed over Korine. Once upon a time, her mother had belonged to the garden club and had grown spectacular roses. Every year she'd thrown a cocktail party to show them off and invited half of Savannah.

After her father's death, her mother let most of the roses go and then the garden.

Although the incident the last time she was at her mother's nagged at her. Why had her mother suddenly been digging where Kenny had buried the doll?

She averted her gaze from Hatcher and wiped at a tear. "Apparently he became agitated during therapy, so I don't know what kind of mood he's in. If he shows up, call me."

Esme assured her she would, and Korine pocketed her phone.

"Your brother checked himself out?" Hatcher asked as he finished his burger.

"Not exactly. He just left."

Hatcher waved the waitress over for the check. "Do you have any idea where he'd go?"

"Maybe to a bar, some place to drink."

"Where does he live?"

"In a loft near downtown."

Korine offered Hatcher her credit card, but he waved it off. "He might pick up some booze and go home."

Hatcher jangled his keys. "Then let's go."

Korine caught his arm, but heat speared her, and she wished she hadn't. The day was wearing on her. Leaning on Hatcher was too tempting.

"Take me home, then I'll go. You don't need to get involved in my personal problems."

Hatcher's eyes darkened. "Stop pushing me away, Korine. If your brother is upset and inebriated, you shouldn't face him alone."

A tiny smile tugged at her mouth at his protective tone. "I am a federal agent," she said. "I know how to defend myself."

He made a sarcastic sound in his throat. "We're supposed to back each other up."

Without another word, he strode toward the door.

Emotions warred inside Korine. She didn't want to face Kenny alone, but having Hatcher so close made her want more.

He was nothing like the other men she'd met. He was strong, brave, protective.

Handsome. Sexy.

He knew how to treat a woman. How to respect her.

How to love her and make her crazy in bed.

If they weren't working together, she might consider sleeping with him again just to feel his hands on her body and his lips touching her intimately.

◆ ◆ ◆

Hatcher had seen too many drunks get violent. He didn't know Kenny Davenport, but a quick background check revealed that he'd been arrested twice in barroom brawls. Apparently he had a temper when he was intoxicated.

He was also angry that Korine had forced him into rehab.

He might turn that anger on her.

The thought of Korine's brother hurting her made Hatcher's stomach knot. Korine was a damn decent woman who took care of everyone but herself.

Someone needed to take care of her, whether she liked it or not.

She gave him the address for Kenny's complex, a series of three brick warehouses that had been turned into lofts. Hatcher wove through Savannah, then veered into the parking area.

"What kind of vehicle does Kenny drive?" Hatcher asked.

"An old Range Rover, but I don't see it here." She unbuckled her seat belt and opened the car door. "I hope he isn't drinking and driving."

Storm clouds darkened as they climbed the steel staircase to Kenny's second-floor loft. Korine pounded on the door. "Kenny, are you in there?"

She leaned her ear against the door and listened. "Kenny?"

Nothing.

She twisted the doorknob, then pushed at the door, but it was locked.

"He's not here," Hatcher said.

"Or if he is, he's passed out or not answering." Korine pulled a set of keys from her pocket, then inserted one and the door swung open.

"You have keys to your brother's loft?" Hatcher asked, surprised.

"One time Kenny passed out in an alley. When I got him home, I made a copy of his key while he slept off his binge. I've called too many times, and when he doesn't answer, I imagine him dead in the streets or in a dumpster somewhere." She shrugged. "At least this way I can check."

She stepped inside, and Hatcher followed her into the room, a large space with an open-concept living, dining, and kitchen area. The bedroom was designated by a platform and folding screen.

From the doorway, Hatcher could easily see the guy wasn't home.

Korine mumbled something that he didn't understand, and he followed her to the table. Dozens of photos of Korine and her parents were spread across the surface . . . except the photos had been mangled and destroyed.

"My God," Korine said as she picked up a picture. Its edges had been jaggedly cut with scissors.

Hatcher didn't know what to say. The pictures were disturbing.

Hatcher glanced at the floor on the other side of the table, and his blood ran cold.

A music box identical to the one Korine had sat on the floor beside a porcelain doll. A doll whose face had been smashed.

A doll with a knife protruding from its chest.

A knife dripping with blood.

A shiver slithered up Korine's spine. What had happened here?

She'd known that Kenny resented her, but the violence displayed in the shredded pictures and in the doll's destruction hinted at more than resentment.

That bloody knife . . . was it from one of their victims?

"I think you should issue an APB for Kenny," Hatcher said. "He appears to be dangerous."

"I can't have him arrested for tearing up some pictures," Korine said, knowing her mother would hate her if she discovered she'd sent Kenny to jail.

Hatcher gripped her arm and forced her to look at him. "Your brother's out of control. He obviously has rage issues. Coupled with drinking or drugs, that rage could escalate." He gently cupped her face in his hands. "I don't want to see him take it out on you."

And the doll was an indication that he would.

Korine didn't like feeling vulnerable, especially in front of Hatcher. She was supposed to be his equal, not a flailing, needy female.

She stiffened and pulled away. "I can take care of myself and my family. If you want to process that knife, bag it."

She headed toward the door. Hatcher caught up with her, his breathing puffing behind her. "Where are you going?"

"Home," she said stiffly. "If Kenny wants to find me, he'll go there. If not, at least I can study that chat room. Maybe we'll get lucky and someone will post about Hortman."

She clamped her mouth shut to stifle a sob as she glanced back at the doll. Kenny knew how much those gifts from her father meant to her.

She hadn't realized how deep-seated his jealousy was.

The fresh air helped to jolt her out of the shock enveloping her as she and Hatcher stepped outside.

"We need to process that knife, Korine. You know that, don't you?"

Tears clogged her throat, and she nodded. "I'll wait. You get it."

He murmured that he would, and she leaned against the railing and drew in a breath.

A minute later, he returned, and they hurried down the steps to his SUV.

She checked her phone for messages as Hatcher drove from the lofts toward her house, but there were no calls from Kenny or Esme.

Hatcher parked the SUV in front of her house. She thanked him for driving her home, then reached for the door handle.

He covered her hand with his. "I'm not leaving until we check out your house."

He let the sentence trail off, but she understood the implication— he wanted to make sure Kenny wasn't lurking around.

At one time, she wouldn't have been afraid of her brother. But after seeing that knife in the doll . . . she didn't know.

"I can handle myself," she said and exited the vehicle.

He didn't say a word, but he followed her up to the front door. She scanned the property, and he did the same, but nothing looked amiss.

Inside, though, the lamp in her bedroom was on.

"I turned off the light in my room when I left." Instantly alert, they both drew their weapons as she fished her keys from her pocket and unlocked the door. The moment she did, she knew someone had been inside.

The entryway and den looked untouched, but a strange scent in the air made her pause. What was it—perfume? Bodywash? Aftershave? Or something else . . .

Straining to hear, she glanced at Hatcher. He raised his brows, and she gestured for him to check her office while she did her bedroom.

One step down the hall, and she glanced into her room. Anger welled inside her as she looked at her bed.

Dozens of broken pieces of doll heads were scattered over the surface.

Hatcher's sharp intake of breath echoed behind her.

She blinked to stem the tears. Had her brother done this?

CHAPTER
THIRTY-SEVEN

Perspiration beaded on Tinsley's forehead as she stared at the image in the Facebook Live post.

A man was tied up, struggling to escape, his face covered by a mask. Things were out of control.

The blog had started out as therapy, a way to help herself and others. But some of her followers had taken it too far.

The federal agents were searching for a vigilante killer. Marilyn Ellis had aired the story on the evening news and hinted that there might be a conspiracy.

Emotions boomeranged inside Tinsley. She didn't want it to be true. Didn't want any of the troubled souls she talked to online to be responsible.

But her instincts warned her they were.

A post quickly appeared beneath the photograph.

> You'll be safe soon, Tinsley. Then the Skull can't
> hurt you or anyone else again.

No . . . Tinsley yanked on her glasses and peered at the man onscreen. His face was hidden in the shadows, also disguised by a skull mask.

The Skull had always worn a mask. She'd never seen his face.

Could this be the man who'd held and tortured her?

She leaned closer, scrutinizing his features. Though he was sitting in a chair, something about him was off. He seemed shorter. More muscular.

And . . . the scar on her abductor's hand . . . the tattoo . . . it wasn't on this man's hand.

He could have had it removed. But why would he do that? She hadn't seen his face, so she couldn't identify him. But the tattoo—she would recognize it.

There was something else wrong, too.

She zeroed in on the man's left hand. The middle finger on her attacker's left hand had been scarred horribly.

This man's finger was smooth.

God . . .

Her heart hammered in her chest. Whoever had taken this man hostage thought he was her attacker. They might have killed three people already. Three who deserved it.

But this time they had the wrong person . . .

Panic surged through her.

An innocent man might die unless she did something to stop it.

CHAPTER
THIRTY-EIGHT

Hatcher cleared his throat. "I'm calling an evidence team to process your house again. If I were you, I'd have a security system installed as soon as possible."

Korine winced. "It's a rental. I'll have to talk with the owner."

Hatcher stepped into the living room to make the call, and she checked the bathroom, closet, and her office to see whether anything else had been disturbed. The family picture she'd hung in the hallway had been removed.

She hurried back to her bedroom and found the picture lying on the floor on the far side of the bed, the frame shattered. The photograph that had been inside was torn into pieces and scattered on the floor.

Kenny.

She'd seen him smash one of her dolls before. But she'd never thought he'd break in and destroy family pictures . . . or leave broken dolls on her bed.

Hatcher inched up behind her, and gently gripped her arms with his hands. "Are you okay?"

She nodded and told herself to pull away from him. But it felt so comforting to have him stroking her arms that she couldn't bring herself to move. "I didn't realize Kenny's resentment ran so deep. He really needs psychological help."

Hatcher rubbed her back. "We'll find him, Korine, and we'll make sure he gets help."

When they did, she was going to insist they talk about the family. If she had to attend therapy with him, they'd get to the bottom of his anger. Neither one of them could go on this way.

◆ ◆ ◆

Two hours later, the evidence team finally finished. Korine had grown quiet, withdrawing into herself.

It was painful to watch.

She didn't deserve this.

"We'll let you know if anything turns up forensics-wise," Drummond said.

"Thank you." Korine forced a smile, but Hatcher knew her well enough by now to realize that she was more upset than she wanted to reveal.

"Did you find the instrument the unsub used to break the dolls?" Hatcher asked.

"No," Drummond said. "He or she must have smashed the dolls somewhere else, then brought them here."

Hatcher grimaced. First those creepy doll heads with the lights glowing in their eyes. Now shattered doll heads. Their eyes were broken, leaving gaping holes, and their limbs were ripped—an arm here, a leg there.

Could it possibly be an indication of what this intruder wanted to do to Korine?

Just like the knife in the doll at Kenny's . . .

The team left with bags of the shattered porcelain dolls and the shredded picture and frame.

Korine stared out the front window. She looked so damn lost that he couldn't leave her alone.

Hatcher made a snap decision. "Pack an overnight bag. You're going to stay at my place tonight."

Korine pivoted, arms folded, eyebrows raised. "That's not necessary, Hatcher. I'm not afraid to be alone."

"Maybe not, but I don't like this situation. Whoever did this is leaving a message. Next time, it might not be dolls he takes a hammer to."

"Kenny wouldn't hurt me," Korine said in a low voice.

Hatcher hated the uncertainty in her voice. He couldn't imagine a family member turning on someone like this. And what if it wasn't Kenny?

"I'm sorry," he said gruffly.

She glanced around the living area, her face strained. "I know. I don't understand, but I'm going to keep pushing until I do."

She disappeared into her bedroom, and he walked to the back door and looked out at the woods. Kenny might be hiding out there somewhere, waiting for Korine to be left alone.

That wasn't going to happen.

◆ ◆ ◆

Korine threw a change of clothes and pajamas in her overnight bag, then grabbed her toiletries. She packed her running shoes and extra ammo for her gun, then checked her phone.

A text from Bellows, wanting to know how Hatcher was doing, if he was drinking.

Hatcher called her name. She'd respond to Bellows later.

She was hoping the rehab center would call and say Kenny had returned, but there was no word. She punched his number and left a message, although she didn't know whether he had his phone with him.

He had turned it in to the therapist when he'd first checked into rehab, so he might be without one.

Hatcher was waiting for her in the living room and grabbed her bag.

"I can carry it," Korine snapped.

"I realize you don't like to accept help," Hatcher said, swinging the bag to his side so she couldn't reach it. "But we're partners and you're stuck with me."

Korine's instinct was to argue, but she was too tired to fight back at the moment. She needed to pick her battles, and this wasn't the one she wanted to tackle.

She followed Hatcher to the car in silence. Fifteen minutes later, Hatcher parked at a cabin on the marsh.

"It's not fancy," he said, "but your brother won't find you here."

That could be good or bad.

Her emotions were running high tonight, something a night's sleep could help. When she confronted Kenny, she wanted to be calm and logical.

More dark clouds hovered on the horizon, casting a grayness over the land that made it look eerie and isolated.

The wind ruffled the dried marsh grass and brought the scent of loamy earth, shrimp, and the ocean.

"You like living alone out here?" she asked as he unlocked the door and gestured for her to enter.

He grunted, a mixture of pain and anger in his eyes. "Yeah."

"I'm sorry," she said softly. "We never talked about the loss of your wife. I—"

"Do not want to talk about her either," Hatcher barked.

Korine froze, her own guilt kicking in. "Maybe not, but I am sorry for your loss. I've felt guilty about that night."

He dropped her bag on the wood floor, then gripped her arms with his hands. "I know you think I lied to you that night, but I didn't. My wife and I . . . we were separated." His eyes darkened. "I'd asked her for a divorce. I'd already moved out and contacted a lawyer."

"But technically you were still married," Korine said. "And I don't sleep with married men."

His expression darkened. "I know you regret it, and so do I. If I'd answered Felicia's phone call that night, she might not be dead."

"But you didn't answer. Why? Because we were together?"

Anger heated his eyes. "It's more complicated than that."

He started to turn away, but this time Korine caught his arm and forced him to look at her. "Tell me."

"She was needy," he said. "Clingy. I . . . at first I thought her constant attention was nice, flattering, but then she became obsessive. She started making up things to keep me close by."

"What do you mean?"

"She'd pretend she was sick so I'd leave work. One night she called to tell me that she'd swallowed some pills and was going to kill herself. But when I got home, I realized she hadn't taken pills. It was just a ploy to get me to drop what I was doing and rush back to her."

Korine sighed. "My God, I'm sorry."

He ground his teeth. "The afternoon before she died, she called and said someone was stalking her."

Korine inhaled sharply. "You didn't believe her?"

He shook his head and squeezed his eyes shut for a moment. When he opened them, emotions darkened his face.

"But this time she wasn't lying," he said in a hoarse voice. "The Skull . . . there were two of them. And one of them was watching her."

The guilt that had nagged at Korine surfaced again, raw and harsh. Hatcher's pain bled into her. The need to comfort him made her reach for him.

"I'm sorry, Hatcher. But under the circumstances, it's understandable that you didn't believe her."

His gaze met hers, turmoil darkening his eyes. "Maybe so, but it's still my fault she was murdered."

♦ ♦ ♦

Grief and self-disgust ate at Hatcher as an image of Felicia dangling from that tree with blood running down her neck taunted him.

"It wasn't your fault," Korine said. "You obviously had reason to doubt her story, and when you discovered it was true, you did everything you could to save her, didn't you?"

Hatcher pinched the bridge of his nose. "I was too late. He had her tied up and he . . . she bled to death right in front of my eyes."

Korine cupped his face between her hands. "She knows you tried to save her. We may be federal agents, but we're also human."

"But if I hadn't been investigating in the first place, he wouldn't have targeted her." Guilt edged his voice. "He took her to get to me."

"He took her because he was a sadistic monster who preyed on women," Korine said softly. "Our jobs put us and anyone we care about in danger. Felicia knew that when she married you."

"I shouldn't have gotten that close to her." Or anyone else.

"Just because you chase bad guys doesn't mean you don't deserve to have love." She cradled his hands between hers. "Your job is part of you. If she didn't understand that and love you for it, then you weren't right for each other."

Her softly spoken words got to him. She'd had a hell of a day and was being tormented by her brother. Yet she was comforting him when he should be the one consoling her.

She stroked his palm with her finger, and his breath caught. The memory of her lips and hands on him teased him. Korine was nothing like his wife. Her strength aroused his admiration. Even mired in her own problems, she wasn't clingy or needy.

He wanted her again. Wanted her now.

The heat in her eyes seared him and stirred his hunger, and he couldn't resist. He pulled her up against him.

Her body felt warm and inviting. His cock hardened. She pressed one hand against his cheek and traced the other along his chest.

He sucked in a sharp breath. Desire heated his blood. She licked her lips, and he lowered his head and kissed her.

One touch of her lips set him on fire. She curled against him, rubbing her body against his.

Their weapons were in the way.

He removed his jacket, holster, and gun, and laid them on the side table, and she did the same.

Then he reached for her. She went into his arms, her breath puffing out. He plunged his tongue into her mouth and tasted her desire, a sweet, fiery need that unleashed his own primitive, raw passion. She met his tongue thrust for thrust.

Pleasure shot through him, and he dragged his mouth from her lips to nibble at her neck. She moaned as his lips and teeth played havoc with the sensitive nub of her ear and her slender throat.

Hunger speared him, and he lowered his hand and cupped her breast in his palm. Her shirt stood between them.

He wanted to touch bare skin. Wanted to tease her nipple with his tongue, draw it into his mouth.

She slid the top button of his shirt open and trailed her fingers across his bare chest. His skin ached for more.

He wanted to be skin to skin. Naked and hot and pumping himself inside her.

Need raging through him, he lifted her shirt over her head and tossed it aside. Her breathing grew rapid. Voluptuous breasts spilled over her lace bra, begging for his hands, and he complied.

She moaned and pushed at his shirt, and he shucked it and threw it to the floor. Then he swept her up in his arms and carried her to his bedroom.

As he eased her onto the bed, she reached for his jeans. Her finger teased his cock as she pushed the jeans over his hips. He kicked them off and removed hers, his pulse clamoring at the sight of those tiny lace panties.

He remembered that about her—she was no-nonsense on the job. Dressed conservatively. Except for her underwear. It was the one area where she was all woman.

With a groan, he pressed his mouth to her heat and nuzzled her through the lace. She lifted her body in invitation, and he kissed her again.

He teased and tasted her, then trailed his lips over her breasts. Her sharp intake of breath drove him mad, and he stripped her bra and looked his fill.

She was the most beautiful woman he'd ever seen. Ivory skin, with luscious coral nipples that stood erect, begging for his mouth.

He'd wanted her every night since they'd parted. Even when he was mourning his wife's death, he'd craved Korine's touch.

It was wrong.

But he couldn't help himself. He was weak.

"Don't think," she whispered as she closed her hand over his cock. "Just feel."

He shut that damn voice of guilt off and did as she said. Then he drew one nipple into his mouth, and pleasure filled him. She urged him closer, her whispered pleas driving him mad with passion.

He lowered his body above her to peel away her panties.

A noise jolted him. His cell phone.

Fuck. He didn't want to stop now, not when Korine was on fire in his arms.

Korine leaned on her elbows, her breath panting out. "You have to answer it, Hatcher."

He gritted his teeth. She was right. He'd lost control again.

What the hell was wrong with him? The last time he'd ignored a call because they were in bed together, his wife had been brutally murdered.

Silently cursing, he eased away from her, then retrieved his phone from his jeans and checked the number. *Cat.*

He connected the call. "Hatcher."

"I think something's going down."

He slid to the edge of the bed and sat up. "What are you talking about?"

"Is Davenport with you?"

"Why?"

"Go to the Facebook page I'm about to send you. It's gone live." Her breath rasped out. "I think a man is about to be murdered on-screen."

CHAPTER THIRTY-NINE

Korine frantically threw on her clothes, horror striking her when Hatcher showed her the picture on the computer.

A man with a skull mask was tied to a chair in the dark room. His head hung down, body limp.

Was he dead or just unconscious?

Hatcher put Cat on speaker.

"When was this posted?" Korine asked.

"About an hour ago."

Korine's phone buzzed, and she snatched it up, half expecting it to be news about her brother. But Tinsley Jensen's name appeared on the caller ID screen.

Did Tinsley know about this?

She quickly connected the call. "Tinsley?"

"You have to do something," the woman said breathlessly.

"What's wrong?" Korine asked.

"Someone from the group . . . they've taken a man hostage. I think they're going to kill him."

Korine motioned to Hatcher and quickly put Tinsley on speaker as well, while Hatcher relayed to Cat that Tinsley was on the phone.

"Hang on, Cat—Tinsley might know who posted this."

"Who's doing this?" Korine asked Tinsley.

"I don't know," Tinsley said. "I swear I don't. I really thought the posts you questioned were just the women's way of purging their anger and bitterness. I never thought any of them would actually hurt someone."

"If you have any idea, Tinsley, you have to tell us," Korine said.

"I told you I don't," Tinsley said. "But it's all my fault. Whoever's holding this man thinks he's the Skull, but he's not."

Hatcher's brow furrowed into a frown. "How do you know that? You said you never saw the Skull's face, and you can't see this man's either."

"I didn't, but I saw his hands." Bitterness tinged her voice. "He touched me enough so I remember . . ."

Korine worked to stifle her own emotions. "Remember what?"

"He had a tattoo on his hand, and the middle finger on his left hand was badly scarred," she said in a pained whisper.

Korine zeroed in on the man in the photo—no tattoos. And no scars on that middle finger.

Her gaze shot to Hatcher's. Tinsley was right.

The vigilante thought he was getting justice for Tinsley, but if he—or she—killed this man, they would kill an innocent.

"You have to stop this madness," Tinsley cried. "I . . . never meant for anything like this to happen."

"It's not your fault," Korine said.

Cat cut in. "Listen, I've been searching the blog comments and message-board conversations and may have found something. Those four women you brought in—Roberts, Grant, Austin, and Willis—they've made some suspicious comments. In one post, Roberts says that the police are asking questions. Austin says they have to do something and mentions the Keeper room. Then Grant and Willis chime in. Grant comments that she's tired of watching the injustices and wants to do something about it. Willis adds that someone has to, that the legal system doesn't work."

Korine chewed the inside of her cheek. "Sounds bad, but they'll insist that the comments are innocent."

"There's more," Cat said. "They talk about meeting at a house on the marsh. I traced the video stream, and it's coming from a house on the marsh as well."

"Send me the GPS coordinates," Hatcher said. "We'll check it out."

Hatcher and Korine rushed to the living area, grabbed their holsters, guns, and jackets and raced outside to his SUV. Hatcher checked the address Cat sent to his phone, started the engine, and was tearing out the driveway before Korine could buckle her seat belt.

"Please don't let anyone get hurt," Tinsley cried. "Whoever posted this thinks they're getting justice for me. He or she may be suffering from PTSD—"

"I understand," Korine said, forcing a calm to her voice as Hatcher sped onto the road. "We'll do everything we can to make sure no one is hurt." She exhaled sharply. "I'm going to hang up now. We'll keep you posted."

"Call Wyatt and ask him to go to Tinsley's," Hatcher said.

She quickly made the call. At first, Wyatt seemed hesitant, but when she explained the situation, he said he'd get there ASAP.

She ended the call, then phoned Detective Brockett and relayed this latest development. "Find the four women we brought in for questioning. If one of them is involved, we have to force them to talk before an innocent man dies."

Brockett agreed, and Korine said a silent prayer that they found the man in time as Hatcher careened around a corner and headed toward the marsh.

♦ ♦ ♦

Hatcher floored the gas pedal, his heart hammering as he raced toward the address. He knew this marshland well. They were only two miles from the place where this man was being held.

"Why did our unsub think this man was the Skull?" Hatcher asked Cat.

Computer keys clicked in the background. "I don't know, but there are photographs of Tinsley all over the wall behind the man."

Hatcher barreled down a winding graveled drive that looked more like a path than a road. Seagulls swooped in the distance, and vultures circled above the swamp.

A Chevy Tahoe was parked at an angle a few feet away from a small white clapboard house overgrown with seagrass and weeds.

Korine pulled her gun as he parked, and he did the same. Then they eased out of his SUV.

He scanned the property in case someone was stationed as a lookout, while Korine inched toward the house. She carefully took cover from tree to tree as she approached. Hatcher went left, cautious as well. His boots sank into the damp soil as he crept toward a side window.

Gun at the ready, Korine remained behind a live oak as Hatcher peered inside the house. The sound of voices echoed from the front, and he stooped down and eased his way to a window and looked inside.

Three women stood talking in hushed whispers beside their hostage.

Hatcher motioned for Korine to join him, and she crouched low and crept through the brush until she reached him.

He held up three fingers, indicating they were dealing with three perps inside, then mouthed for her to back him up.

She gave a quick nod, and he eased toward the door with her on his heels. With every step, he hesitated, listening for sounds that someone had heard them or his vehicle.

But the women inside seemed too busy in their huddle to notice.

Hatcher motioned to Korine that they'd enter on the count of three, then counted down with his fingers. He turned the doorknob, surprised that it wasn't locked, then stepped inside, careful to keep his footfalls light and his gun at the ready.

Korine followed, her gun aimed. He veered toward the living area, then raised his weapon.

"Stand back, ladies."

A sharp gasp punctuated the air, and the women threw up their hands. Not three women—four.

Liz Roberts, Beverly Grant, Laura Austin, and Rachel Willis.

"Don't shoot," Grant said.

Korine inched toward the parole officer. "Put down the gun, Ms. Willis."

Willis's eyes widened, and she glanced at her gun as if she hadn't realized she'd been holding it.

"Do what she says," Hatcher barked. "There's no reason for anyone else to get hurt."

"Set the gun on the floor," Korine ordered.

"Rachel, do it," Roberts said in a hiss.

The young woman slowly lowered her hand, then eased the pistol to the floor. "I wasn't going to shoot," Willis said vehemently.

"It's not what it looks like," Austin added.

Roberts moved toward him, but Hatcher threw up a warning hand. "Don't come any closer."

Roberts froze, her face ashen. "You have to let us explain—"

"It looks pretty clear what you're doing." Hatcher retrieved Willis's gun from the floor. "You're holding this man hostage."

Keeping her gun aimed at the women, Korine crossed to the man and checked for a pulse.

She gestured that he was still alive, then quickly called for an ambulance.

"You thought he was the Skull," Hatcher said. "Tinsley called."

"Tinsley Jensen called you about us," Willis said in a surprised tone.

Grant paled. "We've all tried to help her."

"By eliminating a man you believed hurt her?" Korine asked.

"That's not the way it is," Roberts said.

"Listen to me, you have the wrong person," Korine said. "This is not the man who abducted Tinsley. That's the reason she called."

Shock registered on the women's faces.

Roberts fidgeted. "It's not?"

Willis moved toward Korine. "But—"

"But what?" Korine waved her gun, indicating for the woman to halt.

The parole officer froze, fear flashing in her eyes.

Hatcher wrestled his cuffs from inside his jacket. "You are all under arrest for kidnapping and attempted murder."

More shocked gasps, then Roberts cleared her throat. "Don't say anything, girls. We need to speak to our attorney."

"You're damn right you do. Our FBI analyst traced posts you made regarding this place to your computers and phones. We got you red-handed." Hatcher crossed the room, took Grant's arm and forced her to turn around. "Three murders and now another abduction and attempted murder on top of it."

"We didn't murder anyone," Austin protested.

"Be quiet." Grant tossed a frown over her shoulder at her friends.

Hatcher snapped cuffs around the Grant woman's wrists. Korine cuffed Roberts and Willis while he took care of Austin.

He left Korine reading them their rights while he phoned Detective Brockett and asked for backup to transport the suspects to a holding cell.

While they waited on Brockett and the ambulance, he walked over to the man slumped in the chair.

If this had been the Skull, he might have considered looking the other way. But according to Tinsley, he wasn't.

He shoved the mask off the man's face. Shock slammed into him.

It was Trace Bellamy, who'd been working the crime scenes.

Why the hell had the women thought he was the Skull?

♦ ♦ ♦

Korine met the ambulance outside and led them to the victim. On the heels of the ambulance, the evidence team, Drummond, and another female agent named Carla Watley, arrived along with Detective Brockett. Hatcher was helping him load the women into the police van to transport them to the jail.

The four women had lapsed into silence, their expressions worried but calm as they exchanged furtive looks.

Drummond, on the other hand, was visibly upset. She shifted back and forth on the balls of her feet. "I can't believe this. My God, why would they think Trace was the Skull?"

"I don't know," Korine said. "The suspects aren't talking, but we'll push them for answers at the police station."

Drummond shivered. "Is Trace all right?"

Korine gave her a tentative look. "He's unconscious, but he's breathing. The medics are with him now."

Drummond pushed past Korine to go inside, but the medics rolled a stretcher through the door before she could enter. Trace lay motionless, his complexion ruddy.

Drummond made a pained sound in her throat, then squeezed his hand. "Hang in there, Trace. I'll work here and make sure we have the proof to nail these women for trying to kill you. I'll see you at the hospital."

He didn't respond.

Drummond wiped at a tear that trickled down her cheek as the medics loaded Trace onto the ambulance and raced away.

"How long have you worked with Trace?" Korine asked.

"Almost a year." Drummond heaved a breath. "He's sharp, calm under pressure, and detail oriented. Last week, he told me he wants to be a detective." She dragged a tissue from her pocket and wiped at her eyes.

Korine patted Drummond's arm. "He'll make it. Then maybe he can verify who did this and put an end to this vigilantism."

"I thought you arrested them," Drummond said.

Korine worked her mouth from side to side. "We did. But we need concrete evidence to make the charges stick."

Drummond nodded quickly, her eyes flashing with a mixture of emotions, then she picked up her evidence collection kit. "Then I'd better get to work."

Korine nodded.

A mixture of emotions enveloped her, though, as she glanced at the women. The jobs they did on a daily basis stirred her admiration. She understood the frustrations, too.

But they'd ruined their reputations and lives by committing murder and kidnapping Bellamy.

Still, locking them in prison with hardened criminals somehow seemed wrong.

But they'd crossed the line and come close to killing an innocent man.

For that, they had to pay.

CHAPTER FORTY

Hatcher glanced at Korine, well aware of the tension between them. They hadn't spoken about what had happened between them, but they needed to.

He didn't want to lose his job over it. Or his sanity.

And kissing her only made him want her again, which was totally insane.

Detective Brockett transported the women they'd arrested to the Savannah field office for booking, while Drummond and Watley processed the house.

He and Korine captured pictures of the interior of the house and chair setup, then he combed the rooms in hopes of finding something more concrete pointing to the women and the three murders.

The place looked as if it had been deserted for months, maybe longer. Dust and grime had collected on every surface, and the furniture smelled musty and was threadbare. The kitchen held no perishables, simply a few outdated cans of food and a bag of flour that mice had ripped into.

Drummond found a loose button in the corner of the living area not far from the chair where Bellamy had been secured.

"What can you tell about the button?" Hatcher asked.

"It looks like one from Trace's shirt," Drummond said. "I'll pick up his clothes from the hospital and verify that and also dust for prints."

Korine stepped inside from the backyard with a frown.

"Did you find something?" Hatcher asked.

She shook her head. "No, and that seems odd. We suspect that the murder weapons used on the other three victims were related to the men's crimes—the gavel for the judge, a knife for severing Whiting's penis, an ax or a machete for severing Hortman's hands." She combed the room. "The only weapon here is the gun belonging to Willis." She rubbed her forehead in thought. "The Skull didn't use a gun on Tinsley, did he?"

Hatcher shook his head. "He used assorted tools to torture her. Knives. A tattoo iron?"

"That's right." The images in the photographs of Tinsley after she'd been rescued taunted Hatcher.

"So where are those tools?" Korine asked.

"Good question." Hatcher drummed his fingers on his thigh. The only answer that made sense was that the women had hidden them or that they were in the Tahoe.

Only the evidence team had already searched it and the cabin, and they hadn't found anything.

Unless . . . there was someone else involved. Another woman who'd escaped, or one who hadn't arrived yet.

One who was bringing the tools to their killing party . . .

◆ ◆ ◆

Korine rolled her aching shoulders. It was midnight by the time she and Hatcher left the field office.

Kendall James had shown up and insisted on seeing her clients. When she emerged from the interrogation room where they'd allowed her to speak with the women individually, she looked tired, but she lifted her chin.

"My clients are innocent," she said. "They are model citizens of society with no prior history of any crimes. In fact, they serve the community in their jobs and with very little monetary compensation."

Korine said, "We know where they're employed. But that doesn't give them permission to take justice into their own hands."

"They didn't," James said firmly. "I believe they've been set up."

Hatcher folded his arms. "We caught them standing over their hostage with a gun."

"You're mistaken," Ms. James said. "They were there to try to prevent a crime, not commit one."

Korine's instincts surged to life. "Really? Then they know who kidnapped him?"

Ms. James pursed her lips. "I can't comment on that at this time. However, with your lack of evidence, I'll have them out by noon tomorrow." She straightened her suit jacket. "I suggest that you keep searching for this vigilante killer. My clients are guilty of nothing but being caring, responsible citizens."

"Caring, responsible citizens report a crime and help the police," Korine pointed out.

"Why don't you look at where you're getting your information?" Ms. James checked her watch. "It's late, and we're all tired. Excuse me."

She pivoted, her heels clicking on the floor as she rushed toward the door.

Indecision warred in Korine's mind. Was it possible that the four women they'd arrested were innocent? That they *had* been trying to save Trace Bellamy's life?

If so, why cover for the vigilante killer?

Hatcher wanted the case tied up in a neat bow, but they needed concrete proof. Hopefully they would find it at the house on the marsh, or Bellamy would wake up and be able to identify his captor.

"I'll call Tinsley and let her know we saved Bellamy," Korine said.

Korine pressed Tinsley's number, then put her on speaker. "It's Agents Davenport and McGee. Is Agent Camden with you?"

"Yes, he stepped outside for a minute. What happened?" Tinsley asked, her tone frantic. "Did you find the man in time?"

"We did, and he's safe," Korine replied.

A long sigh echoed over the line. "Thank God. I . . . can't believe this is happening. I meant for my blog to help people, not encourage more violence."

"Don't blame yourself," Korine said.

"Did you make an arrest?" Tinsley asked.

"Actually, we did make arrests," Hatcher cut in. "A counselor named Liz Roberts, parole officer Rachel Willis, guardian ad litem Laura Austin, and court reporter Beverly Grant. Do you know any of those women personally?"

A tense second crawled by. "No."

Hatcher thought he detected a quiver in her voice. "Maybe not, but Ms. Willis had a gun, and the four of them were standing around the hostage. My guess is they got tired of trying to do good and watching the system fail."

Another strained pause. "What's going to happen to them?"

"We'll see. They lawyered up," Hatcher said.

Korine cleared her throat. "Are you all right, Tinsley? Do you want me to come over and stay with you tonight?"

"Thanks, but I'm okay," Tinsley said. "I'm just relieved you saved that man. Please let me know what happens."

"Of course," Korine said. "And don't hesitate to call if you need anything."

Tinsley murmured thanks and ended the call.

But they all knew that she wouldn't rest or be free until the man who'd hurt her was locked up.

At the moment, they had no clue about where he was.

◆　◆　◆

Korine's body ached from fatigue as she and Hatcher entered his cabin. The memory of what they'd been doing before the phone call teased her mind, reawakening her need.

Fool. Hatcher obviously didn't feel the same. His gaze shot straight to the picture of his wife on the mantel.

Determined to preserve her dignity and her job, she grabbed her overnight bag. "If you don't mind, I'd like to shower."

His eyes darkened. "There's a private bath for the guest room. Have at it."

The urge to ask him to join her teetered on the edge of her tongue, but she squelched it and dashed into the extra bedroom. The furnishings were minimal, an antique rope bed covered in a dark-blue quilt, and a pine dresser.

Judging from the lack of personal or decorative touches, it was obvious a woman didn't live here. Then again, her own place lacked decorative personal touches as well.

Remembering that four good women who claimed they were innocent were spending the night locked up raised questions in her mind.

They knew more than they were saying. If they valued their freedom, they would eventually talk.

The sound of Hatcher's footsteps in the living room reminded her that he was only a room away. That they could finish what they'd started earlier.

That she'd wanted him after they'd parted at Quantico, and that she wanted him even more now.

Hoping a shower would cool her desire, she stripped and stepped beneath the spray of water.

But as she ran the washcloth over her bare skin, she could almost feel Hatcher's fingers replacing the cloth, and hunger stirred full force.

♦ ♦ ♦

Hatcher paced to the back porch, desperate to drown out the sound of Korine in that shower. But images of her naked and wet body tormented him.

He flexed his hands and gripped the deck railing, wishing he could touch her again and feel her satiny skin beneath his fingers.

The gusty wind caused the palm trees and seagrass to sway. The cloud cover added a gloomy gray to the swampland and made the water look murky, a breeding ground for mosquitos and a hiding place for the gators.

A reminder that death was a natural part of life. That he'd felt dead since he buried Felicia.

Until he'd touched Korine again.

Suddenly the need to live and feel her beneath him raged through him, and the rational voice that told him to stay where he was faded.

Dammit, he was just a man, and tonight he didn't want to be alone. He needed Korine.

Perspiration beaded his forehead, and he strode back inside to the guest room. The bathroom door was ajar, steam oozing through the room and creating a sensual haze. He stepped inside, his hands fisting by his side.

If Korine asked him to leave, he would.

He took a deep breath, his body hardening at the sight of her naked outline through the fog. "Korine?"

A heartbeat passed. Then another.

Resigned that she didn't want him, he turned to leave the room.

She was the smart one.

Taking her to bed once had wreaked havoc on him for months. It still was.

What would sleeping with her again do to him?

CHAPTER
FORTY-ONE

Korine's voice stopped him. "Hatcher?"

His pulse pounded.

Then she eased open the shower door and waved for him to join her.

Heat surged through him as he shucked his clothes and stepped inside the shower. She was wet and warm and glowing from the soap bubbles dotting her naked body.

He lifted a hand and tucked a damp strand of hair behind her ear, and a shy smile lit her eyes. Shy but needy.

That hungry look . . . nearly drove him to his knees.

She ran her soapy hands over his chest, triggering a hundred delicious sensations to ignite within him. Her touch shredded his reservations, and he reached for her.

But she shook her head and pressed one hand to his chest to slow things down. His chest rose and fell on a strained breath, and he stood ramrod straight, his cock jutting out, hard and thick and aching. His hands itched to touch her all over. His lips craved hers.

Instead of kissing him, though, she soaped her hands and slid them over his chest. Slowly she moved behind him and gave his back the same treatment. Her hands massaged his shoulders, then trailed lower to bathe his hips and thighs.

Soap bubbles dotted her bare skin as she faced him again. Her nipples stood erect, drawing his hands to her. This time she let him touch her, let him tease the silky, slick globes before she cupped his sex in her hand. She stroked him, up and down, over and over, until his cock thickened.

He couldn't take any more.

He wanted her.

But he wanted to pleasure her more than he needed his own release.

She started to stoop down to take him in her mouth, but he captured her hands and forced her against the wall.

It was payback time.

He shoved her hands above her head, watching her carefully to make sure she still wanted him. A smile blended with the hunger in her eyes, and she ran her foot along the inside of his calf.

His legs nearly gave way.

"Korine?"

"Yes," she whispered. "I want you, Hatcher."

Those words were pure music to his ears.

He kneed her thighs apart and rubbed his body against hers as he claimed her mouth in a kiss that started slow but turned fiery within seconds. She plunged her tongue in his mouth, teasing and taunting him. He clenched her hands above her in one of his, then trailed kisses down her neck, tasting the water and her silky skin. His other hand slid to her hips and he yanked her closer to him, stroking her inner thighs with his cock.

She threw her head back and moaned, and he tugged one nipple into his mouth and suckled her. She struggled to free her hands, but he held them firmly and tortured her other breast with his tongue and teeth. Finally, he released her so he could kneel in front of her.

Water cascaded down her body and his back as he teased her thighs apart, then closed his lips over her sensitive nub.

She groaned and pulled at him, but one taste only whetted his appetite for more, and he plunged his tongue inside her and teased her clit until her honeyed release dampened his lips.

"Hatcher, please," Korine said in a ragged whisper.

Body hot with desire, he stood, opened the shower door, grabbed a condom from the drawer, ripped it open, and tugged it on.

She helped him, her fingers stirring the blood in his cock until he thought he would burst with pain and pleasure.

A second later, she parted her thighs, then guided him inside her. He stroked and rubbed her while she cried out and her orgasm claimed her.

Needing more, to be deeper, he lifted her, and she wrapped her legs around his waist, and he impaled her. Her warm body clenched his cock inside her, milking him as she rode him hard and fast.

◆ ◆ ◆

Korine clung to Hatcher and gyrated her hips. Erotic sensations splintered her, making her mindless with pleasure.

The warm water made their bodies slicker, the friction intensifying with each thrust. She nibbled at his neck and tightened her legs around him, wanting him deeper, closer.

Their bodies slapped together in a sensual rhythm that spiked her blood and made her increase the tempo, drawing him deeper inside her as she climaxed again.

He gripped her hips, thrusting in and out and moaning her name as he came.

She buried her head against his wet chest, panting, overcome with sensations and emotions. He spent himself inside her, their bodies still entwined as their orgasms rocked through them.

Slowly, her breathing turned normal, and the water grew cold. Shivering against Hatcher, she managed to turn the water off, then she glided down his body until her feet touched the floor.

He opened the shower door, grabbed a towel and wrapped it around her, then snagged one for himself.

She hugged the towel to herself, brushing water from her hair first, then quickly drying her body. Hatcher stepped onto the floor mat, disposed of the condom, then dried his own hair and tied the towel around his waist.

He looked flushed and sated and so damn handsome that tears pricked at her eyes. His breathing was still choppy, his body hot and hard. She feared she'd see regret in his eyes, maybe even anger, but the passion that had driven him to join her lingered, his eyes dark with need.

His need spurred her own, and she placed her hand against his cheek and kissed him tenderly.

He bit at her lip, then scooped her up and carried her to his bed. Her rational mind whispered for her to protect herself. To stop this insanity.

But she shut out that voice.

Today had been difficult. The dolls. Worrying about her brother. Arresting the women.

Leaving Hatcher's bed was impossible.

He shoved back the covers and laid her on the sheets. Still quivering from their lovemaking, she tossed the damp towel to the floor and opened her arms to him.

He threw his towel onto the chair in the corner, opened his bedside table, snatched another condom, placed it on the table. Then he crawled in bed beside her, pulled her into his arms, and wrapped his hot body around her.

◆ ◆ ◆

Hatcher was drowning in pleasure.

Korine was so sexy and loving, so tender and passionate, that he didn't want the night to end.

They made love again and again, then fell into an exhausted sleep.

But an hour later, the nightmare came again. Felicia dangling from that tree. Felicia screaming for help, pleading for him to save her.

Felicia's blood trickling down her neck and breasts and pinging to the ground. Her last breath as she cried his name and death claimed her.

Riddled with emotions, he slipped from bed, dragged on his jeans, and started into the hallway. Korine's cell phone was on the dresser, a text lighting the screen. Assuming it was about the case or her brother and it might be important, he glanced at the text. The room suddenly grew hot as he read the message,

It was from Bellows. Asking about him—how was he doing? Was he drinking?

God . . . he closed his eyes and swallowed back a groan. How could he have been such a fool?

Korine was spying on him.

Furious at himself, he strode into the living room. His bottle of whiskey sat on the bar, an empty glass waiting.

Why couldn't he have resisted her?

His hand shook as he poured the tumbler half-full.

His mouth watered as he lifted it for the first sip. He missed Jack. Missed numbing his pain and problems with the rich, dark taste.

Missed the warm burn as it slid down his throat. The comforting feel as it seeped into his blood and helped him forget his failures.

He carried the tumbler to the porch, stood, and looked out into the woods.

Felicia's image rose in the murky fog, her hand stretching toward him in that silent plea again, and he turned the drink up and tossed back half of it.

He closed his eyes, savoring the whiskey and waiting for it to begin its magic.

"Hatcher?"

Korine's soft voice jerked him from the bliss of escape.

Her footsteps padded on the wood floor as she walked up behind him. "Come back to bed."

The gentle touch of her fingers on his arm was so tempting he turned to face her. She'd put on his shirt and buttoned it. His clothes on her were even sexier than her being naked.

But she was reporting to Bellows, watching him like he was a damned child.

She saw the bourbon in his hand, and disappointment flashed in her eyes.

"If sleeping with me drives you to drink, then I should go."

He hated the pain in her voice. Pain he'd caused. But anger churned in his belly. "Yeah, run to Bellows and tell him I'm a drunk."

Her eyes flared at his bitter tone, but he couldn't make himself apologize. Sleeping with her had always been a mistake. He sure as hell couldn't afford to care about her.

She bit down on her bottom lip, then took a step away from him.

His phone buzzed, startling them both. Grateful for the interruption, he rushed to answer it.

"Agent McGee, this is Officer Leeks. I was assigned to guard Trace Bellamy at the hospital."

His pulse picked up a notch. "Is something wrong?"

"The doctor said he's out of the woods. He's waking up if you want to talk to him."

Of course he did. "I'll be right there."

Korine was watching him, questions in her eyes. "News on the case?"

"Bellamy is waking up. I'm going to the hospital to talk to him."

"I'll get dressed." She started toward the bedroom, but he wasn't in the mood, not after seeing that text.

"I'm going alone."

Her gaze met his, the turmoil deepening. He was cutting her out, and she knew it.

Before he could give in to temptation and take her back to bed, he strode into the bedroom and dressed. She was still standing in his den when he returned. But her phone was in her hand. For a brief second, he thought regret flashed in her eyes.

"We should talk," she said quietly.

"There's nothing to talk about." He snagged his keys, stormed out the door, and slammed it behind him.

The sooner he closed this case, the sooner he could request a new partner.

◆ ◆ ◆

Korine watched Hatcher leave, her blood boiling. What had happened? One minute she and Hatcher were making wild passionate love and had curled in each other's arms, sleeping. The next, he was up by himself, staring at the woods, drinking.

He had seen that text, too. And he was hurt by it.

She never should have let down her guard. Never should have slept with him again because giving her body to him meant giving her heart.

He didn't want her heart or her as a partner.

His wife had been clingy and needy. She couldn't become that kind of woman.

She lifted her chin, fortifying her resolve, and hurried to get dressed. She wouldn't rely on Hatcher or pressure him for anything.

But she was part of this case, and she wanted to hear what Trace Bellamy said.

Mind made up, she phoned for a taxi.

Just as she was hanging up, her phone buzzed. Probably Hatcher. Maybe Bellamy was awake and had identified his attacker.

She checked the number. Not Hatcher. Her mother's home.

She glanced at the clock. Four a.m.

A bad sign.

She quickly connected the call. "Esme?"

"You've got to come over. Kenny showed up and . . . he's upset," her mother's caregiver said on a ragged breath. "He has your father's gun."

Korine's pulse jumped. "I'll be right there."

She grabbed her purse and jacket, then strapped on her gun and holster.

Armed and ready, she stepped outside to wait on the cab.

Five minutes later, it arrived, and she jumped in and gave the driver her mother's address. Anxiety seized every muscle in her body. It was only a few miles to the house where she'd grown up, but it seemed like it took them hours to get there.

Questions needled her as the driver turned down the drive.

Why did Kenny have her father's gun? Was it loaded? Would he use it?

She handed the driver some cash, then climbed from the cab and jogged to the front door, bracing herself to defuse the situation inside.

To treat this incident just as she would a call on the job, not like it was personal.

But the moment she opened the door and heard her mother's shrill scream, fear flooded her.

Praying she didn't need her weapon, she paused in the foyer to listen. Kenny was shouting something. Her mother was crying.

Kenny's voice was coming from her father's study.

The very room he'd died in.

She didn't want to lose another family member in there.

Easing her weapon from her holster in case she needed it, she held it down by her side and slipped to the doorway.

Her heart stuttered at the sight. Her father's gun was tucked in Kenny's pants, and he wielded a hammer in his right hand—the hand he had brought down to smash one of the porcelain dolls on the floor.

The dolls her father had given her.

Her cell phone buzzed with a text before she could step in to intervene. She quickly glanced at it. Cat.

Traced the Facebook Live post to a phone.

Korine choked on a breath.

The address Cat listed was her mother's house.

CHAPTER
FORTY-TWO

Korine balled her hand into a fist. How was it possible that Cat had traced that Facebook Live post to this address?

Her mother didn't even have a cell phone. Neither did Esme.

And the post had to do with the man the Keeper had thought was the Skull, which had nothing to do with her family or her father's death.

Her mother's cry rent the air. "Stop it! Your dad loves those dolls. He's saving them for Korine."

Esme snatched Korine's hand and pulled her behind the door. "I'm so glad you're here. Kenny is out of control."

Korine touched Esme's shoulder. "What happened to start the argument?"

"I don't know," Esme said. "Kenny just showed up and started talking crazy, and then your mama got upset."

"Stay here. Let me talk to them." Korine held her breath as she stepped into the doorway.

"Mom? Kenny?"

Her mother was sitting on the sofa, eyes glassy, rocking herself back and forth while Kenny paced in front of her. The broken pieces of the porcelain dolls lay scattered across the floor just as they had across her bed.

He raised the hammer and smashed another doll. Her mother screamed and covered her face with her hands as porcelain shards flew.

"Kenny?" Korine eased toward him. "Please put down the hammer and the gun."

Kenny hesitated in front of the fireplace, his eyes wild and unfocused. He kept swinging the hammer back and forth, his body rigid.

"Please, let's sit down and talk."

"Why? All this family does is lie!" Kenny shouted.

"Stop it, son," their mother cried. "Your daddy bought those dolls for Korine for her birthday and Christmas."

Korine hated the pain in her mother's voice, but at least she'd come out of her silent shell and was speaking.

"I know he did." Kenny threw the hammer onto the floor, then grabbed the gun from his pants and waved it in the air. "It was always about Korine, his special, pretty little girl."

"I'm sorry you felt left out," Korine said. "Really. But Dad loved you—"

"I hated him!" Kenny said, venom in his tone. "I hated him and the things he did."

"Because he gave me gifts?" Korine asked quietly. "You were jealous and wanted more of his attention."

Kenny wiped sweat from his brow with a trembling hand. "How can you be an FBI agent and be so stupid?"

Korine gripped her weapon by her side and inched toward her mother. She had to get that gun away from her brother. "Okay, maybe I'm clueless, so why don't we sit down and you can explain everything to me?"

Kenny rubbed his hand over his eyes as if he was debating what to do. Her mother was still rocking herself back and forth on the sofa, confusion clouding her eyes.

Korine patted her shoulder. "I'm here now, Mom, we'll work things out. I promise."

"The dolls, I know you loved them . . . ," her mother said in a low whisper.

Korine gritted her teeth and glanced at Kenny, hoping he'd realize how much his behavior was upsetting their mother. Instead, he looked angry, distant, like a child reliving some horror.

"Kenny, please," Korine said. "Put down the gun so we can talk."

He paced in front of them, his movements jittery. "It's too late to talk."

"No, it's not," Korine said softly. "I love you, and I want to understand."

He spun on her, eyes filled with bitterness. "No, you don't."

She gestured for him to put the gun on the table. "Tell me what upset you so badly that you left rehab. What happened in that therapy session?"

Kenny's face contorted with pain. "They wanted me to tell them everything. But I couldn't talk about it, not with strangers." His body shook as a sob was wrenched from his gut.

Korine took advantage of the moment and eased the gun from him. Carefully, she placed it on the table, then stowed her weapon in her holster. "Tell me, Kenny. What can't you talk about?"

"That night," Kenny shouted. "The doll. And that fucking music . . ."

"You mean the night Dad was shot," Korine asked.

Tears streamed down her brother's face. "I heard the music, and I remembered the other time."

"What other time?" Korine asked, desperately trying to follow the conversation.

"The time with the little girl," Kenny said in a faraway voice. "He gave her a doll just like yours."

Korine struggled to understand. Was he confused? "Dad gave another little girl a doll like mine?"

Kenny nodded, choking on a sob. "He gave a lot of dolls away, to his patients."

Her father had loved children . . . he helped them in therapy. "He gave them to the girls when they were ready to move on from therapy?"

"No, no . . ." Kenny's face contorted in rage. "I saw where he kept them in his office. It was the day fathers were supposed to take their sons to work."

"You were at Daddy's office?"

Kenny nodded, his movements jerky. "He told me to stay in the break room. Even gave me doughnuts. I guess he thought I'd pig out and wouldn't bother him."

A sense of foreboding washed over Korine. Kenny was finally opening up. Although, so far, he wasn't making much sense. "What happened then?"

"I wanted a soda, but there weren't any in the refrigerator so I was going to ask Daddy for money for the vending machine."

Korine nodded. "Go on."

He pulled at his hair, a nervous habit he'd started in his preteens. "I heard the music box playing, and I tried to open the door, but it was locked. Dad was supposed to spend the day with me." His voice cracked. "I was so mad at him. The secretary had gone to lunch, so I found the key to Dad's office in her desk and unlocked the door. I was going to make Dad pay attention to me."

The agony in Kenny's voice tore at Korine.

"I peeked inside. She was sitting on his lap."

A chill shot through Korine. "Who was sitting on his lap?"

Kenny wiped at his eyes. "A little girl," Kenny said, his voice breaking. "He gave her a doll and danced with her, and then . . . then . . ."

Korine glanced at her mother for a reaction, but her mother was staring at her hands, a million miles away.

"He took off her dress," Kenny said, disgust in his voice. "She was crying, but he told her he loved her, and then he touched her all over . . ."

Shock slammed into Korine. "What? No . . . Daddy would never have molested a patient."

Kenny backed up, rage slashing his face. "He did," he said sharply. "I saw him."

Denial stabbed at Korine.

"Then that Christmas Eve, he gave you that doll and the music box was playing, and I looked in and saw you dancing, and I knew what he was going to do—"

Korine shook her head. "Daddy wouldn't—"

"He did." Kenny pulled at his hair again. "He did it with that girl, and then I saw a bunch more dolls and music boxes stacked in the closet in the break room, and I realized he was doing it to other girls."

Nausea flooded Korine. Her father gave music boxes and dolls to other little girls . . .

Kenny picked up the music box and stared at the twirling ballerina. The melody "I Feel Pretty" filled the room. Except this time the music made Korine feel sick inside.

Heart breaking, she took the music box and slammed the top shut, then set it on the coffee table.

"He was going to molest you," Kenny cried. "Don't you see? You were my little sister, and I was supposed to protect you. I had to stop him."

Korine's chest ached with the need to breathe. "Kenny," she said in a raw whisper. "What do you mean, you had to stop him?"

He glanced at the gun, his eyes glazed as if he was reliving that night.

Disbelief and denial made Korine want to run.

But reality held her immobile as she put the pieces together.

The moment Hatcher stepped off the hospital elevator, the alarms were ringing. Nurses and doctors raced into the hallway, shouting orders, and a nurse pushed a crash cart toward a room down the hall.

His gut instincts roared to life.

He picked up his pace, then spotted Officer Leeks.

"What happened?" Hatcher asked.

"I don't know." Leeks jammed his hands in his pants' pockets. "The nurse was in there with him, so I went to take a piss. When I got back, machines were beeping, and nurses and doctors were scrambling around like crazy."

Frustration gnawed at Hatcher. He wanted Bellamy alive and awake so he could identify his attacker—or attackers. Kendall James had probably stayed up all night planning her strategy to get the charges against the four women dropped.

He needed proof, dammit.

"Go get some coffee," Hatcher told the officer. "I'll stay here and find out what's going on."

The officer gave a quick nod. He had been first on the scene when the judge's body was found, and now he was here when Bellamy was crashing.

Suspicion took root in Hatcher's mind. In the briefing meeting, they'd discussed the possibility that someone involved in the case could be the unsub. That they should consider members of law enforcement as possible persons of interest.

Leeks had opportunity.

He stepped into the waiting room, texted Wyatt, and asked him to run a background check on Officer Leeks. Then he made his way down the hall.

A nurse was exiting Bellamy's room.

"Is he going to be all right?" Hatcher asked.

"You'll have to speak to the doctor," the nurse said.

"What happened?"

"It appears that he had an allergic reaction to some medication. The doctor is running a tox screen to find out exactly what substance triggered the reaction."

"Were you aware that he had allergies?" Hatcher asked.

She shook her head. "He was unconscious when he was brought in. There was no family to call, and we didn't find a medical history."

Hatcher thanked her, then knocked on the door to Bellamy's room and stepped inside. A female doctor, probably midforties, stood by Bellamy's bed.

He quickly introduced himself. "How is he?"

"We've stabilized him, but we want to get to the bottom of what caused him to crash."

"You think it was a drug you gave him?"

The doctor pinched the bridge of her nose. "It's possible, although nothing I prescribed should have triggered this type of reaction."

Hatcher's mind raced. Bellamy was waking up, and he might have been able to ID his attacker.

Maybe the unsub knew that and wanted to quiet him. That person could have snuck in and injected him. Yet Leeks was standing guard . . . Unless it was Leeks.

Or someone dressed like hospital staff. Someone Leeks wouldn't have suspected was a threat.

"Let me know what you find out." He studied Bellamy's ashen face. "And alert me as soon as he regains consciousness."

If someone had intentionally dosed Bellamy with a drug to trigger a heart attack or an allergic reaction, that was attempted murder. The four women they'd arrested couldn't be responsible.

Meaning they were innocent. And that the unsub was still on the loose.

◆ ◆ ◆

Korine couldn't believe this was happening. All these years, she'd been determined, driven, to find her father's murderer. Had thought it would give her peace.

But it had never occurred to her that her search would lead to her brother. Kenny had only been nine at the time, a child.

A child who'd witnessed his father do the unthinkable.

No wonder her mother had tried to get her to stop asking questions.

Kenny slumped in the wing chair, his head buried in his hands. From the sofa, her mother twisted her hands in her lap, seemingly lost as tears streamed down her face.

Korine had a sudden urge to run. To forget this conversation and live in denial.

But that was impossible now.

Kenny had been in turmoil for years. Now she understood the reason he'd started drinking.

He'd been plagued by what had happened that night.

But . . . she still couldn't believe that her father, the man she adored and loved so much, would have hurt a child.

Or her.

Slowly, she approached her brother and gently touched his back. "Kenny, you must have been mistaken and misunderstood what you saw. Dad would never—"

"Dad molested that little girl, Korine," Kenny said matter-of-factly. "I saw it. She was naked and crying, but he kept touching her and telling her it was okay, that he was loving her."

Tears burned the backs of Korine's eyelids, fighting to come out. "No, Kenny . . ."

"Yes," he said, his voice resigned now as if he'd finally unleashed a heavy burden. "I never told you because I didn't want to hurt you."

Denial and shock battled inside Korine. "You said you had to stop him?"

Pain streaked his face. "I had to protect you. I . . . ran upstairs and found his gun and . . ."

"And you shot him?" Korine said. "Mom was asleep and you shot Daddy."

"That's not the way it happened!" Their mother lurched up from the sofa and grabbed Korine's arm. "Your brother didn't shoot your father."

Korine was shocked at her mother's tone. "But he said—"

"He was going to, but I woke up and saw him with the gun." Korine's mother's eyes were filled with anguish. "He told me what was happening, but I didn't believe him."

Kenny crossed to their mother, knelt in front of her, and cradled her hand in his. "It's okay, Mom—I saw what he was doing. I wanted him dead. I was supposed to protect Korine."

"I'm sorry I didn't believe you when you first came to me," their mother said in a haunted voice. "But I didn't want to believe it."

Because it was too horrible to believe. Parents had trusted him to help their children in their most vulnerable state.

Yet he had preyed on them.

Her mother pressed her hand against Kenny's cheek. "I was supposed to protect you and Korine, and I failed."

Kenny shook his head, but their mother continued. "I couldn't let you shoot your daddy." She angled her head toward Korine. "So I took the gun, and I ran downstairs."

Korine stared at her mother in shock.

"Then I heard that song." Korine's mother pulled away from him, stood, and picked up the music box.

Raw pain streaked her mother's face as she opened the lid and the music began to play. "I heard the music and your daddy singing, 'You're so pretty, oh, so pretty, so pretty and witty and . . .'"

The song catapulted Korine back in time.

"When I looked in and saw the doll and the two of you dancing, I knew . . . Kenny was right." Her mother's voice broke. "I saw the way your daddy was looking at you, and I remembered one of your daddy's patients. The mother, she came in one day and said he touched her daughter." Korine's mother paused, her body stiffening. "I didn't want to believe it, but later I found more dolls and another music box, and I remembered hearing the music playing one day when I stopped by his office. I was going to surprise him and take him to lunch, but he had the door locked and was in there with that child." Tears rained down her face. "He got so mad at me that day. He told me never to come to the office again."

Korine pressed her hands to her head, willing this to be a bad dream.

But her mother continued, "When I saw him looking at you like that, I . . . realized it was true."

Kenny put his arm around their mother's shoulder. "Mom, don't. It's all right."

"It's not all right. It hasn't been for years. You've suffered long enough. It's time for the truth to come out." She gave Kenny a hug, then faced Korine. "Your brother didn't shoot your father, Korine. I did."

CHAPTER FORTY-THREE

Korine's mother extended her hands, wrists crossed. "Go ahead, Korine. Take me in. I know you have to."

Turmoil twisted Korine's insides as she stared at her mother. How could she possibly arrest her own mother for killing her father when she'd been protecting her? She'd also protected Kenny by keeping him from taking his father's life.

Kenny gently pushed her mother's hands down into her lap. "Korine isn't going to arrest you, Mom."

For the first time in her life, Korine understood Kenny's drinking, his anger, his resentment toward her. Keeping the family's dirty little secret had preyed on him and her mother.

It had also bound the two of them together.

Your brother always took care of you.

Her mother's constant pressure for her to help Kenny made sense now.

A dozen emotions thrummed through Korine. "Why didn't you tell me all this before?"

"How could we?" Kenny asked, bitterness mingling with resignation in his voice. "You adored Dad and thought he could do no wrong."

Kenny was right.

"You were so little," her mother said in a raw whisper. "And I felt so guilty. I should have gotten you out of the room before I shot him, but I was so crazed and out of my mind when I realized what was happening that I didn't think. I just wanted him away from you."

Kenny rubbed their mother's shoulders. "Mom was just taking care of us, Korine. She doesn't deserve to go to jail for that."

"You could have told the police," Korine said. "They would have understood."

"What do you think our life would have been like then?" Kenny growled. "The news would have been plastered all over the place. Everyone at school and in the neighborhood would have gossiped about us."

Korine tried to imagine how her mother had felt when she realized what her father was doing. How shocked and hurt and desperate she'd been to protect her children.

How horrified she'd been, knowing the publicity would ruin them for life.

"I'm sorry, Kenny," Korine said. "Now I see why you hated me all these years."

"I never hated you," Kenny said gruffly. "But I couldn't stand knowing what he was and hearing you talk about him like he was your hero when Mom was the real hero."

Korine wiped at a tear. "You're right about that. And now that I know the truth, I promise to help you. It's time you got your life together and put this behind you." Although she was going to need time to assimilate it.

She didn't know what she was going to do about her mother, though. She'd arrested four women the night before for being vigilantes.

How could she not go to the police with the truth about what happened to her father?

But her mother didn't deserve to be locked away. And she'd never survive in prison in her condition.

"Mom, everything's going to be all right now," Kenny said, his look imploring Korine to play along. "I'll clean up this mess while you rest."

Korine stepped toward the hallway to retrieve her mother's medication. Esme was standing in the doorway, wringing her hands in the bottom of her apron. She had an odd expression on her face.

"You heard?" Korine asked.

Esme nodded. "You want your mother's sedative?"

"Please."

Esme started toward the kitchen, but Korine caught her. "Can we keep this between us for now?"

Esme's dark-brown eyes met hers, turmoil in her expression. "Of course, honey. Of course."

Korine thanked her and waited for her to return. Esme carried the pill inside with a glass of water and a cup of hot tea and settled her mother in the recliner while Kenny cleaned up the doll pieces.

When he finished, Kenny moved to the window, staring out. Korine gently touched his shoulder. "I'm sorry that you suffered all these years, that I didn't understand. It must have been awful, keeping that horrible secret."

A peace like she hadn't seen in years replaced the turmoil in his eyes. "I hated for you to know, Shortstop."

Tenderness for her brother swelled inside her. It had been years since he'd called her that nickname.

She held out her arms, and he pulled her into a hug, and they cried together for a long time.

Hope budded that Kenny might overcome his addiction problem and be able to heal.

The morning sun was streaking the sky as she glanced outside. She'd waited two decades for the truth. For justice.

Maybe justice had been served the day her father died.

◆ ◆ ◆

Hatcher gripped the phone with a sweaty hand.

"Officer Leeks checks out," Wyatt said. "No history of violence. No ghosts in his closet that might trigger him to start vigilante killings. He has a wife, two kids, a mortgage, and visits his mother in a nursing home every Sunday."

He certainly didn't fit the profile of a killer. "Any medical training suggesting he'd know what kind of drug might mimic a heart attack?"

"Nothing to indicate that, but with the Internet these days, anyone can find that information in seconds."

"True." Hatcher tossed the disposable cup of stale coffee into the trash. "Thanks for looking into him. I'm going to request another officer stand watch over Bellamy."

"Probably not a bad idea." Wyatt hesitated. "I'm still researching the women you arrested and their lawyer. So far, they're squeaky clean."

"Thanks, Wyatt." Hatcher ended the call, then phoned the SPD and requested a replacement for Leeks.

He paced the hall outside Bellamy's room while he waited on the officer to arrive. A thirtysomething, slender guy in uniform introduced himself, and Hatcher explained the situation.

"Call me the minute he wakes up," Hatcher said. "And don't let anyone but the staff in the room."

"Copy that," the officer said.

Hatcher headed outside to his SUV, his body tense. He couldn't get Korine off his mind. The sex with her had been incredible.

But that nightmare had plagued him. Then he'd seen the text, and he'd turned to the bottle.

Had she phoned Bellows and told him he was drinking?

♦ ♦ ♦

Korine asked the cab driver to wait while she retrieved her overnight bag. Last night she hadn't wanted to stay alone in her house.

Hatcher obviously regretted making love to her, and she refused to be the clingy, needy woman who begged him to love her.

She rushed inside and was just bringing her bag to the cab when Hatcher drove up. He climbed from his SUV, his expression stony.

"What the hell are you doing?" he asked.

She forced an even keel to her voice. "Going back to my place. I need to clean up that mess."

"You can call someone to do that," Hatcher said.

She lifted her chin. "I know that. But I also have a family situation to handle."

Hatcher slammed his door closed and strode toward her. "Get in. I'll drive you."

"That's not necessary. I'll take the cab." She motioned for the cab driver to put her overnight bag into his car. "What happened with Bellamy? Did he talk?"

Hatcher shook his head. "He had an allergic reaction to some medication and flatlined. The doctors revived him and are running tests to determine what happened. He's still unconscious."

"Do you think someone intentionally drugged him so he couldn't talk?"

"It's a possibility."

"Then the women we arrested may be innocent."

"Or there's another unsub working with them."

Korine tensed. "If so, the vigilante killer may not be finished."

Hatcher nodded grimly. "What's going on with your family?"

Emotions pummeled Korine. She hadn't had time to process the truth about her father and his murder yet.

How could she share something so personal with Hatcher when they had no future together?

◆ ◆ ◆

A pang hit Hatcher in the chest as Korine left. She hadn't answered him.

He supposed he didn't blame her, not after the way he'd stormed out earlier.

What the hell was he going to do about her?

After they'd made love, he'd instantly regretted it. Panicked.

Even though it was the best sex he'd ever had in his life.

He wanted her again, dammit.

But . . . he couldn't take her to bed and not offer her something. But what? A partners-with-benefits relationship?

That would never work.

It wouldn't be fair to either of them. Eventually she'd want more. He didn't have any more to give.

Did he?

Had she ratted him out to Bellows?

Rubbing his hand over his bleary eyes, he went inside the cabin. But images of undressing Korine in the den and carrying her to his bed rose in his mind to torment him.

Fatigue pulled at him, but when he entered his bedroom and saw the rumpled sheets, an image of Korine naked in that bed filled his vision.

There was no way he could sleep.

He cursed, dragged off his clothes, and headed into the shower. The cold water pelted him and woke him up like a shot of caffeine, then he switched it to warm and scrubbed his body. But even as he showered, he remembered Korine's soapy hands gliding over his skin, and his body hardened.

Frustrated, he turned off the water, stepped from the shower, and dried off. His phone was ringing.

Hopefully Bellamy had regained consciousness.

He rushed to answer it, but the name Davenport appeared. Korine had said she was having family issues. Maybe she'd gone to her mother's.

He quickly connected, expecting to hear Korine's voice, but it was the caregiver instead.

"Agent McGee. It's Esme, Mrs. Davenport's caretaker. She wants you to come over."

Hatcher scratched his chin. "Is Korine there?"

A tense second passed. "She left earlier. Mrs. Davenport wants to speak to you in private."

"What is this about?" Hatcher asked. "Is Kenny at the house, giving you problems?"

"Kenny's gone," Esme said. "But it's urgent you come."

Hatcher's blood ran cold. Had something happened to Korine?

"Please hurry."

The phone went silent.

Esme's concerned voice echoed in his ears as he quickly dressed, strapped on his holster and gun, snagged his keys, and raced to his car.

He peeled from the drive and raced toward Savannah and the Davenport estate. The sun peeked through the clouds, announcing morning and a new day, although he felt dismal inside.

The drive took less than ten minutes but felt like an hour. He parked, jumped out, and hurried to the door. Before he even knocked, Esme waved him inside.

"Follow me—she's waiting for you."

Hatcher scanned the living area for Korine or Kenny, but it appeared Esme and Mrs. Davenport were alone. He followed Esme to the living room and found Korine's mother sipping tea.

When she saw him, an odd expression flickered in her eyes, but she looked more lucid than when he'd met her. Esme placed her hand on the woman's shoulder and squeezed. "Agent McGee is here. You had something you wanted to tell him."

Korine's mother stood and walked toward him.

"Thank you for coming."

A bad feeling seized him. He should have called Korine.

"What can I do for you?"

Pain streaked her eyes, and she held out her hands, crossed at the wrists. "It's time I did the right thing. My daughter has worked for years to put her father's killer away. Now she knows the truth, I want you to take me in."

"I don't understand," Hatcher said gruffly. Was she having an incoherent moment?

"I killed my husband," Mrs. Davenport said, her eyes flat. "I did it to save Korine from that horrible father of hers."

"What do you mean?" Korine had sung her father's praises.

"He molested some of his patients," Mrs. Davenport said matter-of-factly.

Again, he glanced at Esme for confirmation, and she nodded.

Hatcher rubbed his forehead. "Does Korine know this?"

"I just told her," Mrs. Davenport said.

Jesus. No wonder she hadn't answered his question.

"She won't arrest me, but I insist you do," Mrs. Davenport said in a no-nonsense voice. "It's time we make things right."

Hatcher swallowed hard. "I think we should call Korine."

Mrs. Davenport's lower lip trembled. "Just take me in," she shouted. "I want to make a statement."

Hatcher glanced at Esme for some clue about what to do, but she looked upset and shrugged.

He took Mrs. Davenport by the arm. He refused to handcuff her. She wasn't dangerous.

Korine was going to hate him anyway when she discovered that he'd escorted her mother to the police station.

CHAPTER FORTY-FOUR

The Keeper had committed too much of her heart and soul to exacting justice to abandon her mission now. The innocent women and children who couldn't protect themselves needed someone to watch over them. Someone to protect them when the police failed.

And they failed a lot.

Agents Korine Davenport and Hatcher McGee were a problem.

She raised her hands and studied them. Clean fingers and nails. No blood on them.

Except she could still see the blood in her mind.

Blood from the evil beings who would have hurt more if she hadn't stopped them.

There were so many more who needed to be reckoned with. Milt Milburn for one.

Korine Davenport claimed she was all about the law. But she was a hypocrite.

She had to die.

Hatcher McGee would have to die with her.

Then the Keepers could continue . . .

CHAPTER FORTY-FIVE

"Mrs. Davenport, you don't have to go to the station," Hatcher said. "Let me call Korine—"

"I'm doing this for her," Korine's mother said. "I know how much her job means to her, and I refuse to put her in an awkward position."

Considering her medical condition, he was surprised at how determined she sounded.

Of course, an hour from now, she might slip back into depression. That could be bad.

"Please," Mrs. Davenport said. "I failed her and the other little girls. I want to make up for it now."

Esme was watching him, her expression concerned.

"What about Kenny?" Hatcher asked. "Does he know what's going on?"

"He was here earlier," Esme said. "But after talking to Korine, he decided to return to rehab. He seemed committed to make the program work this time."

Good for him.

This was the family situation Korine needed to take care of. She obviously didn't want to talk about it with him.

He would help her anyway. Take the choice off her shoulders.

"All right, Mrs. Davenport. I'll drive you to the station to make a statement." Somehow he'd figure out a way to keep her from going to prison, too.

He'd do anything for Korine.

♦ ♦ ♦

Korine hurriedly cleaned up the broken pieces of the dolls, mentally processing what had happened at her mother's.

All these years she'd been angry with Kenny, yet he'd sacrificed so much to protect her. Although those dirty secrets had eaten away at him and nearly destroyed him.

No more. She would do whatever possible to help him.

Although she sensed that unburdening his soul had done more to aid his recovery than therapy could ever do. It had also brought her mother out of her catatonic depression.

She dumped the trash in the bin outside, startling when a noise echoed from the bushes. The limbs rustled.

Instincts on alert, she scanned the area by the house. Perhaps Kenny wanted to talk again before going back to the rehab center.

Her cell phone trilled from inside the house.

Thinking it might be about Bellamy or the women they'd arrested, she raced inside. Hatcher's number.

She pressed connect. "Hatcher?"

"Korine, meet me at the police station."

Fear caught in her throat. "What's going on?"

"Just meet me there, and I'll explain."

The connection ended, and Korine hurried to change clothes. If Bellamy had awakened and identified his attacker, maybe Hatcher had made another arrest, and they could close this case.

Then she could ask for a new partner and forget that she'd fallen in love with Hatcher.

♦ ♦ ♦

Hatcher had hoped Esme would accompany Korine's mother in case she had an episode or became agitated, but Esme seemed withdrawn and declined.

He explained the situation to Detective Brockett while Mrs. Davenport sipped coffee and chatted with the female psychologist he'd requested the moment they'd arrived. Now that she'd confessed, she almost seemed relieved.

Under the psychologist's advisement, Hatcher had obtained Kendall James as Mrs. Davenport's counsel. If she could make the Keepers look sympathetic, she would do the same for Korine's mother.

A mother protecting her child was a solid defense.

Heels clicked on the floor, and Korine rounded the corner.

She looked tired and worried, with no sign that she'd given another thought to their intimate night before. "What's going on?"

He steeled himself against her reaction. "Your mother called me after you left."

Her face paled. "What? Why call you?"

He shifted onto the balls of his feet. "She wanted to make a statement regarding your father's death."

Emotions clouded Korine's eyes. "How dare you not call me. Is this your way of paying me back because you think I was spying on you for Bellows? Because it wasn't like that. He was worried about you. And I didn't tell him anything."

Regret seized him. If he'd ever had a chance with Korine, he'd totally blown it. "I didn't want to bring her in, but she insisted. Maybe she needs to do this."

Korine's venomous expression bore into him. "Where is she?"

He reached out to offer comfort, but she jerked away. "Where is she?"

"In a room with the psychologist and Kendall James."

"Kendall James?"

He nodded. "Considering her medical history and the circumstances, the psychologist and I thought it best to handle this quietly. Ms. James jumped at the chance to represent her."

"Nobody thought to include *me*?" Anger laced Korine's voice.

"Your mother came to me," Hatcher said softly. "She knew you were in a difficult position and wanted to spare you." He reached for her again. "So do I."

"You had no right." She stormed through the door to the interview room where the psychologist and Kendall James were talking to her mother.

Frustrated, he grabbed a cup of coffee, then phoned the hospital to check on Bellamy. Still no change. A few minutes later, Korine emerged with her mother and the lawyer.

Korine avoided eye contact with him and ushered her mother out the door as if she was her guard dog.

It's better this way, he reminded himself. Wyatt would be returning to duty soon, and they would partner up.

Korine would go her own way.

So why did the thought of that make him feel empty inside?

He gave her time to leave the precinct with her mother; then he walked outside and headed to his SUV.

But just as he reached his vehicle, a noise jarred him, and he glanced toward the alley.

A shadow passed, and he sensed someone behind him. Before he could turn to see who it was, something sharp—a needle—jabbed into his neck.

The world spun out of focus. Traffic sounds bleeped and blurred in the background. He clawed at his car door to remain upright.

But he lost the battle, his knees hit the concrete, and everything went black.

◆ ◆ ◆

Korine was furious with Hatcher and with Esme.

She escorted her mother into the safety of her house. Esme was in the kitchen, sipping coffee, baking shortbread cookies.

She always baked when she was agitated. Shortbread cookies, chocolate chip, peanut butter—she claimed her daughter used to love them when she was a little girl.

She'd lost her as a teen, though, a death that had weighed on Esme and brought her into their lives. Esme had claimed she'd needed family.

God knows, when Korine's mother had been diagnosed with severe depression, they'd needed her.

"You're back sooner than I expected." The teakettle whistled, and Esme made quick work of preparing a cup of tea and setting it in front of Korine's mother.

"Why didn't you call me?" Korine said, unable to hide her anger.

Esme fiddled with her apron, then took the cookies from the tray and placed them on a platter. "I did what your mother asked. She felt it was time everything came out in the open, and she loved you so much, she wanted to save you from the pain of doing it." She looked up at Korine, the sadness back. "That's what mothers do. They protect their babies, no matter what."

Tears pricked Korine's eyes. "I wish I'd known what really happened. All these years, I've been looking for answers."

"You were too little to understand," her mother said, her face a picture of normalcy. "It was better you were left in the dark."

Maybe so. But poor Kenny . . . "Why now, Mother?" Korine asked. "Why tell all this now?"

"Kenny," her mother said. "For so long I'd tried to forget that horrible night. I almost talked myself into believing it didn't happen. Then I saw that news story about the vigilante killers. It made me remember . . . everything." Her mother stirred sugar into her tea. "That nice lawyer lady said everything will be okay, though. She's going to make a deal for me, and I can stay home."

Korine admired her mother's courage. "Yes, Mother, it'll be okay. I'll make sure it is."

Korine had never thought she'd cross the line, but her mother had sacrificed so much for her, she'd do anything to prevent her from going to prison and to keep the story quiet.

She waited until her mother settled down with her tea and the sedative was taking effect before she left. Hopefully now her mother and Kenny could both come to terms with what happened and move on.

"Call me if you need anything," she told Esme.

Esme assured her she would, and Korine left to drive home.

Her phone trilled just as she pulled in her drive. Tinsley Jensen.

Instant panic hit her, and she connected as she let herself inside her house. What if the Skull had returned for Tinsley?

She connected the call. "Agent Davenport."

"Someone just posted that the Keepers aren't finished." Tinsley sounded breathless. "He or she also listed the name of the next targets."

A tense second passed. "Give me their names and contact info, and I'll arrange protection."

"The next two names belong to you and Hatcher."

A heartbeat passed. "Have you told Hatcher?" Korine asked.

"I called you first."

"Thanks. I'll get in touch with him."

Korine's other line was buzzing in with a call. "He's calling now. Let me get it." She quickly connected. "Hatcher—"

"He's all tied up right now." A woman's bitter laugh sent panic through Korine.

Dear God. She had Hatcher.

"This is not the way to get justice," Korine said.

"Someone has to do it." This time the voice was shrill, altered electronically. "You call yourselves the law, but you make it worse by freeing hardened criminals and putting them on the streets again."

"The release of those prisoners was not my decision," Korine said through clenched teeth.

"Maybe not, but you're just as bad. You arrest a group of women who've done nothing but help innocent women and children. That's criminal in itself."

"I know the system doesn't always work, but it's all we have." Korine's fingernails dug into the palms of her hands. "Tell me where you are, and we'll talk it out. Just don't hurt Agent McGee."

"Shut up and listen. You and your mother covered up your filthy secrets for decades. Every day has been miserable for me. But you went on with your lives, pretending that everything was fine. You even kept those sickening dolls he gave you. And that damn jewelry box. I've had fucking nightmares of that song ever since he gave me the music box."

Korine swallowed hard.

This unsub, this woman, had been one of her father's victims. No wonder she hated Korine and her mother.

"You're right," Korine said. "Others were hurt because of our silence. But Hatcher had nothing to do with that, so killing him would be senseless."

"Sometimes sacrifices have to be made for the greater good."

The phone went silent.

Korine quickly called Cat for help. This woman was crazy.

She was going to kill Hatcher if Korine didn't find him first.

CHAPTER FORTY-SIX

Korine tapped her foot while she waited on Cat.

A second later, Cat cleared her throat. "I found a post that might fit the unsub. Girl talks about the office space where she was molested as a child. Office belonged to a child psychologist."

A shudder went through Korine. "What else does she say?"

"The psychologist gave her a music box and kept telling her how pretty she was as they danced." She paused. "Jesus, Korine. He also gave her porcelain dolls."

Korine's stomach roiled. That post was about her father.

The girl who'd written it blamed Korine and her mother. She was the Keeper.

She had to be the one holding Hatcher now.

"Do you have an address?" Korine asked.

"Computer was from a coffee shop in Savannah."

"She wouldn't take Hatcher to a public place." Korine's mind raced. "I have an idea. Let me know if you find anything to identify the woman."

Cat agreed and hung up.

Korine entered her father's name into the search engine and found an address for the office he'd used when she was little.

It was a long shot, but she had no other leads.

She looked up the address and silently cursed. That office had been torn down years ago.

She checked the clock. Was Hatcher still alive?

Panic knotted her insides. He had to be.

So where was he?

She rapped her fingers on her desk. This woman might have taken him to the place where her life had fallen apart. Maybe her childhood home . . .

If she only knew her name . . .

The files on her desk and photos on her wall mocked her. Maybe the answer was in there.

Her father had never faced charges, but what if one of his patients had reported him? It might be on file . . .

She grabbed the file on her father and skimmed through it, noting comments from neighbors about what a revered doctor he was.

But there was nothing about him molesting children.

She checked records for complaints about him and found a couple, but the information was sealed. Further digging revealed a lawyer's name.

The lawyer who'd handled her father's estate, the man who'd mentored her and helped her get the assignment in Savannah.

Korine punched the number and explained the situation.

"What's going on?" Blaine Hamilton asked.

"My mother told me about my father."

The man's breath rasped out. "I don't know what you think you know, but—"

"I know my father molested some of his patients. I don't know how many, but he was going to molest me the night he died. He probably would have, except my mother stopped him by shooting him."

Silence stretched between them for an awkward moment.

"You covered up for her, didn't you?" Korine asked. "Is that why you stayed close to the family all these years, the reason you pulled your weight with the bureau to get me assigned back in Savannah?"

"There were extenuating circumstances," the lawyer said. "Your mother was desperate to protect you and your brother, and she's suffered for it. The guilt ate at me, too. You were so determined to find answers that I decided maybe it would be best if you did. Maybe then your mother could let go of the guilt. And Kenny . . ."

Kenny had suffered, too. "What about the other children he hurt? Didn't they deserve justice?"

A deep sigh echoed back. "There were only three. Your father made a lot of money. The families needed it."

"He paid them not to talk?" Korine said in disgust.

"Yes."

Bile rose in Korine's throat. "Do you know what happened to the little girls?"

"Two of them moved out of state. The third one—at first her mother refused the money. But later her daughter started having emotional problems. As a teenager, she was suicidal. Eventually the mother accepted financial help for her daughter's medical bills."

"Where are they now?"

"They moved back to Savannah. The mother took a job as a caregiver."

Korine swayed as the pieces clicked together. "What was the mother's name?"

"Esme. She was a very nice lady, but her husband had just passed, and she had a difficult time with her daughter. The daughter was never right after what happened."

Esme had told her that she'd lost her daughter. Korine had interpreted that to mean the girl was dead. But Esme had never actually used those words. "Do you know where the daughter lives?"

"No," Hamilton said. "Why are you asking about her?"

Korine's mind raced with a possible scenario.

"Korine?"

"You've heard about the vigilante killings?"

"Of course," Hamilton said. "It's been all over the news."

"I think this young woman may be the killer." But she needed more information before she confronted Esme. "I have to go."

She hung up and scrambled to search the cold-case files she'd confiscated from the station. The files blurred as she combed through one after another. Finally at the bottom of a pile, she found notations where a family had made allegations against a prominent doctor.

A psychologist named Davenport.

Korine hurriedly skimmed the contents. It was a complaint filed by Esme and her daughter. The case had been closed when Esme suddenly dropped the allegations.

Korine dug for more information and discovered that her father had provided home visits to the little girl. Her name was Belinda Winters.

Esme used a different last name now.

Her address back then was in Brunswick.

She texted Cat to find out all she could on Belinda and Esme, specifically any properties they owned.

What if Esme was involved? Did she condone what her daughter was doing?

She had to find Hatcher, save him. But if Belinda and Esme blamed her family, Korine's mother might be on the hit list.

Was that the reason Esme had come to work for her mother? So she could get revenge?

Fear flooded her. A text came through from Cat. An address for Belinda Winters.

She had to go.

She punched Wyatt's number. "It's Korine," she blurted out. "I need your help."

"What do you want me to do?"

She gave a quick rundown of what had happened. "I'm checking out an address where the unsub might be holding Hatcher. I need you to go to my mother's. If Esme and her daughter have planned revenge against my mother, she might be in danger."

"I'm on my way. If Esme knows anything, I'll find out."

"Thanks." Korine ended the call, then checked her weapon, grabbed extra ammo, and headed outside to her car. Rain clouds threatened and the wind whistled through the live oaks as she pressed the gas and barreled onto the street.

Please let Hatcher still be alive.

Even if he didn't want her, she couldn't let him die.

Hatcher's head throbbed, and his eyes felt blurry as he struggled to open them. His mouth was dry, like cotton. And the room swayed. He blinked to clear the dizziness.

Where in the hell was he? What happened?

One minute he was heading to his SUV, the next . . . everything went blank. No, not completely blank. A stab in his neck.

Someone had injected him with a drug of some kind.

Shit.

He jerked his hands and arms, but he was trapped. Tied to a goddamn chair.

He had to get free.

Forcing himself to think, he scouted out the room for an escape route. Except for a tiny sliver of light seeping through the boarded window, the room was pitch-black. The scent of rotting wood swirled around him. A mouse skittered somewhere in the distance. Wind whistled through the eaves, adding to the chill in the room.

Who the hell had gotten the best of him? He hadn't seen it coming . . .

Had the unsub gone after Korine?

He banged his boots on the wood floor, rocking the chair back so hard he hoped it would splinter. Instead, it hit the wall and bounced back. "Why don't you show your face?" he shouted into the darkness. "Tell me who you are and why you brought me here!"

Silence met his shout.

Dammit. Where was the unsub? And what did the unsub have planned for him?

Fury fueled his adrenaline, and he fumbled with the ropes. He had to get free so he could stop this maniac. He just prayed she hadn't gotten to Korine.

She was all that mattered.

◆ ◆ ◆

Korine pressed the phone to her ear as she careened up the drive toward the address where Esme and her daughter Belinda had lived.

How would her life have been different if her father had been exposed for the man he truly was years ago? Would Belinda have healed and grown into a happy secure woman, able to love and have a normal relationship?

The wind picked up, gusts blowing leaves and debris all over the place. The house was dilapidated, the windows broken out and replaced by boards, the grass dead, trees withered and tilting at odd angles, others blown down, cracked and rotten from recent storms.

The land looked ravaged, just as Esme's daughter must have felt.

She sympathized with her.

Still, she couldn't condone murder.

And she wouldn't let Hatcher die.

She cut the lights and engine and coasted beneath an overhang of trees about a half mile from the house. Parking in the shadows, she slipped out, checking her weapon as she inched through the bushes toward the house.

A dog barked in the distance. Coyotes howled. A bleak eeriness hinted at the ghosts that wandered the marsh, lost between the tides and day and night.

She crept closer, her gaze scanning the woods. This place had been abandoned at least a decade ago.

But it must hold traumatic memories for Esme and her daughter.

She made it to the porch, but both front windows were boarded over so she crept to the side to find another way in. At least a way to see inside so she could scope out the situation.

Suddenly the brush rattled behind her, and she felt the sharp jab of a weapon in her back.

"Come on in, Korine. Your boyfriend is waiting."

Korine hesitated, her mind spinning. She recognized that voice.

It was someone she'd known all along. Someone who'd helped on the case.

Someone who'd hidden among them to cover for herself and the Keepers.

Someone she'd thought was her friend.

She whirled around and raised an arm, ready to strike a blow, but the sight of the Glock in her face made her freeze.

If she died, who would save Hatcher?

CHAPTER FORTY-SEVEN

The rancid scent of mold and dust and a dead animal assaulted Korine as she entered the dilapidated house where Esme and her daughter had once lived.

She blinked to adjust her eyes to the darkness. A scratching sound came from the corner. She jerked her head toward it and made out the shadowy outline of a man.

Hatcher. Tied to a chair. Not moving. His head slumped over.

Her heart pitched. *Dear God.* He had to be alive.

"What did you do, drug him?" Korine hissed.

The barrel of the gun dug deeper into her back.

"You need help," Korine said when the woman didn't respond to her question. "Belinda Winters . . . I know your real name, but you changed it to Cat. You changed your last name, too."

A sarcastic chuckle. "Do you really think they would have allowed me to join the FBI if they knew my personal history?" She shoved Korine so hard she stumbled forward. She hit the wall, boards splintering beneath her feet from the rotting wood.

"I know you suffered, but I thought we were friends," Korine said.

"Friends?" Cat laughed. "Do you know how hard it was for me to listen to you talk about how wonderful your father was?" She adopted a whiny tone, mimicking Korine. "Daddy loved me. He was such a good man; he helped other children. I have to find out who murdered him."

"I didn't know," Korine said, tears lacing her voice. "Not about the abuse. So stop this now. A jury will understand, and you can get help—"

"I've had *help*," Cat said icily. "All the damn counseling in the world can't erase what your father did to me. That's the downside of having a photographic memory. I could never forget anything, especially the details of what he said when he touched me."

Korine held up her hand. "Maybe another therapist—"

"I don't want a fucking therapist! My mother trusted him, and he locked me in this room and molested me."

"I'm so sorry," Korine said. "I swear I had no idea. My mother didn't either, not until the night he planned to do the same thing to me." She gave Cat a pleading look. "My mother killed him to stop him from hurting me or any more children."

"Yeah, and then he died a hero while they paid my mother to keep her mouth shut."

"I'm so sorry, Cat. Esme should have come forward."

"She needed the fucking money!" Cat waved the gun in her face. "She thought by taking it she was doing the right thing by me, but I knew she was ashamed. She could barely look at me."

Korine reached for her, but Cat swung the butt of the gun up and slammed it against Korine's head.

Pain seared her skull, and stars swam in front of Korine's eyes. "Please, don't do this."

But Cat wasn't listening. She aimed the gun at Korine, then threw a punch to Korine's stomach. Korine grunted, then dove for the gun and wrenched Cat's arm toward the ceiling. The bullet dislodged. Plaster rained down, and Korine lurched toward her and knocked her to the floor.

They fought for the weapon, and it went off again. They rolled across the floor, trading blow for blow. Korine landed a hard punch to Cat's midsection, then knocked the gun from her hand. It sailed toward the wall, and Korine scrambled after it. But Cat jumped her and stomped on her lower back, sending sharp spasms of pain through Korine's kidneys.

Suddenly a thunderous roar rent the air, and footsteps pounded. Cat grabbed the gun, rolled to the left and fired.

Hatcher. He was alive. And he'd gotten free.

He dodged the bullet, then charged Cat. The two of them hit the floor, rolling and fighting for the weapon. Cat slammed her foot into Hatcher's face, then scrambled backward and aimed the gun at him.

Korine crawled to her hands and knees, but Cat swung the gun toward her. "Move and I'll shoot."

Hatcher raised his hands in surrender, and Korine did the same.

Cat paced in front of them, her expression crazed. A moment later, the scent of gasoline filled the air as Cat doused the wood floors and walls.

Korine glanced at Hatcher. They had to act quickly. But the darkness hid his face.

She latched on to a mental picture of him, though. If she had to die today, she'd take that image with her.

Hatcher cursed as Korine tried to get up and tackle Cat. Cat fired at her, then at him, but they both dodged the bullets. A second later, Cat slammed the butt of the gun against Korine's head again, sending her to the floor.

Smiling, Cat tossed a match to the corner near where Korine lay. Flames immediately burst to life, then Cat dashed out the door and slammed it shut, locking them in.

Hatcher raced to Korine and knelt beside her. "Come on, we have to get out of here."

He slid an arm around her waist and helped her stand. She leaned on him as they hobbled toward the door. Heat seared them as the flames climbed the wall and shot to the ceiling. Wood crackled and popped, the fire eating at it as if it were paper, spreading in orange-and-red patches.

Smoke billowed around them, clouding the air. "Stay back," he ordered.

Summoning all the strength he had, he rammed his shoulder against the door.

It didn't budge.

He stepped back and tried again. This time he used his booted foot and kicked with all his might. Korine raised her leg and kicked the door, too. With their combined efforts, the door splintered and cracked.

The fire was spreading across the floor fast. Heat singed his back. Another piece of wood crashed down, then more of the ceiling.

Korine jumped aside to dodge a board, but the ceiling collapsed. She screamed, beating at the flames, as the burning wood fell on top of her.

Fear paralyzed Hatcher. He'd watched his wife die at the hand of one monster.

He couldn't lose Korine.

He snatched the burning boards away from her, beating and kicking at the flames to extinguish the fire. She beat at them as well, grabbed his hand, then they crawled toward the door.

The flames were on top of them, eating at the soles of their shoes as he helped Korine through the hole. As soon as she made it to the ground, he dove through. Panting for air, he grabbed her hand, and they ran toward the marsh.

Firelight flickered against the darkness, illuminating Cat. She stood beneath the live oak nearby, the orange glow accentuating the demented expression on her face. She was mesmerized by the flames, smiling as she watched what she thought was their demise.

He cupped Korine's face in his hands. "You okay?"

Soot and sweat stained her cheeks, but she looked so damn beautiful he wanted to cry because she was alive.

"We have to stop her," Korine said in a gravelly voice.

He gestured toward the opposite direction, back where she'd parked. "Get to your car where you'll be safe."

She shook her head. "We're partners, Hatcher. We do this together."

Their gazes locked, her stubbornness and courage a reminder that she was nothing like his former wife. He could be partners with her.

Not just at work but maybe in life, too.

A loud crash jolted him back to the moment. The entire house collapsed in a burning pile of rubble. Flames shot toward the sky, smoke rising in a thick cloud, sparks flying.

"I'll create a distraction," Korine said, "while you come up behind her."

He nodded, and Korine dashed around the burning house. He ducked low and crept to the opposite side, moving quickly until he had a good view of Cat. Ducking behind another patch of trees, he maneuvered closer until he was only a few feet away.

Korine suddenly appeared from behind a mound of burning wood. "Cat, please, it's over. You can't keep killing people."

Korine's voice startled Cat into spinning toward her. The young woman looked incoherent, lost in her world of hurt and revenge.

As if she was in a trance, she slowly raised the gun and pointed it toward Korine.

Hatcher inched closer, his blood boiling. If this went wrong, he could still lose Korine.

No way would he allow that to happen.

He jumped Cat from behind. She yelped in surprise, and he knocked the gun from her hand and sent it sailing toward a rock. She raised her fists to fight, but he was stronger and shoved her to the ground. He flipped her over and climbed over her, using his weight to restrain her. Then he yanked her arms behind her and handcuffed them together.

Korine retrieved the gun, then walked toward them. Sadness streaked her face as she looked down at Cat. "I'm so sorry for what my father did to you," she said.

Cold hatred streaked Cat's eyes as she glared at Korine.

Hatcher didn't feel as sympathetic. Cat had gotten a raw deal by being abused as a child. But it wasn't Korine's fault.

And neither one of them deserved to die so she could continue killing.

◆ ◆ ◆

The next half hour was fraught with tension as the evidence team arrived along with the fire department.

Watley looked at Cat with contempt. "She tried to kill Trace, didn't she?"

"I believe so," Hatcher answered. "He must have figured out what she was doing, so she wanted to keep him quiet."

Korine gestured to the burning building, then Cat's car. "Get us every piece of forensics you can. We'll need it."

They nodded and went to work. Detective Brockett arrived to transport Cat to booking.

"I have to check on my mother and Esme." When she'd been insistent on pursuing her father's case, her mother always said that not knowing was better.

That comment made sense now.

She stepped over to her car and phoned her mother's number, then Wyatt's.

No answer from either one of them.

Fear crowded her chest and she rushed to Hatcher. "I have to go. Wyatt didn't answer, and neither did my mother."

She might have sent Wyatt into an ambush.

And what would she do if Esme had hurt her mother?

CHAPTER FORTY-EIGHT

Fear wound Korine's stomach into a knot as she raced toward her mother's house. Hatcher insisted on going with her, and she didn't argue.

She might need his help.

Esme had known about her daughter's abuse when she'd come to work for the family. She'd accepted money from Korine's mother to pay for counseling for Cat—Belinda.

Had her mother known who Esme was when they'd hired her?

Had Esme come to work for them to seek revenge against Korine's mother?

Hatcher slipped his hand over her shoulder and squeezed it gently. "It's going to be okay."

She slanted him a dark look. "Not if Esme hurts my mother or Wyatt. I can't believe she's been living in my mother's house all these years and I didn't know her history."

"Did you know she had a daughter?"

A memory surfaced. One Christmas when Korine balked at the Christmas tree and Esme had helped her mother decorate, Esme had talked about how much her daughter had once loved the sparkly ornaments. "Esme said she'd lost her daughter, so I assumed she'd died."

There were so many secrets and lies in her family. Her heart ached. Esme's relationship with them was all born from deceit.

Her stomach churned as she roared down the drive to her mother's house. Hatcher called Wyatt again, but he didn't answer, raising her anxiety.

What if they were too late?

♦ ♦ ♦

Hatcher didn't like the fact that Wyatt wasn't answering. His former partner was a trained, seasoned agent. He knew how to handle himself.

But he'd been injured and was healing, and he could have walked into a damn trap orchestrated by Cat and her mother.

There was nothing a mother wouldn't do for her child. Korine's mother had killed her husband to keep Korine from being molested. Esme may have blamed herself for her daughter's abuse, may have been guilt ridden when the counseling didn't repair the damage.

May have hated the Davenports, who'd paid her to keep quiet.

She might have even blamed Korine because she escaped without being harmed while her own daughter suffered.

Korine barreled down the drive, trees and bushes flying by. Hatcher checked his weapon and scanned the property, looking for trouble. Wyatt's SUV was parked in front of the house. Empty. He had to be inside.

Korine threw the car into park, then jumped out, her hand sliding over her weapon as if to make sure it was still there. Hatcher followed, the two of them pausing on the front stoop to listen.

Voices echoed from inside. A cry.

Korine eased the door open and peered in to the entryway. Another cry. Upstairs.

She inched inside. He stayed close on her heels, gun at the ready.

♦ ♦ ♦

Korine held her breath as she started up the stairs. A sob wrenched the air. Her mother.

Then Wyatt's voice. "Put down the gun, please."

Korine slowly removed her weapon from her holster, then motioned to Hatcher that she was going up. Yet her mind kept going back to Cat.

Cat's law-enforcement training taught her not to leave evidence behind. She could have interfered with forensic evidence by hacking into the lab and altering results. She could have rerouted the posts on the blog to cover for herself. And that Facebook Live post she'd claimed came from her mother's house—Cat had lied about that, too. She had set up the post.

She'd also pointed them in the direction of the four other women to take focus off herself. And she'd probably slipped into Bellamy's room and drugged him. But why go after Bellamy? Had he somehow caught on to who she was and what she was doing?

Hatcher eased up the stairs behind her.

"Just set the gun on the floor." Wyatt's voice echoed from inside the bedroom.

Voices, her mother's and Esme's, then scuffling.

A shot blasted the air.

Fear gripped Korine, and she hastily climbed the remaining steps and rushed to her mother's bedroom doorway.

She swung her gun up, ready to fire, but instead of Esme holding the gun on her mother, her mother had the gun. Korine froze, assessing the situation.

Esme was perched in the wing chair, crying, while Wyatt was trying to convince her mother to relinquish the weapon. "She's okay," Esme said. "She had a nightmare and found that gun again. She wanted me to get rid of it, but it went off."

"Mother, let him have the gun," Korine said firmly.

"I had to stop him from touching those sweet little girls."

"Your husband can't hurt anyone else," Esme said through her tears. "You took care of that a long time ago."

Wyatt eased the gun out of her mother's hand. Her mother cried out and began to wail.

Korine's heart ached. Her mother was going to need therapy now.

Slowly she inched toward Esme. She couldn't let down her guard yet. "Esme, your daughter . . ."

More tears flooded Esme's eyes. "I know, I'm sorry . . . so sorry, all my fault."

Korine did a quick visual check. Esme had no gun, so Korine knelt in front of her and tucked her own weapon in her holster. "It wasn't your fault. And it wasn't my mother's. She didn't know what my father was doing until that night. I'm just sorry that he hurt your daughter."

"She never could move past it," Esme said. "I did everything I could to help her, but she hated me."

"She needs intensive therapy," Korine said. "We're going to get her help, I promise."

Esme nodded miserably. "She did something tonight, didn't she? She tried to hurt you?"

Korine murmured yes. "I'm so sorry, Esme."

"Where is she?" Esme asked. "Is she . . ."

"She isn't hurt," Korine said quickly. "But we had to arrest her. One of our detectives drove her to the police station."

Esme's face wilted even more. "She was the vigilante killer, wasn't she?"

Korine nodded.

"I was afraid it was her, but I didn't want to believe it," Esme said, her voice filled with tears.

"Why did you come to stay here with Mother?" Korine asked.

Esme clasped her hands together. "At first I hated your mama and your father, but when Belinda was little, your mother came to see me. She told me she shot him so he wouldn't hurt anyone else." Esme shrugged. "How could I hate her then? She killed her own husband to protect you and because she was sick about what he'd done to my little girl."

Korine glanced at her mother, who was perched on the side of the bed now, looking miserable but calmer than she had in a long time. Wyatt stood beside Korine's mother, his expression neutral, while Hatcher watched quietly, his big body poised to protect her if necessary.

Esme didn't appear to be dangerous, though. She was heartsick but not a threat.

"She gave you money?" Korine asked, a trace of bitterness in her tone.

Esme nodded. "Not to buy my silence like Belinda thought. To help me pay for counseling for Belinda. She needed it. She had nightmares and . . . she hated people. Hated to be touched. Hated to have me hug her. Hated everyone."

Korine snagged a tissue from the box on the side table and slipped it into Esme's hand.

"The counselor said she had a psychotic break," Esme said on a whimper. "The doctor gave her medication, but the pills either knocked her out or made her sick. Last year, I thought they'd finally gotten her stabilized. She told me she had a good job, and I thought she was happy."

"Then what happened?" Korine asked.

"When those inmates were released, she became paranoid again. She stopped taking her medication. She was following the news, upset about the River Street Rapist trial and that other woman."

"Tinsley Jensen," Korine said.

Esme nodded. "She saw the story about her, and she found her blog and read all those women's stories, and she became obsessive. All she talked about was getting justice."

"I can imagine how much the victims' stories upset her," Korine said softly.

"She came here one night to confront your mama, but your mama was having a bad day and it didn't go well. Belinda laughed and said your mother got what she deserved, but I told her your mama tried to make up for what her husband did, and it was time to forgive."

"She couldn't forgive, could she?" Korine asked.

Esme shook her head, more tears filling her eyes. "She had so much hate inside her. It was eating her up."

Compassion for Belinda/Cat overcame Korine. Yet an image of Hatcher tied to that chair surfaced, a reminder the woman was dangerous and needed to be locked up. At least for now.

"I'm so sorry, Esme. That had to have torn you up. Did you . . . want revenge, too?"

Esme dabbed her eyes with the soggy tissue. "At first, I thought about getting back at your mother. But then I saw the pain she was in, and I heard her crying at night and saw how lost your brother was, and I realized your mama was a victim, too. So were you and Kenny." She drew in a deep breath. "It was odd, but . . . that awful tragedy brought us together." She fidgeted. "Your mama and I were the same—two mamas wanting to protect our babies. I thought I was doing right by Belinda by keeping quiet. I figured your father was dead and telling the world would only bring attention to Belinda. I didn't want her growing up in the public eye, with people and teachers and other kids gossiping."

Korine gave Esme a sympathetic look. No child deserved that kind of life.

Yet keeping quiet had driven Belinda's shame deeper.

The depth of Esme's compassion made Korine's heart well with love and admiration for her.

Korine pulled her into a hug. Esme hugged her back, and Korine soothed her while she cried.

◆ ◆ ◆

Hatcher wanted to take Korine home, but she insisted on staying with Esme and her mother for a while.

The officer guarding Bellamy called with news that Bellamy had regained consciousness.

Hatcher and Wyatt rushed to the hospital, then to Bellamy's room. The young man was awake, propped up with two pillows. He still looked pale, but he was sipping water.

"Can you tell us what happened?" Hatcher asked.

Bellamy pushed the cup of broth they'd brought him away, uneaten. "The past few weeks I sensed something was off with Cat. We went out a couple of times, but she didn't want me to touch her. When those prisoners were released, she was irate. She was always ranting about justice and how often it failed."

Wyatt leaned on his cane. "Go on."

Bellamy rubbed a hand over his face. "The night the judge was murdered, we were supposed to have dinner. But she stood me up. I went by her place, and she acted strange. She seemed agitated and didn't want to talk, so I left her alone." He hesitated. "The night Hortman was killed, she showed up with a pizza. She looked kind of wild-eyed, like she was high. I noticed blood on her shirt, but she said she'd cut her finger." Bellamy fidgeted with the sheet. "Later I realized that the lab result on the blood I collected from Hortman's car wasn't right."

"What do you mean?" Wyatt asked.

"There were two samples," Bellamy said. "I logged them in myself. But the report showed only one. I saw Cat leaving the lab, and I asked her about it. She got really pissed off. Then I started thinking about the things she'd said, the way she tracked down those blog comments so quickly. I know she's a computer whiz, but that's not easy to do. I wanted to ask her how she did it, so I went by her place again, but she wasn't home." Bellamy pressed a hand over his chest as if it hurt. "A window was open, so I went in."

"What did you find?" Hatcher asked.

"Broken doll faces in the living room," Bellamy said. "I didn't know what that was about but remembered those at Korine's, and I realized something was way off." He leaned his head back against the pillow. "Then I found files on Cat's desk. There were pictures of all three murders, the judge, that child molester, the driver's ed teacher."

Hatcher folded his arms. "She took crime photos from the scene?"

Bellamy shook his head. "These shots were taken before the police arrived. The men were still alive, but they were tied up, pleading for their lives."

Hatcher shook his head in disgust. "Trophies. She wanted to relive the crimes."

Bellamy's face went ashen. "Then I opened the drawer, and there they were."

"What?" Wyatt asked.

"The murder weapons. The gavel she used on the judge. The bloody knife she used on Whiting." He scrubbed his hand over his eyes. "The hatchet she used on Hortman."

CHAPTER FORTY-NINE

Exhaustion tugged at Korine as she let herself in her house. The emotional strain of the night had taken its toll.

She flipped on lights as she entered, then undressed and showered, letting the hot water soothe her aches and pains and wash away the soot and stench of the fire.

Slowly, images of Hatcher in the shower with her, running his hands over her, cradling her hips as she wrapped her legs around him and was impaled by him, replaced the gruesome memories.

Only it stirred another kind of tension.

She wanted Hatcher. Again. Tonight.

The temptation to call him was so strong she could barely resist.

But she had to. If she didn't, she'd never be able to give him up.

She scrubbed herself until the hot water turned cold. A quick towel dry, then she dragged on a tank top and pajama pants and padded to the kitchen for a glass of wine.

She took the glass to her back deck, sank into the glider, and stared out into the dark woods. The storm clouds had lifted, and it was a beautiful, clear night. Stars shining. The quarter moon shimmering through the tree branches.

But a dozen thoughts bombarded her—the case, the women who called themselves the Keepers, Tinsley Jensen locked in her own cottage terrified of the man who'd attacked her, her brother Kenny in rehab because of what he'd witnessed as a child, her mother living with the horrible truth that she'd shot her own husband, Esme and her mother's secrets that had tied them together . . .

The justice symbol painted on the victims' faces . . .

Where was the justice in any of this?

At one time, she'd thought finding out who'd killed her father would give her peace.

Tonight she felt anything but at peace.

Instead, she felt torn up inside. And alone. Very much alone.

◆ ◆ ◆

Hatcher and Wyatt got warrants and searched Cat's—Belinda's—house. The pictures, evidence bags, and murder weapons were exactly where Bellamy said they'd be. A search of her computer revealed a list of people they suspected were her next targets.

With Bellamy's testimony, Cat's attack on Hatcher and Korine, and now this physical evidence, they would be able to lock Cat away. Her lawyer would no doubt use her traumatic past and possibly PTSD as a defense.

He and Wyatt had driven back to the field office to interrogate Cat. She'd taken full credit for the vigilante murders and claimed that the other four women they'd arrested were clean. She'd intentionally steered them toward the women to give her time to continue her mission.

The women were being released and the charges dropped.

Hopefully Cat/Belinda would end up in a mental health facility where she could receive therapy.

"What's going on between you and Korine?" Wyatt asked as he parked in front of Hatcher's cabin.

Hatcher bit the inside of his cheek. "Nothing. The case is done. If you're ready to come back and want to work with me again, Bellows will find another place for her."

"I do want to come back," Wyatt said. "And of course I want to work with you."

Hatcher clenched his jaw. "Really? 'Cause I know I let you down."

Wyatt hissed between his teeth. "Get over yourself, Hatcher."

Hatcher's brows furrowed. "What?"

"You are not responsible for the entire world. First you blame yourself for Felicia's abduction, then for me getting hurt."

"But—"

"No buts. We were partners. You did your job, and I did mine. We both know the risks that come with it."

Hatcher's chest ached. Could he really let his guilt go?

"Besides," Wyatt said on a dark chuckle, "I wasn't talking about the job when I asked about Korine. I was talking about the two of you . . . the chemistry."

It felt good, like old times, to be able to talk to his buddy. "I slept with her when I was doing the training at the bureau."

Wyatt's eyes widened.

"In fact, I was in bed with her when Felicia called to say she'd been taken." Emotions made his voice hoarse. "That's another reason I blamed myself."

A tense second stretched between them. "Listen, man, maybe you crossed the line, but we both know your marriage to Felicia was over. That girl had problems. She wasn't right for you."

Hatcher stared at his empty ring finger.

"But Korine, she's a different story. She's tough and strong and . . . hot as hell."

Hatcher couldn't resist a smile. "Yeah, she is."

"If you ask me—"

"I didn't."

Wyatt laughed again. "I'm going to speak my mind anyway. I should have done that when you told me about Felicia. The first time I met her, I knew she was trouble."

Yet Hatcher had been snowed by her attention. Until it had become unhealthy.

Wyatt arched a brow. "Anyway, if you aren't interested in Korine, then you won't mind if I ask her out?"

Hatcher's heart skipped a beat. "Who said I wasn't interested?"

Wyatt punched him on the arm. "That's what I thought. If you are, man, don't let her get away. The good ones are hard to find. Especially ones who'll put up with our line of work."

Hatcher stewed over that comment as he climbed from the vehicle and went inside.

The scent of sweat and burned ashes permeated his skin, so he showered and pulled on a clean T-shirt and jeans.

Although it was way past midnight, he was too wired to sleep. Wyatt's advice kept rolling around in his head.

He didn't want to disturb Korine if she was sleeping, so he texted her with the update on the case, then snagged his keys. He didn't know where he was going, but he ended up at the cemetery, standing over Felicia's grave.

The night seemed still, eerily quiet, the pungent odor of dead flowers and dirt wafting around him. A thin stream of moonlight played across the grave, shimmering off the tombstone.

He usually saw Felicia when he came here. Her eyes glaring at him in shock and blame.

Where was she now?

"I'm sorry I failed you, Felicia," he said softly. "I wish I could go back and change things, bring you back to life."

The wind picked up, tossing leaves across the graves and making the flowers sway. A whisper of a voice calling his name echoed in the breeze and made him look up.

Felicia was there. This time so faint, her silhouette shimmering and fading and more ethereal than before.

"I'm sorry," he said again.

He expected the same angry, accusatory look, but slowly a vision of her hand lifting drifted through the darkness; then a soft smile spread on her face, and she blew him a kiss.

He blinked, certain he was seeing things wrong, but when he opened his eyes, she waved. Then a bright stream of light glowed from the heavens and surrounded her, and she was gone.

Hatcher's chest pounded. So many times he'd seen her, thought she hated him, knew she was waiting to cross. But tonight, she'd looked at peace.

And she'd just said goodbye.

The guilt that had held him back slowly dissipated, and the hole in his heart filled with warmth.

Felicia had died too young.

He and Korine had almost died, too.

He pressed a kiss to his hand, then laid it on the tombstone. She was finally at rest.

His chest felt lighter, too.

His text beeped. Korine thanked him for the information. She was at home. She couldn't sleep.

He climbed in his car, started the engine, and drove from the graveyard. He passed two of his favorite bars in Savannah, but this time he didn't stop. He didn't want a drink.

He knew exactly what he did want, though. And where he was going.

He pressed the accelerator. He couldn't wait to get there.

◆ ◆ ◆

Korine had poured a second glass of wine when a knock sounded. Hatcher had assured her that the case was over.

Still, nerves tightened her body as she rushed to the door and checked the peephole.

Hatcher.

Her pulse quickened.

God, he looked good.

Pulse hammering, she unlocked the door but forced herself not to reach for him when she desperately wanted to drag him into her arms. To hold him and never let him go.

"I couldn't sleep either."

His gruff voice sent a tingle of awareness through her. She gestured for him to come in.

"The case keeping you awake?" she asked, anxious to fill the silence.

His gaze met hers. Emotions mingled with heat, stirring her desires. "No, you were."

She narrowed her eyes. "Me?"

He nodded, then reached for her. "I couldn't sleep until we talked."

She held her breath, waiting, hoping this wasn't goodbye. "I didn't rat you out to Bellows, Hatcher. In fact, I told him that you were the best agent he had and that you'd come back stronger than before."

Emotions flashed across his face and he shifted. "You did?"

She nodded. "I always tell the truth. I also realize Wyatt is about ready to come back—"

"This is not about Wyatt or the case or work at all. It's about us."

"Us?" she asked in a throaty whisper.

He nodded. "I don't want to scare you off, but tonight when we were trapped and we almost died, I realized something."

"We made it out alive, Hatcher. You don't have to feel guilty—"

"I'm done with guilt, too." His gaze darkened as he looked into her eyes. "I . . . I love you, Korine."

A smile curved her lips, warmth spreading through her.

"If you don't feel the same way—"

She pressed her finger to his lips to shush him. "I do."

For a long heartbeat, they stared at each other, words unspoken dancing between them. Then Hatcher dragged her into his arms and closed his mouth over hers.

She kissed him with all her heart, pouring her love into it as his words reverberated in her ears. He loved her.

No promises yet. They'd have to talk about work. Being partners.

But somehow in the midst of murder and dead bodies, of family secrets and betrayals and the ghost of his dead wife, they'd found each other. And they'd found love.

That was all that mattered.

STAY TUNED FOR THE NEXT

KEEPERS NOVEL—COMING SOON

ABOUT THE AUTHOR

USA Today bestselling author Rita Herron fell in love with books at the ripe old age of eight, when she read her first Trixie Belden mystery. Twenty years ago, she traded her job as a kindergarten teacher for one as a writer, and she now has more than ninety romance novels to her credit. She loves penning dark romantic suspense tales, especially those set in small southern towns. Her awards include a Career Achievement Award from *RT Book Reviews* for her work in Series Romantic Suspense, the National Readers' Choice Award, and a RITA nomination. She has received rave reviews for the Slaughter Creek novels (*Dying to Tell* and *Her Dying Breath*) and her Graveyard Falls novels (*All the Dead Girls*, *All the Pretty Faces*, and *All the Beautiful Brides*). Rita is a native of Atlanta, Georgia, and a proud mother and grandmother.